an everlasting bond

Allison Zhang

For my Family

"Friendship is born at that moment when one person says to another, 'What! You too? I thought I was the only one.'"

— C.S. Lewis

one

Sophie

SOPHIE, her eyes nearly covered with her frizzy hair—which was fading from black to brown—sighed as she plopped down on the chair. Its rusting legs and chipping green paint were a sign that the chair was probably as old as the school's founding in 1960. Its strength was also quickly deteriorating, squeaking whenever Sophie shifted her 5-foot 2 frame an inch to the right. Somehow, all the donations from the multi-millionaires that attended Washington High School had better places to be spent than replacing broken chairs. She would move to a different chair, but then she would intrude on someone else's designated spot, and then a whole list of complications would follow. Everyone's seating arrangement would be messed up, and then their attention would be on her. So, with the near-certain ramifications in mind, Sophie decided to continue keeping her body weight ever slightly shifted to the left.

Of course, she could tell Ms. Dretzka, her English teacher, about the long-broken chair. But no, she couldn't do that. She couldn't risk antagonizing her again because she had already flunked her previous grammar test. When Ms. Dretzka had passed back her test, Sophie had looked right past her little, red, rectangular glasses, finding utter disappointment within her wrinkled eyes.

Sophie hadn't cared so much about the score; after all, her parents would never bother to see her grades. And she didn't care if she disappointed them. They deserved it.

Anyhow, Sophie cared more about how Ms. Dretzka had responded. In all her other classes, every teacher loved her. She always turned her homework in on time, studied five hours for each test, and ferociously waved whenever she saw them outside class. She didn't know why she cared so much about the teachers loving her, but she did. Yet, her English teachers never seemed to like her. Ever since she moved from Shanghai to Los Angeles at eight years old, none of them had even pretended to like her. It was a curse, she deemed. A plague that she was forced to carry around begrudgingly.

As a freshman that year, she was determined to break this cycle. However, no matter how much she complimented Ms. Dretzka's jacket or raised her hand to answer questions, each failed test kept her from attaining her goal.

Sophie knew it was her own brain's fault. She wasn't dumb; she could memorize equations faster than the person sitting next to her could finish reading all of them. But it was something about the way that there seemed to be endless possibilities of clauses, commas, semicolons, apostrophes, and conjunctions that made her headache when she stared at them. *Why did some old white man decide one day that all of these grammar structures were a good idea?* She simply couldn't understand why people didn't stick to the old-fashioned independent clauses ending with a period.

"Today, we're going to go over subordinating conjunctions," Ms. Dretzka enthusiastically announced.

Sophie involuntarily let out a large sigh. *Oh no.*

"Is there anything wrong?" Ms. Dretzka asked.

Sophie could already hear her underlying exasperation. *How the hell did I mess up again? I'm an idiot.* "No, Ms. Dretzka. I just didn't get much sleep last night."

"I see." There was an awkward pause, but then, to Sophie's gratefulness, the class resumed.

The clock struck three o'clock, marking the end of the school day. Stuffing her textbooks into the hand-me-down backpack that used to be her sister's, Mackenzie's Sophie pushed open the wooden door and was met face-to-face by Lyla.

Sophie loved Lyla. Or maybe she needed her. When Sophie first moved to Los Angeles and couldn't communicate with anyone, Lyla had found her sitting in the sandbox, etching dim sum onto the ground. Sophie had been hungry because her parents had rushed off to work without packing her lunch. So she had been doing what she always did when these situations happen: Get in her head. She had just been envisioning sitting at Cheng Huang Miao dipping her crab-stuffed xiaolongbao into soy sauce when Lyla jumped onto her engraving. Her tall, lean frame had towered over the tiny sandbox, and Sophie had watched in despair as her dream of the savory soup dumplings abruptly dispersed with the arrival of Lyla's black Converses.

But the loss was worth it. Lyla had given Sophie a green apple lollipop, and they had sat in the dirt together, licking away at the candies while conversing in Mandarin. Both immigrants from China, they had finally found someone to relate to. That day was one of the happiest moments of Sophie's life since leaving Shanghai behind.

Sophie stared at Lyla's hazel eyes, gratefulness brimming in her own.

"Hey. Hey, Soph! Hello!" yelled Lyla as she jumped up and down, trying to break Sophie out of her trance.

"Oh, hi, Lyla! Sorry, I'm here now. What happened?" Sophie kicked herself for daydreaming again.

"There's a party tonight. A huge party. Ashley just told me. Aren't you excited? We got invited to *the* party." Lyla's eyes bulged out of her face as she waited for Sophie's response.

Sophie was stuck. She knew how much Lyla wanted to be friends with Ashley, Katie, and Dylan. But she also despised being around them because she had to hide her true self in a façade of enthusiasm mixed with blissful ignorance.. *Why couldn't it just be me and Lyla?* Not wanting to dishearten Lyla, however, she responded, "Um. Yeah! I'm super excited. I just have to check with my parents whether or not I can go." *Liar.* She knew her parents would say yes; they always wanted her to "broaden" her circle. But it was a solid, typical excuse to avoid responding with a definite yes or no.

"Sounds good. See you later, Soph!" Lyla bounded away, her blonde ponytail swishing back and forth as if a reminder to Sophie that time was ticking, and she didn't have much time to decide whether or not she would go.

It was a Monday, so Sophie didn't have horseback riding practice after school. As a routine, she began her twenty-minute walk back to her house, staring at the lines separating the concrete slabs. She knew exactly which slabs were a bit far apart, due to the ever-expanding roots of the oak trees that dotted her neighborhood in the foothills of LA. Sophie used the time to ponder Lyla's proposal. On one hand, she didn't want to pretend to be someone else while she could stay home and dive into the romance book she had recently started. On the other hand, she didn't want Lyla to resent her for canceling another party. In the past two months, Sophie had made up excuse after excuse to dodge these parties, and Lyla had been getting increasingly frustrated. After all, if Sophie didn't go, Lyla wouldn't go either. They were designated peas in a pod, incomplete without one another. *Why does she always want to go to these parties?* Sophie shook her head, shaking off the negative thoughts about her best friend.

No, I can't think clearly right now. It's fine. It's a Friday afternoon, so Mom should be home soon. I can just follow her instructions.

Upon arriving at her front doorstep, Sophie picked up an Amazon package and unlocked the heavy main door. Almost immediately after taking off her sandals, she was greeted by a bundle of brown and golden fluff.

Bending down to the bundle's level, Sophie exclaimed, "Potato! How has my best boy been?" Potato responded by vigorously wagging his tail and smothering her with sloppy licks. Sophie picked up Potato, using the baggy sleeves of her hoodie as a perfectly sized sling to hold him in.

"Hello? Is anyone here? Mom?" Her words traveled down the hallways that seemed to extend for miles, and they bounced off the modern art pieces that her mother decided were essential to making the house whole. Ironically, the person who deemed that the house needed to be more of a home never seemed to be there to make it one. Her father, likewise, always complained about how they didn't spend enough time together, but Sophie couldn't remember the last time she had sat down and chatted with him. Today was no different.

Even though Sophie was used to arriving at an empty house, her heart still wrenched a tad bit, and it throbbed with unusual pain when she passed by her sister's room. *Mackenzie would have been making me my favorite red bean soup by now. And she would be asking me all about my day at school.* Of course, that was before...

"Oh, Potato, you miss her too, don't you? It's okay, I think we all do." He stared back with sorrowful eyes and stopped panting, which made Sophie feel a bit guilty for not putting on a happier face for her dog.

Arriving at the kitchen, Sophie let go of Potato and cut an apple for herself, making sure to give Potato a slice. Together, they made their way to Sophie's room, walking especially fast when they passed the desolate dining room which both agreed was haunted by previous owners.

After winding up the stairwell and traveling down another lengthy hallway, they finally arrived at Sophie's room. Her favorite and most hated place. She loved the idea of it: a space for her where she didn't have to worry about being judged for not talking, a space where she could forget about the entire world and simply listen to music while staring at the ceiling. And, of course, a place where she would text her pen pal without disturbance. But she despised how it looked: bleak walls devoid of color, sterile pillows bought in bulk from the moving company, and wilting plants she used to cut because of how much they grew. Sophie didn't like to think about how she had forgotten to water them after Mackenzie's death.

At least she still had her pen pal, Anya. But for some reason, Anya hadn't been responding for almost a week, and Sophie didn't want to give in to her darkest thoughts, which was that the person she had relied on for months to vent to had abandoned her.

Sophie lay down amid her blankets, staring at the ceiling blankly. When she reached for her throw pillow, it fell to the ground. *Fuck.* Reaching down to grab the pillow, a tear fell out of Sophie's right eye. *Stop. Don't you dare cry again. Have some self-control.*

Potato barked, and Sophie turned to her window to see the source: a squirrel scaling an oak tree. After waving her hands in Potato's face to stop his incessant barking, Sophie looked at her bedside clock and remembered that the party was in two hours. She had told Lyla that she would arrive at her house at six o'clock, which only gave her an hour to get there. *Shoot.* Quickly wiping away her forming tears while giving up hope on her parents to return home any time soon, Sophie gave in to Lyla's wishes.

Sophie sighed. *Great. Now I have to pick out an outfit.* She usually rotated around five T-shirts, five jeans, and three hoodies. But, for an occasion such as today, she reached past the clothes and found the box that had been stored away for over a year. Opening it, Sophie took out a baby blue dress laced with pink flowers at the collar. The seam cut off at her knees, creating the perfect length where she didn't feel uncomfortable sitting down but didn't make it seem like she was attending a wedding.

Not having grown much in a year, the dress slipped right on, offering her the exact breathing room she had loved when she originally found this dress while shopping with her family. Something about how her body hadn't changed seemed so wrong when everything else about her life had altered. There were no more Sunday afternoons shopping with her family or the ice cream sundaes that followed. There was no more pretending to be a ballerina while twirling around in a new dress. There was no more ecstatic clapping as she finished her "ballerina" performance. *It's for the better, anyway. It wouldn't be the same without Mackenzie.*

After slightly touching up her chaotic hair and using mascara to cover up her puffy eyes, Sophie put on her pair of two-inch high heels. Suddenly, Potato came running from the wine cellar, splotched with dark red patches. *What did he do?* Broken glass was scattered on the cellar floor, her mom's treasured wine spilling out.

Instead of rushing to get a broom, Sophie sat on the floor next to the puddle. Without a second thought, she stuck her two fingers into the wine and brought it to her tongue. *Maybe it's my mind that's my worst enemy. If I could just silence it for a bit...*

two

Anya

OH NO. Anya hadn't done her math homework and had class the next period. Again. It wasn't that she ever forgot; she simply deliberately chose not to do it. She liked to think of it as an act of rebellion. One of those villain-origin stories in the dozens of Korean drama shows she had watched in the past year. Of course, she had watched all these dramas secretly or with her father. Her mother would *flip out* if she found out. She was already mad at her enough as it was.

She hadn't done her homework this time because she hated Mr. Yen, her math tutor. So much that oftentimes she wondered why her sister, Camelia, had disappeared off the face of Earth instead of him. Just thinking about him and his wicked smile as he casually berated her made Anya want to scream, but she didn't want to make a fool of herself in front of Liam when they were in the middle of PE.

"Faster, Anya! I've never seen someone do a sit up so slowly," shouted her PE coach, Mr. A.

"I'm trying!" grunted Anya as she blew her jet-black hair out of her face. She had spent forever in the morning making her hair pin-straight and her foundation seamless, all for it to be ruined in a flurry of sweat.

Under her breath, Anya cursed the dean of her school, who had arbitrarily assigned two of Anya's least favorite classes together.

"Well, try harder. Your mom didn't pay all of this money for you to attend this school just for you to slack off." Mr. A's hot breath reeked of his breakfast of century eggs with porridge.

Anya mustered all her strength to avoid puking, glancing at Liam for inspiration. Since fifth grade, part of her heart and mind had been dedicated solely to him. Everything about him seemed glossy and faultless, even now, when everyone else looked horrendous doing sit-ups. She had never talked to him; she always just gossiped about him with Isabel and Odyssey at lunchtime or after school. It was a ritual at this point; she would find something new about Liam to admire, keep it stored until she met up with her besties, and weave it into her already perfect image of him.

Her parents have never found out about her interest in him. Anya could only imagine what they, especially her mother, would do if they found out that she was increasingly distracted by him as the years passed by. So yes, Anya had a lot of secrets. *But whose fault is that? My mother herself.*

"Ring!" Her phone started blaring just as she finished her set of push-ups. Mr. A looked at her as if to say, "I knew this would happen." Excusing herself from a room full of curious eyes, Anya saw that the caller was her mother. She groaned, knowing exactly what she would say.

Unfortunately, Anya had hit the nail right on the head, as her mother's voice immediately began blaring through the phone. "Anya Chen! Young lady, do you care to explain the five absences from class you have had in the past week?" Her mother's voice pierced through her skull, and Anya, for the second time in a day, cursed her bad luck.

How do I explain this? Better for her to think it's something light-hearted. "Hi, Mom! Please, please don't be mad. I've just found school to be really difficult, so..."

"What do you mean difficult? Do you not know how much tutors, money, and time we've spent to make school easier for you?"

"Mom, if you'll let me finish. I appreciate all the tutors that you've found, but not everyone can easily grasp school."

"Don't you dare end up like your sister."

"Mom! Please. Just let me finish." Anya could already envision the splotches of red that were blooming on her pale face, and she dreaded returning to class afterward.

"Fine. Speak."

"So, as I was saying..."

"Watch your attitude!" barked her mother.

Right. We had a conversation about this before. "Sorry. So basically, I've found school to be really tiring, so I've skipped a few classes to hang out with Isabel and Odyssey. They've helped me during this time. You can ask them yourself. I promise, Mom, I do." *Please don't ask them. Please don't ask them.*

"What do I always tell you? Those girls are terrible influences. All they ever do is make you misbehave. Anya, you have to listen."

Anya quenched her anger before it developed into words. Her mother would never understand her.

"I know, Mom. You're right; this was the last time. I promise."

"Fine. I'm still upset, young lady."

She hung up before her mom could hear her labored breathing. *If Mr. A dares yell at me right now, he won't hear the end of it.* She shook her head back and forth and rubbed her forehead. *Forget about it, Anya. Just be grateful they didn't find out what you truly missed class to do.*

Leaning back against the cement wall, Anya let out breaths of relief, and after taking a short trip to the bathroom to touch up her makeup, she returned to class. However, her mother's words had gotten to her. Not even Liam's presence or Mr. A's shouting could stop her from thinking about Camelia. Memories came back in throbbing waves, curbed only by the figment of her last remaining hope. *Which is now in peril because of that stupid phone call.*

For the rest of the day, Anya couldn't focus. And everything pissed her off.

Normally, she could handle the drama of being friends with Isabel and Odyssey. Often, more than not, she enjoyed participating in it. But today, when Odyssey came to her with "shocking" news that another guy who was already taken had asked for her number, Anya simply couldn't bring herself to care. When Odyssey asked over and over again for advice, Anya tried to show through her brief retorts that she wanted alone time. As usual, Odyssey didn't take the hint and nagged for instructions that Anya knew she wouldn't follow.

So, Anya snapped, "What's the point? Don't you know he's got a girlfriend already?" Which was something that Anya, in hindsight, probably shouldn't have said and regretted saying right afterward. But she had spoken her truth, and it was already out there. Thus, when Odyssey had sniffled and stormed off, Anya had comforted herself that someone had to tell her someday.

Then, upset that her best friend didn't understand her and dreading the impending piano lesson after school, Anya's day was thoroughly ruined. Nobody dared to talk to her as everyone, including teachers, feared the deathly silent, pursed-lip self that Anya became when upset. Paired with her thick eyeliner and bangs that reached almost over her eyes, Anya managed to scare off even her supposedly fearless classmates.

The school bell rang, and instead of rejoicing like other students, Anya groaned in dismay. There wasn't one day when she had free time after school, as her parents ensured she had plenty of extracurriculars to fill the time. Even when Anya told her parents repeatedly about her dislike of playing piano, they always insisted that she loved it since birth. So, according to their logic, she should love it now. "Plus, it's good for college admissions" is what Anya thought they wanted to truly say. She knew that they didn't care about her passions. For all she knew, they probably thought that her passion was just scrolling through WeChat and listening to pop music. Which it probably was. Unlike her sister, who wanted to travel the world and save animals, Anya had no interests. No subject interested her except if one. Art. Maybe in another life, she could've developed her passion for art further, but art was out of the picture when all her parents did was stick her in tutoring classes and other extracurriculars that Anya had no interest in. Even if she carved time from talking to her friends, her parents would simply tell her how useless her sketches in her notebook were. *If they had thought that Camelia's noble goals to save the world were stupid, what would they think of mine?*

So now, she was stuck with Dr. Wu for the next two hours while she could have been searching for Camelia. Instead, she resorted to skipping classes and enduring her mother's wrath for it.

"Did you not practice again?" Mr. Wu was a patient old man, but Anya had worn his patience thin.

She felt a little guilty. Every time, she told him she would practice for the next class. She always left the class with that promise. But she broke it again. "I'm sorry, Mr. Wu. I have a lot of things going on right now."

He sighed but relented, something Anya knew that he only did because he had a grandson that he assumed was going through the same phase as her. "It's okay. Let's start with the right hand first, then."

Despite her urge to fall asleep over the piano keys, Anya played with all her heart so he wouldn't be disappointed. She could tell that Mr. Wu wanted the best for her, and it hurt her to see his downcast eyes when she hit an F note instead of a B note twice in a row.

After a grueling two hours, Anya finished playing the last note and politely said goodbye to Mr. Wu without staying longer than necessary.

Just as Anya turned away from Mr. Wu's house, she saw her father waving to her from the end of the driveway. As her piano teacher's house was only a ten-minute walk from her house, Anya had planned to walk by herself home, but now that her father had come, she smiled and ran to him.

"Hi, Dad! What are you doing back from work so early? I thought that you had work until 7 pm today?" Even though Anya loved talking to her father, especially when they ranted together about her mother, she had simply looked forward to some alone time to smell the aromas wafting from the restaurants. But she would never pass up a chance to talk with her father.

"Hi, my daughter! I left work early because I finished checking up on all my patients. Most of all, I wanted to check up on you. It feels like ages ago when we last talked. Every time I return home, you're always doing homework." His voice once again made that melancholy sound that always made Anya sad.

"I know, Dad. I'm sorry. It's not that I don't want to talk with you anymore. It's just that…"

"I understand. You're in high school. You should be focused on your studies."

"Right. Right." Anya had meant to say something else, but since her father assumed the typical, she just let it go.

"Just make sure to tell me if you need anything, okay? I'm always here for you. I know your mother can sometimes be, well, you know."

"Haha, yeah. I will, Dad. Don't worry about me." More than anything, Anya wanted to tell him about all the crazy events in the past week, but a gut instinct told her to keep them secret for now. She would tell him in due time after she learned more herself.

Arriving home, her father made them some potstickers. Seeing that her mother wasn't home yet, they relaxed and turned on the TV to watch the latest K-drama.

While quickly grabbing some soy sauce to pair with the potstickers, a thought suddenly popped up in Anya's mind. "So, Dad. Isn't it your birthday soon? Are you planning anything?"

Mr. Chen sighed. "It is. I'm turning fifty-four this year. Time passes too fast."

"Stop being like that. We *need* to do something. Remember that year when Camelia and I performed a whole debut of Black Pink songs for you and Mom?"

Chuckling, Mr. Chen replied, "How could I ever forget? You guys even choreographed an entire dance. For once, your sister out danced you that day."

"She really did. Afterward, she kept telling me how she would forever be embarrassed by the recording of her dancing. But I think she secretly loved it and just used that video to remind everyone of how she beat me." Anya smiled.

"You and your sister. Always competing against one another."

"Thinking back on it, we were quite competitive." Anya added, "Even though I don't miss that part of our relationship, I still miss her. I wonder how she's doing now."

The room turned quiet as they paused to think about Camelia. A thick, suffocating air of words left unsaid hung over the room, but without wanting to dive deeper into their shared loss, the two commenced watching the TV. Few words passed between Anya and her father as both sat in reminiscence.

Promptly, at six o'clock, Mrs. Chen returned home from working at the hospital. Anya helped set up the table and nervously ate dinner with her parents. Not a word passed between the family as Mrs. Chen still was ticked off at Anya while Mr. Chen didn't want to further provoke his wife. Just ten minutes after Anya sat down to eat, Mrs. Chen rushed her to complete her homework. So, Anya returned back to her room, plopping down on a cushioned chair. She leaned over her desk and played with a pencil while procrastinating on homework. Too unmotivated to do work and not wanting to scroll on her phone, she blankly stared in front of her for ten minutes. Suddenly, just when she felt like falling asleep on her desk, a thought jolted her awake. *Ah! My pen-pal! How could I forget? It's been so long since I last responded! Oh no, she probably thinks that I ghosted her. This week has been so busy, but still! How could I forget?*

Wide awake now, Anya opened up her laptop and started to type away.

three

Sophie

WHAT AM I DOING? After tasting the acrid flavor of the wine against her tongue, Sophie immediately recoiled and ran to the kitchen to drink some water. *How do Mom and Dad like this stuff? How did Mackenzie like this stuff? I better clean this mess up.* Moving Potato away, Sophie quickly mopped up the spilled wine and picked up the shattered glass shards, leaving the room exactly as she had previously seen it. Flushed, Sophie quickly called an Uber, rushed out of the house, and set off to the party at Ashley's house.

When she arrived at the party, Sophie lost her breath to the dazzling decorations that sprawled from the front door to the driveway. Letters spelling "Happy Birthday Ashley" were staked into the freshly mowed grass, and the water fountain had been redesigned to have purple and blue undertones. Even the bushes had been trimmed to spell out Ashley's name. *Wasn't this party supposed to be low-key? I thought that Ashley didn't want to repeat her last birthday party. Huh.*

"You're finally here!" Lyla ran to Sophie, and once again, Sophie was shocked.

Lyla had meticulously curled her hair until its usual shoulder-length had become almost bob-like. Her red dress shone under the moon's glow, and even her shoes seemed to dazzle. Sophie couldn't help but feel a twinge of shame for her messed up hair and sneakers, which she had decided to change into at the last minute. For some reason, she thought most people would have worn a T-shirt or sundress. So, she had purposely not worn high heels to avoid being an outcast. But now, looking at Lyla, Sophie regretted not trusting her first intuition.

"Hi, sorry. I'm so, so sorry. I got caught up with my parents."

"Your parents? They're back from work already? I thought you would just call them for permission." Lyla's voice sounded dubious, and Sophie cringed. *Why did I say that? Lyla knows that my parents don't come home until late.*

"Yeah! They came home early today because they had to bring Potato to the vet."

"Oh. Is he okay?"

"Yeah, yeah. He's fine. He just stopped eating for a while. It's probably a stomachache." *When did I start lying so much?*

"Poor puppy! I'll go over to your house tomorrow to see him. But let's go in for now. The party has already started for a while. Come on!"

The inside of the house seemed even more grandiose than the outside. Chandeliers hung from the top of the three-storied ceiling to right above Sophie's head, and table after table of charcuterie boards lined the dining room.

In an enthusiastic voice to cover her secret jealousy, Sophie implored, "Lyla, do you see all of this? This party must have taken so much time to decorate." *How do her parents have so much free time?*

"I know, right? If only my parents would do something like this for me. They just baked me a cake for my last birthday party." Lyla didn't even try to hide her envy.

Both of them sighed.

To cheer Lyla up, Sophie said, "Let's say hi to Ashley."

As they entered the living room, the party's main room, they saw the group of girls—not exactly besties with Ashley's friend group but also considered to be on their "level"—wearing alluring gowns that radiated off the dazzling lights. Yet, amid all the faces in the room, they couldn't find Ashley anywhere.

As they planned to give up and settle onto the couches, Katie appeared, and right off the bat, Sophie could tell that she was worried.

"Have any of you seen Ashley? I can't find her anywhere." Katie's voice was at a higher pitch than usual.

Sophie responded, "Lyla and I were just looking for her. How long has she been gone? She might be in the bathroom."

Shook her head, Katie sighed, "I've already checked there. Dylan's going around asking other people if they've seen her. It's already been twenty minutes. She would never be gone that long from her own birthday party."

Lyla pitched in, "How about Ashley's parents? They should be here, right? Ashley is probably talking with them in another room."

Katie's eyes brightened at this thought. "Good idea. Knowing them, they'll probably be in the study room. Let's go."

With Katie leading the way and Sophie and Lyla sprinting behind her, they arrived at the room instantly. However, Katie faltered upon standing in front of the grand door.

Confused, Sophie asked, "Are you okay? Shouldn't we go in?"

"Sorry, guys. It's just that her parents are a bit... never mind, let's head in." Katie gently pushed the door open.

What could her parents be like? Sophie glanced at Lyla, confirming that they shared the same worries.

"Hello? Who is it?" A lady's voice, high-pitched to the ear, rang from behind a bookshelf.

Katie responded, "Good evening, Mrs. Miller. We were looking for Ashley. Have you seen her anywhere?"

Mrs. Miller immediately jumped up. "What? Don't tell me you haven't seen her. Oh no. Shouldn't she be in the living room? I haven't seen her at all. She never usually comes into this room. Hold on, let me call my husband. It'll take too long for me to go all the way to my bedroom to get him. He was planning to sleep soon, but he might know something. How could you guys lose her?" Her voice became even more high-pitched, further stressing everybody in the room.

The phone rang, and Mr. Miller's voice shared the same amount of anxiety as Mrs. Miller's. Nobody had seen her.

Lyla tried to calm her down. "Don't worry, Mrs. Miller. She's probably just taking some alone time."

"Alone time? You expect me to believe that? What if she's passed out somewhere? I knew I shouldn't have let her out of my sight." She began to pace the room, waiting for her husband to arrive. Everyone else didn't dare to breathe out of fear of agitating her more.

Footsteps thudded down the hallways, and the door slammed open. Mr. Miller had arrived.

"Where is Ashley? Where is she?" If possible, his voice sounded even more urgent than his wife's. He had yet to change out of his purple pajamas.

In an exasperated and nervous voice, Mrs. Miller said, "Why would we know? That's why I called you in the first place."

"I know. I know. I'm just worried. Ashley wouldn't disappear like this. Do you think something happened to her?"

Sophie gulped. *What if Ashley's actually in danger?* Even though Sophie didn't know Ashley well, she still hoped with all her heart that she would just show up again. *Please don't let her be hurt.*

"We should call the police!" exclaimed Mrs. Miller.

Mr. Miller nodded in agreement, acknowledging that the police could more easily find Ashley than anyone else.

As Mrs. Miller dialed 911, everyone else forced themselves to sit down on the ground so that they would stop pacing. Mr. Miller held his stomach, looking as if he would puke. Katie also didn't look great; her perfectly-tied braid had become a jumble of knots. Nobody dared to talk as they nervously waited for the police to arrive.

Knock. Knock.

"Guys? What happened?"

Everyone's mouth dropped open in shock. There, standing at the door, was Ashley.

"Why do you guys appear so surprised? I just went out for some air. The room got a bit stuffy with all those decorations and people. Sorry if I scared you guys." Ashley's voice seemed too normal, too placid.

Without speaking, Mrs. Miller, Mr. Miller, and Katie hugged her. Sophie and Lyla let out a huge breath and walked over to welcome Ashley back.

In a teary voice, Mr. Miller said, "Oh, my daughter. You have no idea what happened during the time you left."

Mrs. Miller added, "Yes, honey. We even called the police. Oh, shoot! The police!" She rushed over for her cell phone, but it was too late. Sirens rang down the street, stopping in front of the house.

Ashley's parents sprinted downstairs to address the police, leaving Sophie, Lyla, Katie, and Ashley to talk.

"Girl. What happened?" Katie, after calming down, spoke in a pissed tone that largely varied from her worried one before. "You scared the hell out of us."

Ashley defensively responded, "Why? I can't just go out for a walk? It's my birthday, and I can't even do that?"

"What do you mean? *You* invited all of us over and then just left. Without a word. I know it's your birthday, but that doesn't mean you can leave us all here."

"*I* didn't even want this. I didn't want any of this. I never asked for our entire grade to show up. So excuse me if I want some alone time."

"What do you mean? Your parents did all this for you, and you say you didn't want it?

Both Katie and Ashley seemed to be on the verge of bursting, so Sophie interceded. "Hey, guys? Should we return to the living room? Everyone is probably wondering what's happening right now." *Shit. I shouldn't have said that.*

Katie and Ashley whipped their heads around, giving Sophie a death glare. "You go handle it then!" both of them shouted. Terrified, Sophie took Lyla by the hand and left the room.

"What was that?" muttered Lyla.

"I shouldn't have said that."

"No, no. Not that. What does Ashley mean she didn't want this party? How could she not want this party?"

"I think I know. Did you see how much her parents decorated this place even though Ashley explicitly told them she didn't want it?"

"I know. But, still. She should know how lucky she is."

Sophie sighed, "She really should."

Returning to the living room, they saw nearly everyone had left. Apparently, Ashley's parents had called everyone else's parents to pick them up. Just like that, the party was over.

Sophie suddenly whipped around. "Lyla, does that mean they called my parents?"

"Yeah. Why do you ask?"

"I didn't tell them I would come."

"You didn't? I thought you asked for permission at home."

"Right. So, I might have lied to you earlier. Well, it was kind of a lie. I was planning to tell them. But then they weren't home. I had planned to call them next, but I was mad at my mother for not keeping her promise to be home."

"So you just came? Oh, Sophie. You better pray that they don't kill you."

"Haha. Very funny." Internally, Sophie was a mess with worry. This event was the first time that she had snuck out. And look how it ended up.

"Oh shoot, my parents are calling." In an apologetic tone, Lyla said, "Sorry to leave you, but I have to go."

"Wait!" But Lyla had already bounded off, leaving Sophie to face her parents alone. *Oh no. Please don't leave me to be the only one!* Turning to stare at her desolate surroundings, Sophie suddenly felt a wave of embarrassment and sadness that her parents were the last ones to arrive.

Fifteen minutes passed, but they still hadn't shown up. *Where are they? Did Ashley's parents not call them?*

Just as Sophie thought she could call an Uber and was off the hook, a car honked outside. She recognized that sound.

She slowly approached her parents' car, her feet trailing on the ground. Sophie had seen this scene in the movies before and braced herself for a car ride filled with berating.

"Hi, Mom. Hi, Dad." Sophie tried to see their faces through the rearview window to no avail.

Mrs. Zhou replied, "What were you thinking? How could you do this without talking to us first?"

Immediately, Mr. Zhou added, "Sophie. You know you can't just go places without our permission, right? We taught you that. You of all people should know better"

"I know. I'm sorry. I will never, ever do this again. I promise you."

Mr. Zhou exhaled. "I wish you would talk to us. Do you know how much I work to give you the best life possible? Why did you have to sneak out?"

Because you guys weren't home. "Mom, Dad. I'm really, really sorry. I swear in my life I will never sneak out again. I swear."

"Fine. Let's just forget this ever happened." With that, Mrs. Zhou ended the conversation, and the car ride commenced in silence.

Home. At last. Having felt like she was about to suffocate in the car, the sight of her house had never been so appreciated. Apologizing again and saying a quick goodnight, Sophie ran back to her room and quietly shut the door behind her.

For thirty minutes, Sophie read her book to calm down. It worked. As she let herself fall into the story, she finally released the tense breath that had been stuck in her chest. *Today was truly something else. My first taste of alcohol and sneaking out. Wow.*

Before sleeping, she propped open her computer. *Just in case.*

four
Anya

ANYA WOKE up and immediately realized that the night before, she had impulsively sent Sophie all the details about what had happened in the past week. *Did I tell her too much? Especially for someone whom I've never met in person? Oh well. It's better this way. She lives in California, and I live all the way in Shanghai. She can't actually hold this information against me.*

Full of adrenaline, Anya ran around her room, trying to calm herself down but failing. Not having school didn't help either because she had even more time to panic about what she had just done. *Should I check my computer? It should be her night time right now, so she probably saw it a little while ago.*

"Anya! Are you up yet? It's already almost 12 pm!" Mrs. Chen's voice rang down the entire hallway, and Anya could hear her impending footsteps.

"I'm up! Don't come in; my room's really messy!"

"Well, clean it up right now and come out! You have an appointment with Sunny!"

"Got it! Will be out in ten minutes!"

Anya smiled. At first, she had begged her parents not to bring her to a therapist. They had been adamant, insisting they could not have her turn out like Camelia. In an act of retribution, Anya hadn't talked to her parents for days. But, when she met Sunny, her therapist, she had fallen in love with the meetings. In those one-hour periods, she could vent about everything and never fear judgment. Instead, Sunny always simply listened and passed Anya tissues when she cried. Now, Anya considered them best friends, even though they had only known one another for a little bit over a month.

After getting ready, Anya went to her computer to respond to Sophie. However, before reaching her table, Mrs. Chen yelled, "Hurry up!" *It's okay. I'll respond to Sophie later.*

"Coming!" Anya yelled back.

On the car ride over, Mrs. Chen barely said a word to show the anger that she still held about Anya skipping class. Thus, Anya stared outside the car's window, mindlessly taking in the view as they made their way through the traffic. Her eyes had grown used to driving past these buildings and street vendors for over the past ten years, so when she saw that her favorite potsticker place had shut down, she audibly gasped.

Mrs. Chen whipped around. "What are you making that sound for?"

"Lucky Breakfast closed down!" Anya hadn't gone to this restaurant for a month due to all the chaos that had occurred. However, she had no idea that her favorite restaurant would suddenly close.

"Why are you so surprised? We were always the only customers." Anya cringed at her mother's stoic voice.

"But how could people not love it? They had the best potstickers ever."

"Ay, Anya, look around you. Compared to the new buildings around this restaurant, can't you see that it lacked renovation for a long time?"

Anya didn't know what to say, so she stayed quiet. Thinking about her mother's words, she began to examine her surroundings. *So much has changed.* Because she had lived in the same city for her entire life, she had never seen how it had slowly but surely developed. She wanted to grasp onto her past, to return to the little vendors lining the streets instead of the modern skyscrapers that now took their place, but she couldn't anymore.

"Good afternoon, Anya and Mrs. Chen!" Sunny walked up to greet them.

"Good afternoon, Sunny!" Anya, out of habit, sank down on the leather couch.

Mrs. Chen sighed at Anya's action but didn't say anything. "Thank you so much, Sunny. Please be patient with her; she's quite a handful."

Sunny chuckled, "It's completely fine, Mrs. Chen. I am her therapist, after all. We've also grown quite close."

Mrs. Chen replied, "That's good to hear; I thought she would also be rebellious here. You can never trust her."

"Mom!" exclaimed Anya.

Mrs. Chen stuck her tongue and took a look at her watch, "I need to run to the hospital, so I'll see you guys later, then."

Anya breathed a sigh of relief. *Now I can actually talk to Sunny.*

After Mrs. Chen shut the door behind her, Sunny turned to Anya and said, "Is it just me, or does Mrs. Chen seem upset at you today?"

"Don't even get me started. She's been pissed at me from yesterday morning to today."

"What happened?"

Anya hadn't seen Sunny since a week ago, so she had yet to update her on the major event. "Well, it all started with a letter..."

Without interruption, Anya told her story. Sunny would be the second person she ever told about this event.

Finally, after twenty minutes, she finished. For a while, Sunny sat in thoughtful silence. Then, she asked, "So you're sure that the person who wrote to you was your sister?"

Anya responded, "I recognized her signature, and she addressed me in the first line as 'Sponge,' which was a joke we had since elementary school. So I knew immediately that it was her."

"And she just told you where she was? Nothing else?"

"Well, she also told me happy birthday. But besides that, nothing else."

Sunny thought for a moment. "I wonder why she only wrote this letter to you and not your parents. I know that she had a tough relationship with them, but still. Why give her address to you?"

Anya exclaimed, "That's what I thought at the time, too! If she had just wished me happy birthday, I would have been surprised but would have just dropped the subject. But to give me her address? I'm not too sure anymore."

"Have you written a letter back?"

"Yes. I wrote a letter right away. But she still hasn't responded."

"I see. And you keep searching downtown because she had a lot of friends who graduated and live there. Hmm." As Sunny paused, Anya nervously tapped her feet.

"The thing is that when Camelia had first left, I hadn't thought too much of it. I missed her, but I thought that her departure was justified. She deserved to leave to pursue her dreams. But then, when she told me her address, without any other information, I had grown nervous. Previously, when she had written to me, she always used a random location. But this time, she had explicitly told me where she was. I thought that had to mean something."

Sunny nodded. "I can see where you're coming from. That is quite strange, indeed. Have you had any luck with the people you visited?"

Anya shook her head. "Almost everyone has turned me away. Expect one person. Her old best friend from high school."

"Tell me more about this person."

Suddenly, just as Anya was about to open her mouth to answer, Mr. Chen's voice rang outside the room. "Hi, Anya and Sunny. Are you guys almost done?"

Shit. Anya wanted to continue discussing the event with Sunny more than anything, but she also didn't want her father to find out.

"Sorry, Sunny. I have to go."

"Okay. But make sure you don't get yourself in trouble. Maybe slow down on visiting all these houses. Wait a while longer for Camelia to respond. And we can continue this conversation next week."

Anya knew that the chances of her sister responding before next week were rather low, as these letters seemed to take forever to reach her. Still, Anya agreed with Sunny and said goodbye.

Seeing her Dad's smile, Anya desperately wanted to tell him everything she had just told Sunny, but she knew she couldn't. She couldn't risk it, not when he could potentially reveal it to her mother and ruin the entire plan. So, even though all Anya could think about on the car ride home was Camelia, she kept a stoic face and carried on like any other day.

As soon as Anya arrived home and grabbed a goldfish snack, she ran upstairs and into her bedroom. *I have to see if Sophie responded.* Opening her laptop, Anya internally celebrated when she saw that Sophie had responded. Secretly, she had feared that Sophie would think of her as weird and stop texting her. After all, they had only briefly talked about Camelia and kept most of their conversations to lamenting about their schoolwork or parents.

The text, which Sophie had written in multiple messages, read:

"What! There's no way! That's a good thing, right? Wait. I'm not sure. That seems off. Something's off. But you're so brave for trying to find her. I applaud you. You're forgiven for not responding for A WEEK. Is there anything you need me to do? Maybe research?"

Anya chuckled. She had forgotten how much fun she had talking with Sophie in all the chaos. There was just something about how she could tell Sophie about the parts of her life that she couldn't talk about with her other friends. *Maybe it's because she lives in an entirely different country so there's no "liability." Or is it because we truly click?*

Anya responded, "Haha, I'm not brave, but thank you. I hope that something comes out of this. My mother is really upset. If you don't hear from me next time, she has probably bitten my head off."

Anya knew that Sophie hadn't woken up yet, so she shut her computer and called Odyssey to hang out and, most of all, apologize.

Odyssey picked up. "What do you want? I'm quite busy right now."

Part of Anya wanted to just not even bother consoling Odyssey, but the better part of her made her reply, "Hi, Odyssey. I'm sorry I acted like that yesterday. I had just gotten into a major argument with my mother, which put me in a bad mood."

Odyssey sighed. "Fine. I understand. Your mother can be quite a handful at times."

Anya cringed at Odyssey's blatant criticism of her mother, but she played it off cheerfully. "I know, right? So, are you available to meet up sometime? Maybe with Isabel as well? We can go to the new boba shop that went viral on Little Red Book."

"Oh my god. Yes! We need to go there. I'll text Isabel right away. Let's meet up in thirty minutes at your house."

"Sounds great! See you then!" Anya let out a breath of relief. Being friends with Odyssey and Isabel was amazing but tiring at the same time. Recently, it has been on the more tiring end of the spectrum.

As Anya hung up her phone, Mrs. Chen walked in without knocking.

"Anya. You are not hanging out with your friends after skipping your classes. I will not permit this."

"Mom, were you secretly listening to my conversation?" Anya, hurt that her mother would purposely eavesdrop on her conversation, wanted to scream but held herself back.

"Yes, I was. So what? I'm your mother. I can do that."

"Mom. You can't just spy on me."

"Watch your language! Do you want to be grounded for even longer?"

"Since when was I grounded?"

"Since I called you yesterday! Are you stupid?"

Feeling tears emerging into her eyes again, Anya grabbed her computer and ran out of the room.

Mrs. Chen yelled, "What are you taking your computer for? Don't you dare go out!"

Anya yelled back, "I'm taking it for homework!"

Reaching a safe distance from her mother, she texted to Odyssey and Isabel, "Can't go. Grounded."

Isabel responded, "Oh no! What did you do?"

Right. I haven't told either of them why I missed class. Shit. "You know. My mom. She happened." Not wanting to tell them anything further, Anya shut her phone off. Soon, she found herself in her safe spot: Camelia's bedroom. Nobody had lived in the room for a month, but nobody had the heart to clear it out.

Anya loved every aspect of the room, from the light coming in from the open ceiling to the carpeting, making it the perfect spot to sit down for hours on end. The best part was that Mrs. Chen never entered the room; it seemed like she purposely avoided even being near it.

Snuggling against Camelia's Costco bear that Anya had bought her for her seventeenth birthday, she opened her computer.

Hm. Research? Should I? Inspired by Sophie's text, Anya decided it was time for her to do some digging.

five

Sophie

IN THE MORNING, instead of groaning at the sound of the neighborly finch waking her up, Sophie jumped out of bed and threw open her windows. Saturday had at last come, and she couldn't be more grateful. She already particularly enjoyed the weekends, but combining a *Saturday* morning with knowledge of Anya's reply made this day even better.

I should see what Anya has said. Opening her laptop, Sophie was immediately hooked.

Instead of her short texts, Anya had written an entire paragraph.

She read it out loud, softly so as not to be heard.

"I have so much to tell you. After reading your text, I started researching more about Camelia's location. And guess what I found out. She's in Costa Rica! Which, I know, is far away. But that also probably means she's carrying out her dreams. Ah, I'm so proud of her. Based on her letter, she's on the island of Tortuguero, so I assume she's participating in conservation efforts. It's almost summer, so I would love to go. The only problem is that the flight is twenty-three hours, and I know my parents would flip out if I asked them to go with me. What should I do? Should I ask Camelia to meet up somewhere closer? What if she moves to another part of Costa Rica before I go to Tortuguero? Please help!"

Sophie tapped her feet, unsure about how to respond. No matter how much she thought about the situation, it seemed off. *Why would Camelia tell Anya her location if she knew that the travel time was nearly an entire day? Surely she knew that Anya can't simply ditch her life behind to travel there? Did she do this for secrecy? Or did she just want Anya to be assured that she's doing okay? No, if that was the case, then she would have elaborated further on her career there. For now, I should just respond to Anya so that she doesn't freak out and do something impetuous.*

As Sophie's finger nearly hit send on her reply, she came up with a better idea. *What if we called? We've been texting for months but still haven't seen each other's faces. Plus, I think it's better if we discuss this topic over call and not just text. We'll never reach a solution solely by texting.*

Sophie deleted her previous message, replacing it with a new one. "Hey, Anya. I know this might sound crazy, but what if we met over Zoom? I think it would work better. It's totally fine if you don't want to."

Almost immediately, a text bubble in reply started forming. *Did I go too far?*

Anya's text completely contradicted Sophie's worries. "Wait. That's such a good idea! Why did I never think of that?"

Sophie smiled. "Haha, me too! I just thought of it now."

"Oh, my goodness. And that means we finally get to meet! Well, sort of."

"I mean, I guess we can count calling over Zoom as a meeting? When are you available?"

"I'm so excited! Ah, shoot. I can't call right now though. My mother is pissed at me, and she can definitely hear me if I start talking to you. And then I'll be screwed."

"Damn. I wish you the best of luck!!!" Sophie almost sighed in relief. Although she wanted to meet Anya, she also greatly appreciated having a little bit of time to think over what she would say.

Walking out of her room to grab some breakfast, she expected both of her parents to be at work, as they constantly worked even on weekends. So, when she saw them both sitting at the kitchen island, Sophie jumped back in surprise. *What are they doing here? Do they want me to do something? Are they still upset about yesterday? Shit. I'm screwed.*

Nervously, Sophie asked, "Good morning, Mom and Dad. What are you guys doing here? I thought you would be off to work already?"

Mrs. Zhou sternly responded, "What? Did you want us gone so that you could sneak out again?"

Sophie cringed. "No. No. I would never do that again. I promise."

Mr. Zhou responded, "You better. I already have enough to worry about at work, and your mother too. Both of us know that you would never do that. You're Sophie, after all. Our perfect daughter."

Sophie, without thinking, responded, "Why do you think I'm perfect?"

Mr. Zhou, shocked that his daughter would ask such a question, responded, "Why, you're Sophie. You've never acted up since birth. Don't tell me you're going to start acting up now. You're already fifteen years old for goodness sake."

Sophie nervously chuckled and said, "Right. I will forever be your perfect daughter." She made sure to keep her tone sincere, knowing that her father was completely capable of blowing up if she sounded sarcastic.

As Sophie sat down to eat with her parents, she couldn't stow away the part of herself that wanted to rebel and act out simply to prove that she *wasn't* perfect. But she couldn't do that to them, not after they had already lost one of their daughters. So, plastering on a smile, Sophie put her chocolate croissant in the microwave, apprehensively staring at her parents' facial expressions. However, before the one-minute timer of the microwave even stopped, both her parents stood up.

Mr. Zhou spoke up first. "Okay, good chat. I need to go now, though. You know. Extra work stuff."

Of course. What did I expect? "No worries! I'll see you in the afternoon?"

Mr. Zhou said, "Don't wait for me. I'll be back sometime later."

Sophie silently nodded. She already had a routine on Saturdays: go horseback riding and then spend the day with Potato. *Speaking of which, I should go wake him up.* "Alright, then. See you later then. Mom, we should leave for horseback riding soon."

Mrs. Zhou responded, "Let's go in thirty minutes. I have to respond to an email from a client first."

"Sounds good."

Reaching the "sunroom," the brightest room in the entire house, Sophie found Potato asleep with his feet sprawled in the air. *He's been sleeping like this for six years.* Not wanting to disturb Potato from his peaceful slumber, Sophie quietly filled up his food bowl and tiptoed out of the room.

Already in her horseback riding outfit, Sophie spent a while thinking about what she would talk about with Anya. *Should I research more about Tortuguero?*

Pulling out her phone, Sophie searched for this name. *Huh. I mean, it looks beautiful with all its river canals and trees. And it only has 1500 residents! It's definitely very different from Shanghai.* Sophie could see the appeal of the village, but she also couldn't wrap her head around how Camelia would suddenly go from the bustling city life of Shanghai to the placid nature of Tortuguero. *I wonder if she's been there all of these months.*

"Sophie! Let's go!" Mrs. Zhou's voice echoed from outside the house.

"Coming!" *I'll find out more about this later with Anya.*

For now, Sophie looked forward to horseback riding. Even just two days from not visiting the barn seemed too long, and she missed her horse, Cassie.

Arriving at the barn, Sophie took a deep breath. The barn, located in the middle of a valley and surrounded by mountains, always offered her a serenity that she never felt anywhere else. Even when nobody was riding, there were the constant sounds of birds chirping and horses snorting. Even the grass seemed to be alive, especially when it reached spring. Having come to this barn since she arrived in the United States at just under eight years old, Sophie had fallen in love with it, and it had become her true home.

She took a deep breath and walked down the cobblestone path to her horse's stable. Her mother never followed her inside, always claiming that the barn would "stink up her new clothes." Sophie never understood her logic; to her, the barn simply smelled of a mixture of spring.

Reaching Cassie's stall, Sophie proceeded with her normal routine: scrub off Cassie's pelt, comb out her hair, and put on the saddle and bridle. This procedure was already ingrained in her head, but she never found it boring. This was something that she and Mackenzie always had in common, which was that they loved animals. *Or else we would never have gotten Potato. Mom and Dad would certainly have never agreed to it without our persistence.* Sophie smiled at the memory as she couldn't stop Cassie and let the wind blow into her face.

Too soon, the ride was over. After untacking Cassie and feeding her molasses treats, Sophie took one last wistful glance at the barn and walked back up to the car. *I wish I could stay forever. It's okay though. I'll be back tomorrow.*

As she approached the car, Sophie expected to see her mother in the car, but she wasn't there. *Where is she? She's usually always in a rush.* As Sophie made her way to the other side of the car, she found her mother behind a tree talking to someone on the phone. Seeing that her mother hadn't yet seen her and not wanting to disturb her call, Sophie awkwardly waited for her to finish.

Just expecting it to be a call about work, Sophie stared off into the distance and let her mother's words blur into the background. However, when she heard the word "Mackenzie" come out of her mother's mouth, Sophie audibly gasped.

Mrs. Zhou whipped her head around, and seeing Sophie, immediately hung up. "Sophie. What are you doing back already? You didn't even make a sound."

"Mom. Why did you say Mackenzie's name? Who were you talking to?"

"I was simply talking with a friend about her. Why do you ask?"

Sophie opened her mouth to ask why she sounded so nervous but decided not to poke deeper if her mother truly didn't want to say anything. "Oh, nothing. Sorry for asking."

"It's okay. I'm sure you miss her. We are all still letting her go."

"Right. We are." *But why do you sound so nervous? What are you hiding?*

Mrs. Zhou cut off Sophie's thought by saying, "Don't forget. You need to call your grandparents soon. They miss you."

"Yes, Mom. I'll call them either tonight or tomorrow morning. Don't worry."

"Good, good. Let's go home now."

Knowing that her mother would not open up again about the phone call no matter how much she asked, Sophie decided to slip the event to the back of her head. *I'll try to find out more later.*

After a quick shower and changing into her comfortable sweatpants and T-shirt, Sophie sat down to finish some homework. For an agonizing five hours, she worked on the same English assignment, only intermittently halted by lunch and playing with Potato. The entire time, Sophie waited for Anya's reply. *I wonder how upset her mother is with her. At least my parents aren't that angry at me. They were surprisingly okay with everything. Huh.*

As the clock struck five o'clock pm, Sophie's laptop buzzed.

Anya had replied. "Sorry! I just woke up, and I'm so groggy because I barely got any sleep last night. Speaking of last night, sorry that I didn't have a chance to get back to them. My mother was watching my every move. But they sleep in on Sunday mornings, so I'm good to call now. Are you available?"

Pushing aside her English worksheets, Sophie quickly responded, "Yes. I have around an hour before my parents call me to dinner. Let's call Zoom now." Both on edge and excited, Sophie opened up the call.

six

Anya

"Hi!" Anya first noticed Sophie's frizzy hair, remembering how her friends mocked anyone with slightly messy hair. Despite the instinct being instilled in her that she should only have straight hair, Anya couldn't help but think that this hairstyle actually suited Sophie's rounder face. It made her look natural and almost kind.

"Omg, hi! I can't believe we're finally meeting!" Sophie's genuine enthusiasm shone through, which made Anya smile. *Odyssey and Isabel would never act this way in front of someone they've never met. They would be way too embarrassed.* Anya didn't mind it though. *Finally, someone who I might be able to stand being around.*

Anya enthusiastically replied, "I know, right? We've been texting each other for *months*, but we've only just met. I have so many questions I want to ask."

"Right? I feel like I know you from all our texts, but I don't truly know you. For some reason, I expected you to look a lot more..." Sophie's voice cut off.

"A lot more what?" Anya cocked her head.

"I don't know. I just thought that with all your sister stuff... you would be sadder looking? If that makes sense. Sorry, I didn't mean to say anything mean. It's just that I feel like losing a sister is so…"

"No, no. I get it. To be honest, I thought that you would appear sadder as well. I think it might be that we've only shared our sorrowful stories with one another." *Huh. We thought the same thing even though we live across the world from each other.*

Sophie's face looked flushed. After a quiet pause, Sophie responded, "Sorry to bring this conversation off track. Let's go back to what we called for. We should focus on finding your sister. That's if you still want to, of course."

Anya sighed before responding. "Yes, we should try to find her. I've been going around asking her old friends, but they haven't received anything from her."

"Nothing at all?"

Anya hesitated for a moment. "Well, there was this one girl. She was Camelia's best friend. She was the only person who didn't immediately wave me away. I think that when Camelia left, they stayed in contact for a while."

"Did she say anything helpful?"

"She told me a little bit about Camelia's plan." *Thinking back on it, I'm her sister; I should have known more than her. But I don't.* "All I know from this friend is that Camelia's with her boyfriend."

"She has a boyfriend?!"

"Yes. Well, nobody was supposed to know. My parents don't even know. I only found out because I caught Camelia texting him late at night when I snuck into her room for snacks. And only then did she explain it to me. But she made me swear that I would never tell anybody. So I've kept it hidden until now."

Sophie nodded.

"Her boyfriend is still on social media; his name is Nathan. He's pretty recognizable: curly brown hair and round-shaped glasses that don't truly suit his face. Wait. Here's his WeChat." Anya cringed at seeing his face, partially blaming him for Camelia's disappearance. *Why did he have to convince her to leave behind everything she knew?*

"How do you even have his WeChat?" Sophie leaned closer to the laptop.

"So... I might have forced Camelia to give me his contact. I said it was for emergency purposes. In case I couldn't reach her." *I just wanted to see who she was dating by scrolling through his post page. Who knew that I would actually one day not be able to reach her?* "Anyways, I haven't reached out to him in a while. I don't think he likes me very much."

"How do you know that?"

Anya scoffed. "How do I know that? He's disliked me from the very beginning. I think he associates me with my parents. Like I'm harming my *own* sister or something. Which is completely untrue. I couldn't be more different from my parents." Anya had an inkling that her perception of how Nathan saw her was only fueled by her hatred for him, but she squashed it before it could develop into a full thought.

"I mean, at least that means he only wanted the best for Camelia, right? Or else he wouldn't have cared so much about her personal life. He was probably trying to protect her."

Anya could feel her blood boiling, so she took a deep breath. *It's not Sophie's fault. Don't get angry at her right now. Damn it.* "Well, he sure did a great job of protecting Camelia. She's forever gone from me now." *Oof. Was that too harsh to say? Why do I always lash out so much?*

Anya looked at Sophie's facial expression, expecting her to have the identical look as Odyssey the other day. However, Sophie remained stoic, and oddly even more excited than before. Sophie responded, "Wait. I have an uncle. He works in Shanghai as well. He's really adept with technology and works in IT, so he might be able to link Nathan to your sister. I think he'll be able to find their location as well."

Anya sat straighter in her chair. "Really? Wait, where does he work? I might know the place."

"He works at Yitu. It's an AI company. He specializes in software development, but I'm sure he also has proficient knowledge of other technologies. I'll give him a call today."

"You're the best. Thank you so much. This way, we'll know where Camelia is for sure." Anya tapped her fingers together excitedly. *This is a good start.*

"Of course, I'm happy to help."

Anya, realizing that she hadn't given Sophie anything yet, inquired, "You're doing so much for me. Is there anything I can do for you?"

Sophie paused. "No. I think that helping you is like helping myself if that makes sense. I've always harbored regret about Mackenzie. I should've been there for her, but I wasn't. I wasn't even truly aware of anything." Sophie's voice cracked.

"I'm sorry."

"No, no. Don't be sorry. Just think of me helping you as a way to alleviate some of that regret. So we're even. We don't owe each other anything."

"Alright. Nevertheless, thank you. You're the only person, besides my therapist, who has heard me talk extensively about Camelia. It feels like we've known each other for so long already." *I haven't even told my parents anything yet.*

Sophie sighed. "Me too. I haven't talked to anyone about Mackenzie. Well, I tried. And failed miserably. Anyhow, it's remarkable how we suddenly found each other online and then connected about our sisters."

"It really is." *How did that even happen? Must be really good luck.*

Sophie glanced toward her door, "I think my father is finally home. We're going to eat dinner now. Talk to you later?"

"Talk to you later." Anya waved goodbye and hung up. As she leaned against her cushiony headrest, a wave of exhaustion suddenly washed over her. *If I feel like absolute chaos all the time, I wonder how Sophie feels. At least I have a chance. Her sister is dead. Gone. How does she even manage to get up from bed each morning? If Camelia were dead...* Anya shuddered.

Mrs. Chen's voice echoed, "Anya! It's time to go to math class!" For once, Anya didn't mind her mother's voice, as it helped drag her out of the spiraling chain of thought. *I need to think more positively.* Shuddering once again, she left her room.

Anya stood outside Mr. Yen's office, located in a high-rise building facing the Huangpu River. *What if I just fled? Run into the elevator?* Every inch of Anya's body yearned to take a few steps away from the dreaded class. But, knowing that she did not have any room to provoke her mother, she begrudgingly stepped inside.

Mr. Yen looked up. "Hi, Anya. Did you do your homework this time?"

Wow. The first thing he asks. Great. "Yes, Mr. Yen. I did my homework."

"Really? That's surprising. I see you're finally trying to be different from your sister. You're finally growing up."

Anya recoiled. *I want to snap his snobby head off. He's lucky my mother is like a hound and would kill me if I even slightly stepped one foot out of line during class.* "Can we not talk about her? Let's just go over the homework."

"Right. Let's see what we should work on in this class. Pre-calculus questions, I'm assuming?" His condescending tone usually made Anya seethe, but she held her temper today.

"Yes. I have a test coming up on Tuesday, which I need to prepare for." Anya tried to make her voice sound angelic and peaceful. *Someday, I'll take revenge for me and Camelia. But not today. I need to stay on my mother's good side.*

The class started. For the next three hours, Mr. Yen breathed down Anya's neck, watching her every stroke of the pen. Occasionally, when Anya's head started throbbing, she stared at the Huangpu River, wishing that the carrier ships could stow her away from this tortuous place. *Maybe even bring me to Camelia.*

Despite believing that the class would never end, it did. Anya curtly said goodbye, releasing the burden of the class. *How could such a man work in such a beautiful office?* As she closed the door behind her, she longingly stared at the glistening stars floating atop the river. *He doesn't deserve this view. Not after how he berated Camelia during each and every lesson that she used to come here for.*

Reaching the building's lobby, Anya looked around yet couldn't find her mother anywhere. *She's usually never late. Oh well.*

At first, Anya didn't mind. After all, the lobby was truly one of a kind: a cascading waterfall, marble flooring and tabletops, and white, plush couches. Sitting down on one of the couches, she scrolled on her phone for a while. Twenty minutes passed, then thirty minutes.

Okay, maybe I should call my mother. But when Anya called her mother repeatedly, she didn't pick up. Although Anya didn't particularly mind staying in the lobby longer, she also wasn't used to her mother being late or not picking up her phone. *We're on bad terms, but I hope she's okay.* Anya sat up straighter on the couch, wondering what she should do.

I should probably call my father. It's the weekend. Unless he has golf, he should be free right now. Just as Anya's fingers prepared to press his phone number, she stopped herself.

Maybe the rest of the day's events would have played out entirely differently if she had just moved her finger one inch closer. But no. Perhaps stirred by Mr. Yen's comments or motivated by Sophie, Anya decided that she would use this time to find Camelia. So instead of calling her father, Anya called out for a taxi. Sitting in the car and headed for the other side of the city, Anya stared out the window as the familiar dipped into the unfamiliar. *Shit. I'm going to be in huge trouble after this. Oh well, it's the only time I have.*

seven

Sophie

AFTER WAKING up from her restless sleep tormented by dreams of her sister, Sophie woke up in a jolt. *I haven't had such a vivid dream of her in a long time. The memories must have been stirred from my conversation with Anya.* Although she had never seen her sister's corpse, her dream had painted a picture of Mackenzie lying on the sidewalk, arms sprawled to the sides. Sophie shuddered, hugging her blankets tighter to her chest. *Maybe it was for the best that my parents didn't show me her death. I don't know what I would have done.*

Sophie stayed in bed longer, letting her dream dissipate with the sunlight peeking into her room. *What if I just stayed in bed today? No, I have a job I need to complete. Talk to my uncle. Right, I told Anya that I would contact him.*

While brushing her teeth, Sophie suddenly noticed her dark eye circles. *How? I'm only fifteen years old. It's probably from all of the nights of restless sleep. Think of it, my sleep recently has really degraded.* Sophie tried to scrub her eyes with cold water but couldn't make them any lighter or less puffy. *What are my parents going to say when they see me? Shit. I don't have any makeup to cover it up either.*

Knowing that her mother always used makeup, Sophie decided to go take some from her ensuite. Gently nudging her own door open, Sophie crossed the long hallway and peered inside her parents' room. *It's empty. They're probably at work again. They sure have a lot of extra work this weekend; it's only 8:30 a.m. Better for me, I guess.* Reaching the restroom, Sophie rummaged through her mother's makeup box. *Mackenzie and I used to always play dress up with her makeup.* Sophie, dabbing some foundation under her eyes, smiled at the memory of her sister trying cherry lipstick for the first time.

Just as Sophie prepared to leave the room, a piece of yellow paper on her parents' bedside table caught her eye. *It's probably just one of Mom or Dad's work documents. I should probably just leave it. But...* Sophie thought back to her mother's behavior yesterday at the barn.

Hesitantly, Sophie grabbed the paper and flipped it over.

Andy Mao? Is he just a work person? Intrigued, Sophie read further until she suddenly stopped at the date: 2/7/24. *Wasn't that just a week after Mackenzie died? Who is this guy? Have my parents been meeting with him? Is this the guy that Mom was calling yesterday?*

Taking out her phone, Sophie jotted down his office address and his phone number. *I'll find him later. First, my uncle.* Sophie placed the paper back on the table exactly as she had found it, crouching down to eye level with the desk to ensure that it was at the exact angle as before. Satisfied, she left the room.

Returning back to her room and placing Potato on her lap, Sophie started scrolling through her phone contacts and finally found her uncle's. *Aha. I haven't talked to him in forever. How should I start the conversation?* Leaning back into her bed, Sophie thought about her last conversation with Uncle Wang. *He probably still remembers our last conversation. But then again, he wouldn't have had to face my screaming that time if he hadn't told me right after Mackenzie died that my parents can't be blamed for what happened. Like, how the hell did he even know? He's not even a part of our lives. Is it because he graduated from MIT that he believes he's all that?* Sophie sighed. *Now I have to suck up to him. Great. This is about to be the most awkward conversation ever.*

Hearing her uncle's voice through the phone, Sophie put on her sweetest tone.

"Hi, Uncle Wang! How are you? It's been so long since we last talked!"

"Sophie? That's you? Why are you calling me? Did something bad happen?" Her uncle's voice sounded genuinely concerned.

Sophie cringed. *He's probably still a little bit traumatized from the last time we met.* "No, no. Everything's great. Mom and Dad are doing great."

"Good, good. Is your mother still on those pills?"

"No, she stopped a while ago. At least, I think." *To be honest, I'm not even sure. They're gone most of the time.*

"That's good to hear. What about you? How are you doing?"

"I'm doing fine. School's fine. Friends are good. Life's moved on." *Yeah, right. Nobody in this family has moved on.* "What about you?"

"I'm doing better now, too. It was definitely a shock to this entire family to lose Mackenzie." Her uncle's voice turned quiet. "We all loved her."

How did you even love her? You barely visited her. You haven't even come to see me once after Mackenzie's death. Putting on a pleasant voice, Sophie responded, "We did. We'll forever miss her."

Her uncle cleared his throat before continuing. "So, what did you actually call me for? I know you didn't just call to check up on me. Not with your busy, high school schedule."

He's smart. "Okay, you saw right through me, although I actually missed you, believe it or not."

Her uncle chuckled. "I missed you too. But get to the point; I don't have all day."

"Alright. It all started three months ago, shortly after Mackenzie's death..." Sophie quickly summarized all the events that had occurred with Anya while her uncle quietly listened.

After Sophie finished her last word, Uncle Wang asked, "So, you want me to track this guy?"

"Yes. I know that it seems crazy and kind of creepy, but I really need you to do so." *Please, please say yes.*

Her uncle paused for a moment before saying, "Fine. But only because you said that it would make you feel better about Mackenzie. And I don't want you to be in danger. No crazy shenanigans with this information. Just relay it to Anya, nothing further. Understand?"

What does he think I'm going to do with this information? Fly across the world?

"Of course not, Uncle Wang. I won't do anything that makes you worry about me."

"Good. Or else your mother..." He didn't have to say anything further for Sophie to understand.

"I understand. Okay, I won't take up more of your time."

Expecting her uncle to quickly say goodbye, Sophie was startled when he said, "Wait. Before you go, I wanted to apologize for not visiting you guys all these months. It's been quite difficult, especially when I see my own little sister losing all her spirit. I know that it was irresponsible of me, and I probably hurt your feelings. But I just wanted you to know that I do care. Anyhow, I'm truly sorry."

Damn. Did I judge him too early? Sophie thought back to how she had treated him the last time they met, cringing at how she had thrown accusations at him for not caring at all about her family. "I'm sorry too. I shouldn't have said all those words to you last time. I was in a lot of shock and spewed basically everything out. Even if I didn't mean it."

Her uncle slightly smiled and nodded reassuringly. "It's okay. You were just a child, and I was a grown adult. I should have cared more. I'll start visiting you guys more often." He paused, rubbing his chin before talking again. "In fact, I was planning with your aunt about flying to visit you guys in LA in a couple of weeks."

What? This is huge. Sophie exclaimed, "Really? I had absolutely no idea. You best not be lying."

Her uncle shook his head. "Nope, you can ask your aunt if you would like."

"Ah, so it is true. Well then, I'll hold you to it, and I'll start preparing your favorite watermelon to snack."

Her uncle laughed. "You still haven't forgotten about what I told you when you were a baby."

"How could I? You told me over and over again that I should open up a watermelon farm just so that you would have endless watermelons to eat." Sophie relished that memory for a while, remembering how her uncle would help her scrape up every piece of watermelon.

Her uncle interrupted this memory. "Hey. By chance, do you know who your parents have been visiting?"

Hesitantly, Sophie responded, "What do you mean?"

"Well, I'm sure it's nothing. But occasionally, when I called your mother, I heard your father's voice as well as another man's. And when I asked her, she always told me that it was nothing."

Could this man be the Andy guy? "Did she not even tell you what his name was?"

"No. That's what made me curious. Your mother usually tells me everything."

Sophie muttered under her breath, "I think I might have an idea."

"What did you say? Speak up."

I probably shouldn't tell him yet. I don't want to cause any misunderstandings. "Oh, nothing. Mom and Dad have seemed quite normal recently." *I'll tell you more after I figure out who this Andy guy is.*

"Maybe I'm just overreacting. It's probably nothing if you haven't even noticed it. I'm probably still a bit paranoid." Her uncle's voice sounded relieved.

Sophie felt a little sorry for him. *He probably worries a lot for us but doesn't know how to help us.* "Yeah, I wouldn't worry about it. Anyhow, thank you so much for doing this."

Her uncle replied, "No problem. I'll get it back to you tomorrow. In two days at the most."

Sophie said goodbye and hung up the phone. For the first time in a while, it felt like the puzzle pieces were coming together, like she wasn't completely useless, and her family cared about each other. The feeling, soft yet refreshing, gave Sophie a source of energy that she hadn't had since her sister's death. *Maybe it'll all be okay.*

Yet, she couldn't shake off the underlying feeling that her parents were hiding something important. *Should I tell Anya about it? I mean, she told me everything. So, why shouldn't I tell her?*

Sophie typed up the message, hovering her fingers over the send button. *But what if telling her takes away from her attention to finding Camelia? What if she misses the chance to find her sister because she's too busy helping me? When I don't even know what I saw is anything of significance?* Sighing, Sophie shut her computer. *I'll just have to do it myself. But how?*

eight
Anya

NOW THAT ANYA was standing outside of Olivia's house, she just realized what she had done. Her head started spinning. *There's no way. Did I just go all the way to the other side of Shanghai? To Pudong from Puxi?* She could already imagine her mother sprinting into Mr. Yen's office and biting everyone's heads off for letting Anya out of their sights. *I don't even want to imagine how upset she will be with me. But it's too late. I'm already here. I need to see what Camelia's best friend knows.*

Anya gulped and knocked on the door. "Hello? Is anyone home?" *Shit. I don't even know if Olivia is here. What if she's at her part-time job right now? No. It's pretty late. She should be home by now. Please.*

"Hello? Who's there?" A man's voice made Anya jump.

A man? I don't remember Olivia having a boyfriend. "Hi! It's Anya. I'm here to talk to Olivia. I'm a friend of hers."

Gruffly, the man responded, "I don't remember her saying anything about someone coming over. Are you sure you have the right address?"

Anya rechecked the address, having written it down on her phone. "Yes. I'm sure. I was here before as well. If you don't mind, could you first open the door, and then we can talk? It's quite difficult to talk with a door between us."

"Fine." The door swung open.

Anya, upon seeing the man's face, took a step back. *What the hell?* In front of her stood an old man, perhaps in his seventies. He leaned on a wooden cane, and his rectangular glasses were nearly slipping off his nose. His face also scrunched upon seeing Anya, and both of them stood in an awkward silence.

The man was the first to speak. "You look young. Too young to be Olivia's friend." Pointing his cane right at Anya's chest, he demanded, "Who are you?"

I could ask the same thing. "Sorry. I'm not actually Olivia's friend."

"Ha. I knew it."

"I'm her best friend's sister. Do you happen to know Camelia?"

It was the old man's turn to step back in shock. "Camelia? Of course, I know her. That's who Olivia ever talks about. Camelia this and Camelia that. She's even gone crazy and left for Costa Rica to find her. That's why I'm here to look over the house. I'm her grandpa."

"WHAT? Are you serious?" Anya's face turned pale. *There is no way.*

"Of course, I'm serious. I'm the one who told her over and over again not to go. But she kept on insisting on the card. I can't really remember what she said. But she always brought back the card. That darn card. I should have burned it." The old man grimaced and looked down at the floor.

So she got the card as well? What the hell is going on? What should I do? Anya responded, "I got the card as well. That's actually why I'm here in the first place."

"Well, it's too late now. She's gone, and she isn't picking up my phone calls. It's only been a day, but I'm so worried, you know? She really hasn't gone anywhere that far before."

Anya nodded her head. "I understand why you're worried, but at least she's an adult now. And if she doesn't respond in a few days, we can figure out a plan together."

"Okay, okay. I'm still worried though. She's an adult, but she doesn't often act like one. She's still a kid to me."

That's true. She's only in college. "Don't worry. Here, I'll give you my phone number. We can keep each other updated. I promise we'll contrive a plan if she doesn't call back in two days." *What plan though? The only possible solution that I can think of is...* Anya didn't even dare breathe it.

"Thank you, young lady. Taking a deep breath, the old man said, "Oh, I'm so sorry. You've been standing at the door this entire time. Do you want to come in for a cup of daffodil tea?"

I would love to, but my mom would kill me. I'm probably already dead in her eyes. "Maybe next time. My mother expects me home soon, so I have to go now. I'll keep in touch though."

In a sad tone, the old man replied, "Okay. Let's hope that we don't have to come up with a plan."

Yes, let's hope that we don't have to ever come up with a plan.

Despite Anya's protests, the old man walked her all the way down to the car, seeing to it that she was in the car before he said goodbye. As he waved, she waved back, hoping he wouldn't have to worry much longer for his granddaughter.

As Anya got into the taxi, she tried to relax but couldn't help but think about Olivia. *I just saw her less than a week ago. Was that what she was trying to tell me back then before we got interrupted by my mother's call? That she got the letter? So now, she's gone to find Camelia? Should I do the same? Is Camelia trying to tell me something? Is she trying to get me to go? By myself?* Anya shook her head. *No. no. I'm going crazy. Today's events have just been too much.*

Pulling out her phone, Anya suddenly remembered her mother. *I'm so screwed.* As she checked her phone call history, though, she saw that nobody had contacted her. *Is my phone broken? There's no way.* Anya restarted her phone, but no new notifications popped up. *My phone should be blown up by now. What is going on? Did something happen?*

"Hi, driver. Could you please bring me to my destination faster? It's quite urgent."

As they sped across the bridge connecting the two sides of Shanghai, Anya couldn't stop herself from worrying. Not once in the past few years had her mother not contacted her every few hours, not even when they were on good terms. Perhaps it was because of Olivia's disappearance or any of the events that had happened in the past few days, but the usual quiet that Anya usually relished seemed suffocating as she gazed out the window.

Anya arrived home to an empty house. Frantically looking through all the rooms, Anya realized all the lights had been left on, but not a soul was to be found. *What the hell? Where are Mom and Dad? I should try calling Dad. Maybe he'll pick up.*

But when Anya dialed his number, it went straight to voicemail. At this point, Anya thought she had gone crazy. *Am I dreaming? Is this even possible?* Just as Anya was about to sink down on the kitchen floor, she found a pink sticky note on the fridge.

The cursory note read, "Your father is at Jiahui Hospital. He passed out. I'm going to be with him."

Upon reading these words, Anya stepped back in shock, ramming into the kitchen counter. *There's no way. I just saw him this morning. She's got to be joking. Is this some sick joke to get me back for being such a terrible daughter?*

Despite Anya not wanting to believe the message, before another ten seconds passed, she was already sprinting out the door and calling another taxi.

For the second time in a row, she found herself begging the driver to go faster even though she knew that it was nearly impossible in the traffic of Shanghai rush hour. *It's taking too long. At this point, I won't be at the hospital for another hour even though it's only a few miles away.*

Before she knew it, she found herself leaving the car in the middle of the street and rushing into the Metro. She had only gone on the Metro twice before, both times with her grandfather. Thus, she always relied on him to navigate the snakes of tunnels that each led to vastly different destinations.

As Anya stood at the entrance of the Metro, her thoughts jumbled amidst all the faces of people rushing to return home, and she could barely move despite numerous people yelling at her to stop blocking the path. *Okay, Anya. You're on your own now. Think.*

Anya remembered what her grandfather had told her before. "If you don't know what to do, ask the concierge located at each station." Quickly, Anya started looking around and, after a minute or two, found the concierge. *Thank goodness for Grandpa's tips. I need to hurry though. I've lost enough time as it is.*

After receiving a map of where she should go, Anya set off. The next twenty minutes passed in a blur as Anya counted down each station until the hospital. The entire time, she kept on checking her phone, but her mother still hadn't contacted her. *If Dad's actually sick, I don't know what I will do. What Mom will do. His father had a brain tumor... No. I can't think like that. Anyhow, I'm about to see him.* Anya had at last arrived at the hospital.

"Excuse me. You can't run in the hospital!" A nurse's sharp voice stopped Anya in her tracks.

"Hi. I'm sorry. Where's the front desk? Please, it's urgent." Anya tried to control her labored breathing to no avail.

The nurse's voice turned softer, and she put down her papers. "Here, just follow me."

"Okay."

After receiving directions from the front desk and saying a quick thanks to the nurse, Anya finally made her way to her father's room. Sliding the door open, Anya gasped.

Before, she had always thought that her father was impenetrable. He was the one in the family that never fell ill, the one that never complained about soreness. He was the one who cooked porridge for everyone else when they became sick, the one who massaged his wife's shoulders even after coming home late from work. But as he laid in the hospital bed with a pale blue gown on, he looked weak. Like all the energy that he had dedicated to others had finally been drained. Anya could barely even recognize him.

She looked at her mother, who clutched his hands and barely looked up when Anya came in.

In a shuddering voice, Anya asked, "Mom, what happened?"

"Oh, you're here? How long has it been?" She also seemed frail, not the usual assertive woman Anya knew.

"Well, it's already almost 9 pm."

"It's been that long?"

"Yes, Mom. What happened to Dad?" Anya's eyes fluttered between her mother and father, not knowing where to look when everything seemed so utterly wrong.

In a cracked voice, she responded, "He just passed out. It's my fault." She looked up, and Anya could see the tears forming in her eyes.

"What do you mean it's your fault?"

"We... We got into an argument in the car. And then when we got out of the car at the destination, he had only taken a few steps before suddenly dropping to the ground. I thought he was faking it at first. You know... being dramatic and all to make me feel upset. But when I shook him, he wouldn't get up." Her mother's tears started running fast now, and Anya hurried to hug her.

"No. I'm sure it's not your fault. And he'll wake up. He just needs some rest." *I hope I'm telling the truth. I've never seen either of my parents like this before.* As she held her mother in her arms, Anya realized something. *My parents aren't as strong as they seem to be. I've always thought of them as these unbreakable machines. How wrong I was.*

Wiping her tears away, her mother choked, "It is my fault. Your father is good at hiding his stress, so I always thought that he could take my harsher words. I always let him take care of me, never the other way around. And now look at what has happened."

"Mom. Dad's just like that. He likes taking care of people. To be honest, our entire family has taken more from him than given him anything. So it's not only your fault. Don't do that to yourself."

"Oh, my daughter."

Together, mother and daughter cried, comforted each other, and anxiously waited for the patient to wake up.

nine

Sophie

PLAYING with Potato in his room, Sophie was bored out of her mind. Her parents had said that they would return at the latest by two o'clock, but they were nowhere to be seen. Sophie didn't care though; her parents never actually returned home at the time they said they would. When they had first started doing it, she had freaked out and called her parents continuously to ask them when they would return home. But now, being at least the twentieth time they were late, Sophie could care less. *They'll probably be home at six or seven o'clock. Who knows? All I know is that I'm so bored. And Anya's sleeping, which means I can't talk to her. Hmm... should I check up on Lyla? I haven't really talked to her since Friday.*

Just as Sophie was about to pull out her phone, Lyla's text popped up, saying, "Sophie! Guess what I found out! Ashley and Katie had a huge argument and now they're spewing hate at each other left and right on Snapchat."

Sophie, having absolutely nothing else to do, decided to engage in this conversation even though she knew that it was just another one of the trio's dramas that would eventually lead to a heartfelt reconciliation that would echo throughout the entire school. *I've seen this scene play out way too often. It's just going to be another fight over a silly topic that results in the next day with them walking hand in hand. But, if Lyla's so interested in it, I might as well see what's happening as well.* Sophie texted back, "Really? Is this from the party on Friday night? If it is, they will probably make up soon."

Lyla immediately started texting back, "No. It's bigger than that. Apparently, Ashley doesn't want to associate with Katie and Dylan anymore. She says that everyone's fake. I'm not sure."

"Huh? Didn't Katie freak out over Ashley's disappearance?" *It certainly looked real to me.*

"I know, right? But I think Ashley wants to cut everyone off. I'm not sure what's happening with her, but she doesn't even want to talk to her parents anymore."

"Did something happen to her? Something she's not telling anyone about?" Sophie couldn't help but think that Ashley, the girl who always appeared to school with flawless outfits and hair, wouldn't simply cut everyone off that easily.

Lyla responded, "That's what I was thinking as well. But nobody can get through her. And Ashley's been making it really public that she's cutting everyone off. Really public. Just see Snap."

Sophie quickly checked her Snapchat and saw that Lyla wasn't joking. Ashley had posted dozens of private messages that said she was done with everything. In return, Katie and Dylan had commented, spewing lines of confusion and anger. It was an utter mess. "Do you think that Ashley is leaving next year? There's no way that she can stay in school at this rate."

"She is. Apparently, she's going to a boarding school on the East Coast."

Ah, so she's leaving her parents too. There has to be something deeper behind all of this than what we see on the surface. "I hope she's doing okay, but there's really nothing we can do to help. We're not even that close to her."

Lyla took a while to respond, finally texting, "You're right. I might try to talk to Katie and Dylan right now. I'm pretty close with them, at least more so than Ashley. Plus, I feel quite sorry for them too. They're being attacked out of the blue."

How do you even know that? And when were you ever close to Katie and Dylan? Despite her confusion, Sophie responded, "That sounds like a great idea. I think you should do that."

Putting down her phone, Sophie ruminated a while over what she had just learned, but decided it best to put it off for now. *I'll talk to Lyla more about it later. For now, seeing that it's only three o'clock and I don't have anything else to do, maybe I should try to find this Andy Mao guy.*

Not having any particular lead on how to find Andy except for the yellow slip of paper, she decided to use the information on that paper for now. *A phone number. That seems quite useful. Should I dial it? What will I say if he picks up? Oh well, I might as well give it a try.*

Dialing the phone number, Sophie anxiously waited for a response.

After a few seconds, a man's voice came through. "Hello? Who is this?"

Not actually having expected someone to pick up, Sophie was at a loss of words. *Shit. What should I say? What should I say?* "Hi. This is Mrs. Zhou. I changed my phone number, so that's probably why you don't recognize my phone number." *What the hell am I doing?*

"Oh hi, Mrs. Zhou. I'm sorry, how are you?"

"I'm great, how about you?"

"That's good to hear. I'm fine as well. What are you calling for? Do you need to move your and your husband's clinic date? It's set for tomorrow morning, can you not make it?"

What the hell? What clinic is he talking about? "Oh no, I don't need to move it. I just wanted to say hello, that's all." *What kind of lame answer is that? I need to get better at lying.*

"Oh, thank you then. I'll see you tomorrow if there's nothing else?"

Sophie promptly replied, "Yes. See you tomorrow!"

Hanging up the phone, Sophie let out a huge breath that she had been holding for the entire call. *What have I just done? What if he asks my parents about this call tomorrow? How will I get my way out of this? I can only pray he doesn't bring this up tomorrow.*

Despite Sophie's fear of being caught, she realized that the phone call had allowed her to discover something. *So they have a meeting tomorrow. If only I didn't have school... What if I missed school to follow them? How could I even do that? I have to find a way.*

For the next hour, Sophie made up plans, scrapped them, and redid them until she finally came up with one that might work. But it would have to wait until the next day and, until then, she had to pretend she knew nothing at all. *Just be like you always do. It can't be that hard.*

Yet, when her parents finally returned home, Sophie couldn't see them the same anymore. At the dinner table where her parents had brought back some takeout, Sophie asked, "Where have you guys been?" *There's no way you guys were at work this entire time.*

Her father responded, "We were looking at new houses. Your mother and I think that it's time to move. You know, start again?"

Sophie, in shock, looked to her mother, who quietly nodded. *There's no way. They have got to be kidding me.* "What do you mean, start again? I feel like this house is perfectly fine."

Her mother still remained silent, so her father spoke up again. "Don't you think it's hard to let go of the memories of Mackenzie here? We think that it's time we let her go."

It's only been a few months, and they already want to let her go? There's no way. "But... but we've made so many memories here."

Mrs. Zhou finally spoke up. "We have. But most of these memories have been sad ones, haven't they?"

Realizing what she said was mostly true but not wanting to accept the reality, Sophie snapped back, "So what? You're just going to forget all the years we spent as a family?"

Mrs. Zhou sighed and then responded, "No, of course not. We could never do that. But lately, it seems that the bad seems to overpower the good."

Well, you both have certainly been making that obvious. None of you have even tried to make it better. Not once. "Whatever. Do whatever you want. I don't care anymore."

Sophie stood up and took her plates with her, no longer having an appetite.

Her father called out to her, "Where are you going? We aren't done with dinner yet."

Sophie, without looking back, said, "I have some homework I need to finish. You guys enjoy your dinner."

As she walked away from the kitchen, she kept on expecting her parents to call out to her. To tell her that everything was going to be okay. To perhaps even get upset at her for speaking to them like that. But there was nothing. Absolutely nothing at all.

Sophie slammed her room's door and sat down on her bed. Her first instinct was to text Anya about this event, but she stopped herself when she remembered that Anya already had her fair share of troubles. Her next instinct was to text Lyla, but for some reason, after their morning conversation, she didn't want to anymore.

So, Sophie just laid on her bed and wallowed in anger and self-pity. *How could my parents do this to me? To Mackenzie? All they've wanted to do since Mackenzie died was to move on. It's like their entire life—including me—died with Mackenzie. They probably wouldn't have even told me about moving houses if I hadn't asked them about it.*

A tear almost fell out of Sophie's eye, but she stopped herself. *No. This should instead give me further incentive to see who this Andy guy is. Since they obviously don't want me to know about him, maybe I can get some revenge by exposing who this guy is and what they have been planning all this time without me. They deserve it, after all.*

Sophie thought for a moment about how her parents would be upset but quickly shook the thought from her head. *No, I don't care anymore. I'm exposing them tomorrow.*

As Sophie had already finished her homework, she took some downtime to read, which was interrupted by Lyla's text.

It read, "Sophie! I texted Katie and Dylan, and I think something's actually wrong with Ashley. Apparently, they did nothing, but Ashley's just freaking out for no reason."

Of course, they would say that they're completely innocent. There's no way that Lyla's falling for that trick. "Are you sure they didn't do anything to provoke Ashley?"

"I know it's unbelievable, but I probed quite hard. And they seem completely innocent. They didn't try to defend anything they've done. They seem just as confused as we are."

"So why did they write all that hate on Ashley? Seems pretty guilty to me."

"Duh. They have to respond. Otherwise, it would seem to the school they could be easily pushed around. And they would never let another person have the upper hand over them."

"I guess that's true. But then that makes it really weird because Ashley would never do something like that to tarnish her reputation."

Lyla responded, "I know. That's why Katie and Dylan are upset, but they're also worried."

What sort of friends are worried for their friend but then post all those hateful comments? "I see. And are they able to reach out to Ashley?"

"Nope. Not at all. I'm not even sure if she's going to school tomorrow. If she does, it will be extremely awkward."

At least I won't be there for the beginning. But no. I can't tell her my plan. It has to work. "Let's hope that it's all nothing and they reconcile soon. But if it is something big and I see Ashley around, then I will try to talk to her." *Like she would even talk to me.*

"Okay, thank you. You're the best."

Sophie chuckled. *I'm probably going to be of zero help.* "Haha, I'm really not. But anyways, goodnight."

"Goodnight!"

Sophie read a little bit more and then went to bed. *I need to rest up for my big day tomorrow.*

ten
Anya

WAKING up with her head on her mother's lap, Anya initially thought she was dreaming. Nothing was believable. Not the blue hospital light. Not the cold floor. And especially not her being so close to her mother. But as Anya's eyes came into focus, and she saw her father lying on the hospital bed, everything came crashing down. *Dad passed out.*

Making sure to not wake her mother up, Anya quietly checked the time. *Only 6 a.m. When did I even fall asleep? I can't remember anymore. Mom and I were talking for so long.*

Anya tiptoed toward her father. *I don't think he's woken up yet. Should he be up by now? What if he won't wake up? Should I call the doctor?*

Just as Anya was about to step out of the room to call a doctor over, her father called out, "Anya? Is that you?"

Anya whipped her head around and saw that her father's eyes had opened. Running to his bedside, she yelled, "Dad! I've been so worried!" With one arm around his neck, she used her other one to wipe a tear away before he could see her crying.

Weakly, he responded, "Worried? About me? No, never."

"Oh, Dad! Promise me you'll never do that again. Mom and I nearly died waiting for you to wake up. We were so, so worried."

At the sound of the commotion, Mrs. Zhou also woke up, immediately saying, "Honey? You're up?" Her voice sounded strong, but Anya could see the slight tears forming in her eyes.

Mr. Zhou responded, "Of course, I am. What, did you expect me to lie here forever?" He chuckled while Mrs. Zhou ran to hug him.

Good. He still hasn't lost his sense of humor.

After all giving each other hugs, finally letting out everyone's tears, and calling in the doctor to give Mr. Zhou a checkup, Anya decided it was finally time to address how her father had passed out.

"So, Dad. I would love to know why you suddenly passed out."

Mrs. Zhou responded in the same way. "Yes. We can't have that ever happening again."

Mr. Zhou didn't respond at first, but when Anya gave him a stern look to tell him that he had to respond, he finally said, "I... I didn't want to worry you guys."

Mrs. Zhou gasped, "Are you sick?" Her shaky hand immediately went to his head. "Is it something bad? Not cancer, right? Oh no, this is so, so bad."

Anya tapped her mother's lap, kindly reminding her not to interrupt.

Mr. Zhou, giving Anya a grateful glance, said, "No. Don't worry, I'm not. It's just that I've been really worried lately. I know that I shouldn't, but I keep on thinking about Camelia. I wonder if she's okay, if she's eating well, if she's taking care of herself. I mean, she's barely an adult, and she's already gone." His voice cracked, but he continued. "I've tried my hardest to never talk about her; I know how much it hurts both of you. And it hurts me so much to see you two be on bad terms."

He paused, and Anya held his hand tighter. Once again, tears bubbled to her eyes, and she averted her eyes from his gaze. Noticing that his breath was shallow, she said, "Do you want a break, Dad? You just woke up."

With tears in her eyes, Mrs. Zhou added, "Yes. You should rest for now."

Despite the mother and daughter's efforts, Mr. Zhou responded, "No. I'm fine. I just need to say a few more things. Who knows when we'll be like this again? Anyhow, I want to say that I'll be better. I want to organize family trips and make an actual movie room where we can all sit together and watch TV on Friday nights."

I would love that, but I don't know what Mom will say. As Anya warily turned to look at her mother, she saw her nodding.

Mr. Zhou asked Mrs. Zhou, "What do you think?"

Mrs. Zhou responded, "I see where you're coming from. Let's do that."

She didn't even take a second to think it over. Anya knew how much her mother had to change from her usual self to allow this, but she also hoped that this conversation would mark a turning point in their relationship. *I haven't felt at ease around her for weeks, months even. Would this be a good time to tell them about Camelia?*

Anya looked around at her parents, who were hugging each other. Their arms looked frail by themselves, but interlocked, they finally looked strong. *No, I shouldn't. I can't ruin this beautiful moment. I'll just have to tell them another time. For now, I should solely focus on my parents.*

Mrs. Zhou took a look at her watch and saw it was already almost eight a.m. "Anya, don't you have school? It's Monday. I nearly forgot!"

Shoot. I nearly forgot as well. "Yes, I do. But I can call a taxi. You stay here with Dad."

Her mother, taking a glance at her husband still lying on the bed, said, "Okay, Anya. If you don't want to go, you don't have to. I know you've had a big day. And if you do go, I'll be there to pick you up for math class afterward, so you don't have to worry about that."

Glancing at her father, Anya saw him waving at her to go. "Dad, are you sure I should go?

He firmly responded, "Yes. I've taken enough time out of your days. I don't want you to be falling behind classes because of me. We can hang out tonight and any other time. Go. Hurry."

Taking one last wistful glance at her father, Anya replied, "Okay, then. Take care, Dad." Looking at her mother, who sat hunched over his bed, Anya said, "Mom, take care too. Get some rest, okay?"

Her mother didn't look up but just continued to tend to Anya's father.

Anya, nearly out of the room now, ran back to give both her parents a huge hug. "Love you guys."

Her mother looked up now. "Love you, my daughter. I'll be fine, you go to school now, okay?"

Anya gave each of them another small hug and hurried to make it to school on time.

The rest of the school day passed in a flurry as Anya felt like a huge burden had been lifted off her shoulders. *Mom and I are finally on good terms again. Dad's going to be okay. And Camelia... I'll figure that out too, I'm sure.*

She was so content that although Odyssey and Isabel barely expressed concern about her father's condition, Anya simply brushed it off and carried on joking around with them. But as she sat in her mother's car to Mr. Yen's class, she kept thinking back on how her childhood best friends had talked about her father for twenty seconds and then started talking about their love life. *I shouldn't even care. They've always been like this, after all. But still. I don't think that Sophie would ever be like that. And I've only known her for a few months.* Anya sighed.

Her mother asked, "What is that sigh for? Are you still worried about your father? He's doing fine, don't worry."

"No, no. I'm just tired. Sorry."

There was a pause before her mother asked, "Do you want to buy some ice cream to eat before your class? You can't miss Mr. Yen's class or else you'll fall behind, but the cold ice cream might give you an energy boost. We have some time before your class starts."

Is she being for real? She never lets me eat ice cream. I thought only fruits were an acceptable snack according to her standards. "I would love that."

As they sat down next to a convenience store to eat their Godiva ice cream bars, Anya suddenly felt a bit awkward. *We haven't simply hung out in so long. What should I say?*

Her mother beat her to it. "So, how has school been going? Not academics, but your social life?"

She's really trying to make a change, isn't she? What should I say? "It's been going fine. Just hanging out with Isabel and Odyssey, that's all."

"That's it? Nothing else to tell me?"

"Well. I recently had an argument with Odyssey, I guess."

"What was it about?"

Well, it was kind of because of our argument that made me stop thinking of my words when I talked to Odyssey. But I can't tell you that. I guess I can tell you another truth. "It just seems like my friends are not like how I used to think of them. Or maybe I'm changing. I'm not sure."

"What do you mean by that?"

"It's just that..." *Should I tell her? Is she even going to care about what I'm going to say? Whatever, I'll just say it.* "I've recently started to notice how my friends don't actually care about me. I think that I knew it before, but now that I've made a new friend..." *Oh no. She doesn't even know about Sophie.*

"Who is this friend?" Her mother glanced at her.

"It's an online friend. She lives in the U.S."

"Really? You've never told me! Why didn't you tell me?"

Anya thought for a moment about why she hadn't said anything but couldn't pinpoint the reason. "Don't worry about it, Mom. I haven't told anyone about her yet. Not even Dad. Plus, I'm not even sure if Sophie and I are that close."

"So then how can you say you feel like she's better than Odyssey and Isabel?"

I don't know either. "She just seems to care. Like truly, truly care. Like she'll be the one to first ask me if I'm okay." Now that Anya had said it out loud, she realized just how much she had begun to rely on Sophie, especially during those days when it seemed that both her best friends and mother couldn't even look at her.

Finishing her ice cream, Anya's mother patted her on the back and sighed, "We need to go, but before we do, I just want to say it doesn't matter that you've been friends with Odyssey and Isabel since elementary school; people change, and sometimes we have to move on. So if Sophie truly makes you happy and the other two don't, don't force it, okay?"

Wow. When did she become so philosophical? "Sure, Mom." *Easier said than done though. I can't just abandon my friends.* "Mom. What happened when you were in high school? I feel like you've never told me about your younger self. Or about yourself at all."

She sighed. "Ay, we can talk about me sometime. We've all finished our ice cream, let's go to class now."

Anya knew that her mother was just avoiding the subject as she always did when it came her turn to talk about herself. But she let go of it for now. She didn't want to ruin the recently mended relationship. "Okay, Mom. But I'll find out one day, I'm sure."

"Maybe one day. But for now, focus on yourself and your studies, okay? You don't have time to be hearing my silly stories. What a waste of time, right?"

"Mom, don't say that!"

"Whatever, whatever. Let's go to your class now, or else we might actually be late."

She never lets me have it my way. So frustrating. But I suppose she does truly care about me. As Anya watched her mother throw away their ice cream sticks, she smiled.

Mr. Yen's class went the same as before, and Anya, despite her best efforts, again couldn't resist snapping at him whenever he brought up Camelia. She wished that she would never see his dreadful face again, but she also realized how much her mother had put into this class. *She had talked about this renowned class for years. When we finally got it, she had nearly passed out with joy. It would be too cruel to quit, despite my intense hatred of Mr. Yen. I can take the snarky comments every now and then if this class truly improves my math skills and makes my mother happy.* She told herself this line over and over until the class finally finished.

Returning home, Anya sat down to eat dinner with her parents, and the food seemed especially delicious as she sat across from her father. *I hope he never grows older. Just stay like this for a moment.* She also saw her mother looking at him, a slight glint in her eyes. *Perhaps she's thinking the same thing.*

She wanted to stay longer and talk to him forever, but glancing at the grand clock that stood at the end of the room, she realized with a sense of disappointment that it was already almost eight p.m. *Shit. I have so much work to finish.*

"Mom, Dad. I have to finish my homework."

Her father put down his chopsticks. "You have to go already?"

Her mother looked at the clock and said, "No, no. She's right. At this rate, she'll never finish her work."

Seeing in her father's gaze that he wanted her to stay longer, Anya comforted him, "Don't worry. We can hang out any other day. Movie night, Friday?"

He brightened up. "Yes, let's do that."

Anya walked back to her room, feeling energized from the day's turn of events. As she opened her laptop to begin working on her Chinese essay due the next day, she saw Sophie's text pop up.

Clicking on it, she saw that it read, "My uncle thinks he found the location. Do you want to go check?"

eleven
Sophie

SOPHIE COULD FEEL her hands trembling as she exited from text messages and put her phone back in her pocket. *At least if everything goes wrong today, I will have helped out Anya with finding her sister.* Peaking outside her door, she saw that her parents were eating breakfast. She took a deep breath, trying to calm herself down so that she could think rationally. *It's okay. Just follow the plan.*

Holding her hand to her head, Sophie walked toward her parents. A bead of sweat dripped down her forehead as she prayed for the plan to work.

In the most fragile voice possible, Sophie said, "Hi Mom. Hi Dad. I don't feel so great. I think I must've caught that cold going around in school."

Her father stood up and replied, "Oh no. Do you think you can still make it to school? Or do you want to stay at home?"

That was surprisingly easy. "I think I need to stay home."

Just as Sophie was about to walk back to her room and carry out the next part of her plan, her mother stopped her by saying, "Wait. Let me check your temperature. If you don't have a fever, you can still go to school."

Ah... not as easy as I originally thought. It's okay. I prepared for this. "Mom, you don't even have to take my temperature to see that I have a fever. Just feel my head. It's burning up."

Her mother placed her hand atop Sophie's forehead and immediately nodded. "Okay, you definitely have a fever. Yes, you stay home today. Unfortunately, I can't stay with you today, but I'll get you some Tylenol. I'll keep the bottle on your bedside table, so make sure to take a pill each time you feel the fever coming back, okay?"

"Yes, Mom." *Thank goodness she didn't insist on using the thermometer. That hair dryer must have worked really well.* Sophie's hand remained in a tight fist as her parents resumed eating their breakfasts.

Okay. Step one finished, but I have to hurry now. Can't waste any time, or else this plan will all fall to pieces. Sophie made her way around the corner, outside of her parents' sight. There, she opened her palm. Inside were her mother's car keys. *Good. They were so distracted by my "fever" that they didn't notice me stealing Mom's car keys from her pocket.*

Sophie took a deep breath, shaking her body to rid of her jumbled-up nerves. *Now I just have to unlock the car, put the keys back in the house, and get in the back trunk. Easy.* Sophie felt like she was going to pass out.

Opening the garage door, Sophie made her way to her mother's car. As it was parked behind her father's car, she could only hope that her parents would most likely take this car and not the other one. *Please, please, please.* The beeping of the car unlocking made Sophie cringe. After tensely waiting for ten seconds for a possible reaction, Sophie didn't hear anything. *Okay, good. They shouldn't, anyway. The garage is almost on the opposite side of the kitchen.*

Just as Sophie relaxed and was about to resume her plan of putting the keys back, she heard her parents' voices through the door. *Shit. Was that too loud?* Realizing that her plan was about to be ruined, Sophie had no other choice than possibly the worst one possible.

As her parents' voices became increasingly louder, Sophie tossed the car keys to the edge of the garage and rushed into the back seat. She rolled onto the ground of the back seat and crammed herself as far as she could under her front seats so that her parents wouldn't see her. *This definitely isn't as safe as the trunk option; but it will have to do for now.*

Peeping from the car's window, Sophie could see her parents opening the garage door and walking in. She could also hear them talking about the clinic but couldn't entirely distinguish what they were talking about as they were talking in hushed voices.

Suddenly, her mother exclaimed, "My car keys! I swear I just had them."

Sophie perked up, nearly revealing herself through the window as she waited to see if her parents would suspect something.

Her father's keen eye saved Sophie, seeing the car key where Sophie had thrown it.

Breathing a sigh of relief that her father was now in possession of the keys, Sophie pressed her ears to the door and heard him say, "Honey, did you accidentally drop it here? You probably dropped it here yesterday when you came back from work."

Her mother replied, "Oh, thank goodness you found it. I must have dropped it, then. I'll be less clumsy next time."

Her parents had fallen for her trap, but it still wasn't over. Sophie laid down, pressing herself as far down as possible under the back of the car seats so that her parents wouldn't see her from the rearview mirror. *Almost to the final step. Please don't fail me now, plan.*

Along the car ride, Sophie nearly suffocated from holding her breath. Despite her feeling of suffocation, Sophie didn't dare take in a deep breath in fear of being caught. The minutes seemed like hours, and each silent red light seemed like eternity.

Finally, after Sophie had already lost count of time and was lacking so much oxygen that her eyelids became heavy, she heard her mother say, "We're here."

Sophie's eyes opened up wide, and she waited for her parents to first leave the car. When they did, Sophie crawled to the front of the car and gently opened the door. She quietly tracked behind her parents as they made their way toward the elevator sign. At each corner, Sophie lightly paused to make sure she wasn't too close to her parents. *Aha. Just as I thought. They're going to go up the elevator. After they do, I'll track the level they're on and then go to the same one.*

But Sophie had thought too soon. Right after spotting that her parents had reached the area of the elevator, they disappeared from sight. *What the hell?* Flustered, Sophie impetuously risked showing herself in order to see where her parents had gone.

As she whipped around the corner, she saw a side door. *That's the only place they could've gone.* The door had no window, so Sophie first tried to listen for any sounds. *Nothing. Nothing at all. Shit. How did they just disappear like that?* Her mind spinning, Sophie had no other choice except to open the door.

When she did, she saw that it was a stairwell leading both up and down. Her parents were nowhere to be seen. *Okay, Sophie. Think. The elevator's working, or else they would have put signs saying that it was broken. And I'm sure that we are at B2 from all the descending when I was in the car. That means that if I check downstairs, I will probably only have to check a few levels, whereas if I go up, who knows how many levels I have to check?* After weighing the odds, Sophie decided to head downstairs.

The staircase was barely lit, and Sophie couldn't shake off an ominous feeling she had inside. Her gut instinct told her to quickly turn back around, but she combatted that fear with the willpower to find out what her parents were up to. *Get it together, Sophie. This is L.A. You'll be fine.*

When she reached the bottom of the stairs, she saw that it was the last floor. The only object in sight besides the tight wall was a door. Stepping closer, Sophie saw through the crack underneath the door that it was lit on the other side. *Is that where my parents are? How do I even check when there isn't a window?*

Desperate to see whether or not her hunches were right, Sophie shimmied up against the door, but it was too thick to hear anything. Sophie tried to hear through the crack of the door, but she could only hear muffled voices. *What should I do? I didn't come all the way here to just not learn anything. There's no way, right?*

Sophie played with her fingers, wavering between leaving without anything or barging in to see what was happening. *Ah... maybe, in hindsight, it would be better for me to just leave. This seems extremely, extremely sketchy.*

However, before she could turn to leave, her phone, placed in her pocket, started ringing. *What the hell?* Sophie frantically tried to stop the ringing sound, but in the process of panicking, she didn't focus on what was happening on the other side of the door.

Click. From the other side, the door opened and closed. Before Sophie realized what had happened, it was already too late.

Standing there, mouth agape in shock, was her mother.

Oh my god. I am so screwed. What do I even say in this kind of situation? Act cool. Right. "Hi Mom. What a surprise to see you here!"

Her mother, mouth still open, didn't respond for a solid ten seconds as Sophie stood there waiting. *I'm so dead.* Finally, she said, "Sophie Chen. What are you doing here? What the hell have you been up to? Have you been stalking your father and me? Don't you dare lie to me."

Shit. Shit. Shit. Sophie brushed away the sweat forming on her head. "No, Mom. Of course I wouldn't stalk you guys. Well, technically no. So, actually. Um."

"Exactly. You can't explain yourself, which means that what I said was true. And if I hadn't come out to use the restroom, you wouldn't have ever told me about you ditching school and stalking your own parents?"

Sophie's mouth cringed at the words, each one truer than the next. *Okay, since defensive is obviously not working, it's time to shift to offensive mode.* "Well, it's not like you're exactly being all blatant and everything."

Her mother, now in a more defensive tone, said, "What do you mean by that?"

Aha. I got you now. "Don't lie, you've been all secretive ever since that phone call at the barn."

"What phone call?"

"That phone call where you brought up Mackenzie. And then when I asked you about it, you said it was nothing. And so much other stuff as well, like that piece of paper..."

Her mother cut Sophie off. "So you've been stalking me this entire time? What has gotten into you for you to think that it's okay?"

"That's not the point of what I'm trying to say."

Her mother, with her tone becoming more and more defensive as well as upset, said, "So then what are you trying to say? That your father and I can't have our own private lives? That we can't even visit a therapist without telling you everything?"

Sophie took a step back in shock. *A therapist? There's no way. They would have told me then if it was just a therapist.* "I don't believe you. Show me then."

"Of course, you don't believe me. Why would you believe me? We're in a basement, for Christ sake."

"Exactly, you are in a basement. So, show me then."

"Fine, if that's how you want it, I'll show you. But everything, and I mean everything, about this interaction has just been wrong. Do you at least understand that?"

Sophie blankly nodded, waiting for the reveal of the "therapist." *Is she actually telling the truth? If she is...* Sophie gulped in anticipatory guilt.

Walking into the room, she saw two couches and an armchair. On one of the couches sat her father, who now looked at Sophie in absolute shock. On the armchair sat a man, perhaps in his fifties, who wore spectacles, and a name tag titled Dr. Mao. *Oh my god. She was telling the truth.*

Turning to her mother, all Sophie could say was a meek "sorry."

Wave after wave of guilt hit Sophie, condemning her for suspecting her parents and not realizing the pain that her parents had been in after Mackenzie's death. She clutched her stomach, feeling bile forming in her stomach and moving to her mouth. Meanwhile, everyone in the room just stared blankly at her.

Dr. Mao broke the silence by saying, "Ah, so this was the mystery caller you two were talking about earlier. I was wondering who would pretend to be Mrs. Zhou. This makes much more sense now that I've seen this scene play out."

Oh my god. I'm even more screwed now. Sophie couldn't deny the truth now, so all she could say again was "sorry."

Neither her mother nor father uttered a word, until her father finally stood up, grabbed Sophie by the arm, and dragged her toward the room's exit. To Mr. Mao, he calmly said, "So sorry about this, doctor. I hope that your office upstairs is soon fixed. Goodbye, then."

But, as they exited the room, he muttered underneath his breath to Sophie, "What the hell did you do?" Sophie gulped, trying to swallow the bible that felt like it was going to spurt out of her mouth any second.

The car ride back home was absolute torture. Sophie sat in the back seat while her parents didn't utter a single word. Each time her parents let out a sigh, Sophie wanted more and more to bury herself in the car seat and to never show her face again. *How did I mess up this much? Why did I think that... when they were literally seeing a therapist because of Mackenzie? What kind of fucked up daughter am I? Are they going to give me the silent treatment until forever? I know I said previously that I didn't care, but I feel so, so guilty. Oh dear.*

twelve

Anya

ANYA, having skipped the first class of the day, stared at the building in front of her. She rechecked the address to ensure that she had the right one. *Yes, this is the one.* It was a tall building in the bustling center of the city, which meant that it had only taken Anya around ten minutes of biking to get from her school to this building. *Which also means that I can hopefully make it back to school before the second period begins. Let's hope that Mom doesn't mind too much about me just missing one period of class. I can say that I forgot and was instead doing homework. She probably won't believe me, but an excuse is better than nothing.*

As Anya was about to walk inside the building, she realized that she stuck out like a sore thumb within all the people filing into work. While she was wearing a backpack, everyone else had briefcases slung over their arms. And while she was in her school uniform consisting of a polo shirt and a skirt, everyone else was wearing suits and pants. Taking a glance at the security guards who stood right outside of the sliding doors, Anya could feel her palms becoming sweaty. *What if they see that I'm an anomaly and then kick me out? What do I do then? Should I just call Sophie's uncle instead of going there myself? But no. Sophie told me that I should go see him, which means that she thinks I'll be fine. Plus, if she wants me to go see him, that probably means she had a reason for wanting me to meet him face-to-face instead of just over the phone.*

Mustering up her courage, Anya blended into the barrage of people entering the building and managed to slip right past the guards' gazes.

The inside of the building was even more intimidating than the outside, as it was lined with rows and rows of people on the phone. *Probably accountants, I'm guessing.* Seeing that she had to be on the fifth floor, Anya gradually followed the crowd, going left and right until she finally made it into the elevator.

On her way up, Anya tried to think about what to say when she saw Sophie's uncle, who she had never met and didn't know of his personality whatsoever. *What if he's upset that he had to spend time tracking down somebody for someone he's never even met?* Anya consoled herself that Sophie wouldn't send her straight into a deathtrap, but she still couldn't push down the underlying nerves. Each time the elevator stopped at a level to let people off, Anya increasingly tapped her feet in anticipation.

The elevator dinged. Anya had reached the fifth floor.

She stepped off and right in front of her was labeled "Dr. Wang's Office." *Okay, I'm here. Deep breath. I'll be fine. I hope so.*

Knocking on the door, Anya heard a man's voice say, "Come in!" She stepped inside.

To her shock, the room, in stark contrast with the outside, seemed like a normal, household room. There were couches, pillows, books, fruit, and mugs. On top of that, there was a sense of coziness that filled the entire room, perhaps evoked from the vanilla incense that was burning on the tabletop.

"Hello. You must be Anya."

In the process of examining her surroundings, Anya had forgotten to actually look at the person standing right in front of her. *Shit. I've really been doing too much undercover stuff lately.* "Hi, Mr. Wang! Sorry, I got a bit flustered coming into the building. Anyhow, thank you so much for having me here. It was probably a hassle, what I asked you to do." *I thought he would look scarier, but he kind of looks like a grandfather. Huh.*

Anya's observation was made even more strengthened when she he spoke in a tone similar to that of her own grandfather's: steady and calm. "Ah, don't worry about the hassle. I'm very glad to have finally met one of Sophie's friends. I told her to tell you to come over so that I could meet you face-to-face. Or else I don't think I would have ever met one of her friends. She's always so secluded."

So that's why I'm here in-person. "Haha, yeah. Sophie's one of my best friends, but she really doesn't tell much about her life to anyone." *She probably knows so much more about me than I know about her.*

"Yes, that sounds like her. She really has grown up recently, though. Anyhow, where are my manners? Would you like some pear? I recently got a huge box from one of my old friends, and I can't finish all of it myself."

"No, no. It's okay; I feel bad that I didn't bring anything."

"No, I insist, or else my niece will accuse me of being cold again." He chuckled, and Anya relaxed. *He really does seem quite nice, not at all who I envisioned him to be.*

Anya replied, "Thank you, Mr. Wang," and she sat down on the couch.

He paused. "Hold on, you look kind of familiar. I swear I've seen you somewhere."

"Huh?" *What could he possibly mean? I'm sure that I've never seen him before.*

"Wait, can you say your last name?"

Hesitantly, Anya said, "I'm Anya Chen. Why do you ask?"

"Your last name is Chen? Oh my goodness, I'm pretty sure my wife is best friends with your mother."

"What?" *Oh wait...* "I think I've seen her before; I just didn't corre-late Mrs. Wang with you." *There's no way. How is the world so small that we ended up like this?*

Mr. Wang sat down on the armchair, crossing his legs and putting his hands together. He said, "Well, then. That's definitely a surprise. I suppose you're the youngest daughter?"

"Yes, Mr. Wang. My older sister is Camelia."

"Ah, I see. And since you're a family friend, please do call me Uncle Wang. It seems way too formal to label me as *Mr.*"

Anya chuckled. "Okay, then."

Uncle Wang continued, "So, now that I just had a huge revelation, we should get talking about that friend of yours you were asking about. I know where he is."

Anya leaned forward in her chair in excitement. "Where is he?" *Yes, everything might click together now.*

"I can't tell you right now."

Anya tilted her head. "Why? Did you not actually find him?"

He laughed slightly. "No, of course I found him. Or else I wouldn't have called you over to just disappoint you. But I will need some information in return."

What kind of information could I possibly give someone who has access to nearly everything? "Sure, tell me, and I'll see what I can do."

"Well... you see, Sophie doesn't really tell me anything. I guess that's partly my fault..."

Anya cut him off, saying, "Wait. If you want me to tell you anything about Sophie's personal life, I can't tell you that. I would never do that to her."

"No, I would never ask that of you. It's just that I don't believe this whole friend act. I've seen these types of scenes play out before, and they're never that simple. Sophie told me that it was just to check his safety, but why would a young girl like you ask about a full-grown man's safety? It just doesn't check out."

Ah. He's nice, but he's intelligent. "You're right. We weren't telling the truth before. But if I tell you, will you promise to keep it a secret? I can't have anyone else learn from it, or else my plan might be ruined."

"Yes, I promise. I wouldn't have anyone to talk to about this plan, anyways. So, what's your plan?"

"Well, my plan is to find my sister." For the next twenty minutes, Anya once again told her story, the third person she had truly told besides Sophie and Sunny. He would intermittently pause her to ask some clarification questions, but he stayed relatively quiet throughout the entire talk, which Anya appreciated.

After Anya finished and took a sip of green tea that he had poured for her earlier, she asked, "So, what do you think?"

He didn't speak for a while as he leaned against his hands. Finally, he said, "Wow. That's a lot. I suppose you haven't told your parents about this yet, am I right?"

"Yes. Actually, the entire reason why I need to keep it a secret is so that my parents don't find out. If they do, I might as well give up all chances of finding my sister."

"Why is that? Wouldn't they want to find your sister if they knew where she was?"

Anya shuddered at the thought of it. "No, you don't know what my mother is like. After Camelia left, she literally can't even talk about her without freaking out."

Uncle Wang cocked his head.

"My mother's crazy." Anya thought for a moment before correcting herself. "Well, she's not necessarily crazy. She's just, how do I say it? Overly obsessive. She put all her heart into Camelia getting in a good college, and I mean her *entire* heart. She went to such extremes that she would literally plan out each of my sister's meals so that she would have the best food for her brain 24/7. Like she literally would wake up at five a.m. each day to cook variances of fish because she saw online that fish is good for the brain. And so although my sister wanted nothing more than to have what my father and I had for breakfast, she always had to have her own. And it got even worse when the test was coming around the corner. I could go on, but then I would talk for the entire day." Anya took another sip of the tea, her mouth parched from talking so much. *How the hell did I just tell a stranger who I have never even met before so much? I must be going crazy myself.*

Uncle Wang nodded. "One last thing to ask you, and sorry for making you speak so much. This part is just for my curiosity, so you don't have to respond if you don't want to. What I wanted to ask is how come your sister didn't fight back? Did she just stay silent the entire time?"

Anya sighed. "That's just who my sister is, and I suppose that's part of the reason why everything happened the way it did. See, my sister is almost completely unlike me. Me, I'll talk back to my mother whenever. But my sister, on the other hand, was always the docile one. I don't think in all of my years living with her that I ever heard her say a word back to my mother. To anyone, actually. She always hid her deepest thoughts so that she wouldn't hurt anybody. So when my mother started pressuring her to do well on the test, Camelia knew that large tests weren't her forte, yet she didn't say anything. For days on end, she would lock herself in her room to study, only coming out a few times a day to grab some food. But as the test day arrived, the pressure must have been too much, and not wanting to disappoint Mom with a bad test grade, she must have fled. I think that she was like a balloon: slowly and quietly building up pressure until the day when everything popped."

After she finished, Wang took a moment of silence and eventually replied, "I'm so sorry. That must have been so hard on Camelia. On your entire family. My wife never told me anything about this."

Anya didn't respond, just staring at her feet. The conversation had brought memories flooding back, particularly the ugly ones that she always chose to shove to the back of her mind. She could envision herself knocking at her sister's door, pleading with her to open it and come out to talk. She could feel her anguish when her sister hadn't responded, only coming out an hour later to grab a glass of milk for further studying.

Too many memories barraged their way into Anya's heart, and she quietly wiped away at a tear forming in her eye. "Sorry, I'm just getting a bit emotional."

Mr. Wang rushed over to hand her a tissue. "I'm so sorry. I shouldn't have asked you something so personal. Here, take this tissue."

Anya looked up, embarrassed at how she let her emotions get the best of her. *Why am I always crying? I really need to get it together.* "I'm fine now. And you don't have to be sorry; that was actually a good question. I think that recently, I've almost forgotten *why* I want to find my sister because I've been so focused on the *how*."

Mr. Wang patted her on the back. "It's always good to let out your locked-up emotions. It's also about time that I told you that her boyfriend's in Costa Rica. Do with that information as you will."

thirteen

Sophie

SOPHIE NOW SAT in her seat, once again in English class. Although the topic of discussion today was about literature, her favorite topic to talk about, Sophie's gaze kept blurring over as she thought about her parents. She thought back to their absolute silence as they drove her back home to grab her backpack and then send her off to school. Her parents didn't yell when they got upset, they just got silent. And the more silent they got, the angrier they were. *I hope that this time isn't like when they just completely stopped talking to me for two entire days. But then again, they do have reason to be really, really upset at me. I can only hope that their anger doesn't last more than a week.* Sophie reminded herself that she was supposed to be upset at her parents, but she only felt dejected. *If I had known it would turn out like this, I would have never done such a thing.*

Sitting on the car ride over to the barn was not much better either. Although her mother still took the time out of her work day to come pick Sophie up, she was completely silent the entire car ride. Sophie sat at the edge of her seat, praying that the car ride would soon end.

When Sophie exited the car to go ride, she mustered up the courage to say to her mother, "You can go if you want. I'll just call an Uber back home."

Her mother just sighed and said, "Just go and be quick."

Sophie winced at her despondent tone and lightly closed the car door behind her.

The ride also went unusually terrible, as Sophie continuously miscalculated the striding to the jump. Her trainer, realizing that she would fall off if she continued this way, stopped the lesson early and told her to come back another day when she was better prepared. Sophie left the ring absolutely disappointed in herself, as she had let her horse and trainer down. *Why can't I do anything right these days? From sports to academics to family, absolutely nothing is working out for me.*

Arriving back home at around 4 pm, all Sophie could do was stare wistfully at the door of her mother's office, desperately hoping that her mother would eventually open the door and start talking. *Dad's not even home yet; I wonder what he'll be like when he gets back from work. Do I even want to see what he will look like? He'll probably be the exact same as Mom, if not worse.* Sophie had only seen her father angry twice in her life: once when Mackenzie and Sophie had started physically fighting and another when Sophie's grandparents had been scammed over a hundred thousand dollars. So, for Sophie, she was even more afraid of her father's anger than her mother's.

As she heard his car pulling up into the driveway, she jumped up. *Why is he back from work so early? It's only 4:30 pm; he doesn't usually get back until at least 6:30 pm.* Startled, she lost all her courage to address her parents and instead ran into her bedroom. Leaning against the feet of her bed, she could feel tears welling up again. Even when she picked up her favorite book as a way to calm down, thoughts of how she had betrayed her parents kept on spiraling inside her head until she thought she would go insane. *No, I can't keep going like this, or else I'll forever be stuck this way. But I've never felt this guilt before. To accuse my parents of something like...? This is way worse than when I snuck out. Way worse.* Sophie didn't even want to say it in her head, as it sounded even absurd now. *How the hell did I think my sister could be alive? I must have gone absolutely crazy from listening to Anya talk about her sister. Should I just confess to my parents that I had gone crazy?*

Sophie shook her head and decided to divert her mind using another method. *It's been a while; I should see what Anya has been up to, even if all the talk around her sister might actually be driving me insane.* When Sophie opened her computer, numerous notifications started buzzing, all texts from Anya.

Sophie took a minute to read all the texts and noticed that many of them repeated, perhaps out of excitement or shock. After reading all of them, she sat back, recognizing that she had expected this outcome but that it was still surprising all the same. *So he's in Tortuguero as well. That should confirm it then. Camelia's in Costa Rica.*

Seeing that Anya wanted to call, Sophie wavered for a moment. *My parents just got home, which means that it would be the perfect time to apologize to them about my actions. But also, Anya has probably been waiting on my call for a long time, as this news could mean something huge for her.* Sophie looked between the door and her laptop, and finally decided to keep her laptop open. She comforted herself that Anya needed her more right now. *And I get to avoid my parents' wrath for just a tad longer.*

Hearing Anya's excitement was like a sip of ice-cold water during a sweltering day. Her entire energy radiated hope and passion, which made Sophie focus her attention solely on Anya instead of herself.

Anya kept on saying, "Omg, I can't believe it. It's actually true!"

Meanwhile, Sophie kept on repeating, "Yes, it's actually true! Congrats!" A smile came to her face, something that hadn't happened in a very long time — not since the *incident*.

Finally, after Anya had calmed down, she asked, "So, do you think I should tell my parents? I mean, they should have a right to know, right?"

Sophie, reflecting on her terrible relation with her parents due to a lack of communication, responded, "Yes, you definitely should. They'll be ecstatic to know."

"I know, right? I bet they'll be so excited that they might even forget about my academics." Anya chuckled and Sophie laughed along with her.

She seems to have everything figured out now. Good for her. Sophie looked out her window with a twinge of envy, hoping that the same would happen for her. *Please, please, please let my parents forgive me.*

Anya, a little quieter and more hesitant this time, added on, "Do you think she'll want to return back home? No, on second thought, I don't even need her to return home. She can go wherever she wants. I'm just worried that if she escapes... she doesn't want us to find her."

Sophie could see the worry painted on Anya's face, so she comforted her, "No, no. Don't think like that. If she sent that letter, then I'm sure she would want you to find her." *That has to be the case, right?*

"That's true. But still, the letter was so encrypted that I'm not even sure if she sent it. I mean, I'm pretty sure that she sent it, but..."

She thinks that her situation is too good to be true. "Anya, listen. You're only worried now because you have everything you want. Think about it. Isn't it so much more likely that she sent it than some random person? You said you recognized her signature, correct?"

Perking up at this reminder, Anya replied, "Yes, that's true. I need to stop being irrational and just look at the facts in front of me."

Sophie nodded, glad that she had succeeded in at least making one person feel better.

Anya said, "I think I'm going to tell my parents after this call. I didn't originally tell them about the letter because I was unsure about the situation, but I'm going to tell them now." She paused for a moment. "Also, after my father fell ill for a day, my mother's became more welcoming, so I think that the timing would be perfect."

Sophie smiled and gave Anya a thumbs up.

After hanging up the phone, Sophie shook her body to release her bundle of emotions. She was more than excited for Anya's success and joyous at her for mending her parental relationship. Yet, despite how much she tried to stop herself, she couldn't help but feel jealousy. *It seems that she has everything while not only did I not take a step forward, but it seems that I took ten steps back. Why couldn't life be more equal? Why did*

Mackenzie have to die? Why couldn't she have just run off like Anya's sister? Why do my parents have to be so mysterious all the time? And gone?

Realizing that she had let her dark thoughts flood in, Sophie stood up. *No, it's because I need to take action myself. I can't just sit here and rot away while hoping for change. I have to talk to my parents.*

Exiting her room, Sophie beelined to the kitchen as she expected her parents to be preparing for dinner. But when she arrived there, she saw that her parents weren't there. *Did they go back to their offices to do more work already? What is happening today to make everyone so... weird? Did something about work arise?*

Sophie decided that she had to talk to her parents today, even if that meant she would intrude some of their work time. *I'll start with Mom first; she might be easier to talk to than Dad.*

As Sophie neared the office, which was on the complete opposite side of the house, she heard both her mother and father's voices. *Why are they in a room together? This will make talking to them so much harder because they can each back up each other. Shit. It seems that the world really doesn't want me to confront them today.* Just as Sophie was starting to think about turning back to return to her room, her father's shout echoed through the corridor, making Sophie jump back in shock.

Right after the shout, the room went dead silent. Intrigued and half worried by what had occurred, Sophie walked closer to the office. Realizing that she was treading on her tippy toes so as not to be caught by her parents, Sophie thought to herself, "What the hell am I doing again?"

But curiosity dragged her closer and closer to the room until she was almost at their office door. From there, she could hear hushed yet urgent voices. *What are they whispering about? Do they not want me to find out?*

The more her wild thoughts ran, the closer Sophie got to the room until her ears were right against the door. There, she could hear her parents quite clearly.

fourteen

Anya

AFTER HANGING UP THE CALL, Anya's head was in a complete spiral. During the school day, she had only felt excitement. Thoughts about finally seeing her sister again made her especially eager whenever her friends talked to her, and even Liam commented on how much she was smiling throughout the day. Nobody had questioned her missing the first period of class, as they all assumed it was because of a doctor's appointment or her sleeping in. Her mother also hadn't questioned anything, as Anya had made a perfect excuse of taking a makeup test during that period due to missing all the days of school before.

So, Anya, after finishing the call, knew that she should be more than ecstatic for the news on her sister. Yet as time ticked on, she began to increasingly realize the stakes of the situation. *What if Camelia doesn't want me to find her? What if she's upset that I told my parents? Should I even tell my parents? But if I don't, how will I ever find her?* Sophie's words had calmed her down a little bit, but as her comforts wore off, Anya's deepest worries arrived one by one.

Anya also had another point of worry, which was how her parents would react. *I know they'll probably be extremely happy, or will they?* She couldn't exactly place what she was worried about; it was just a gut feeling that this news would throw off their recently mended relationship. *I haven't been this close to my mother for so long. I really don't want to go back to how it was. But at the same time… I need to see my sister again.*

Her mother called out to her, "Anya! It's time to go to your chemistry class!"

Anya sighed, realizing that she had forgotten all about the class in the day's excitement. "Coming!" *Is this when I tell her? Should I tell her sooner or later?* Anya left her room.

On the car ride over, Anya's mother talked to her a few times about school and her social life, but Anya barely responded.

Her mother, after repeatedly not receiving a full answer, finally asked, "What is going on with you? Why do you not want to go to class today?" She sighed before continuing. "Hold on before you answer. I need to correct myself. I understand that you have a lot on your plate right now, and you probably don't want to go to class after what happened to your father. But… just understand that this is all for your good. Okay?"

Anya finally diverted her glance from the window to her mother. *Shit, have I been blanking this entire time?* "No, sorry Mom. Yeah, it's just been a lot. But I'm doing fine. And yes, going to class today is just fine with me."

"Okay, that's good to hear. Do you have anything you want to talk to me about though? You've been awfully quiet."

"Well, actually…" *No, I should wait until both Mom and Dad are present to tell them. That way, if Mom gets upset or something like that, I'll have Dad to back me up.* "It's nothing."

Her mother gave her a weird side glance but said nothing more.

Anya resumed looking out the window. Her thoughts drifted between Camelia's and her parents' reactions, until she finally decided that she could wait no longer. She had to tell her parents during dinnertime, or else she would never muster up the courage to do so.

The chemistry tutoring passed rather quickly, with only a few hiccups when she had to turn in her uncompleted homework and when she was called to the front of the five-person class to write down Boyle's equation. But for once, Anya didn't want the class to end quickly, as that meant one step nearer to telling her parents.

Yet, no matter how much she wanted to stay seated in her little, uncomfortable desk pod, her mother's phone call came. She had arrived downstairs.

Anya, deciding that she had to be on her mother's good side before she revealed the situation, asked her mother in the car, "How was your day, Mom?"

Her mother responded, "I'm doing fine. Why do you ask?"

Shit. Did I just make the situation more awkward? No, this is good. "Well, I feel like you've been kind of taking all the pressure on your own shoulders after your father got ill. You haven't even said a word about how you were fending. So I just wanted to ask you to check in."

Her mother didn't respond at first, but Anya could see her slight smile through the mirror. Finally, she responded, "That's very nice of you." She paused and Anya let out a sigh of relief. *Crisis averted.* But then, she gave Anya a weird glance through the mirror. "But that's very unlike you. You would never care what I'm up to. Not at your age. Hmm... I wonder what you're up to now." She chuckled, and Anya gulped.

Have I been that bad of a daughter? Anya thought back to the previous months, and she realized that she hadn't asked her mother that question in months. It had always been her mother asking her about her day. Never the other way around. *I've been complaining so much about my mother, but maybe I need to focus more on bettering myself as well.* Seeing that her mother was glancing at her through the mirror, Anya let out a weak smile.

Upon arriving home, Anya would have normally just gone to her room. This time, however, she chose to help set up dinner.

Not having done so since she started high school, her mother at first shooed her back to her room, saying, "No, no. You have to focus on your studies. You can't be doing foolish stuff like this."

But each time, Anya bounced back, replying, "No, Mom. I insist. It'll only be for thirty minutes. And plus, I don't have too much homework today. I'll be fine."

Finally, upon Anya's third insistence, her mother relented, "But stay away from the stove, okay? I can't have you burning the entire house down."

Anya, realizing the unfamiliarity of all the kitchen tools, also agreed with her mother. "I'll just help out with the plating then."

Together, one cooked and the other plated. Although the final outcome didn't look as great as usual, as Anya had spattered sauce everywhere, both Anya and her mother smiled at their hard work displayed on the table. *It actually feels so rewarding to help out Mom. I should definitely do it more often instead of just fleeing to my room all the time.* She also realized that she hadn't spent any time fretting over the confrontation while she was helping out, as her mind had solely been focused on the task in front of her. Her previous nerves had calmed down as she waited for her father to return home from work.

So when her father pulled into the driveway, she put on her brightest smile and went to open the door for him. As her father walked out of the car and saw her waiting at the door for him, he also smiled wide and shouted, "Hi, Anya!"

"Hi, Dad! Come in; we've prepared dinner already!"

He quickly went up to his room to change his clothing from working at the hospital, and everyone was soon sitting at the dinner table. Anya let everyone eat for a while, as she wanted to ease into the topic.

After she had seen everyone eat a bite from each dish, she decided that it was time to speak up. *How do I even introduce this? I should probably start with something they'll be okay with.*

"So, Mom and Dad. I wanted to talk to you about something."

Her father put down his chopsticks. "Yes, Anya? Sorry that I haven't been speaking much. I've had so much work while catching up for the time lost when I passed out."

Anya's mother, in reply to what the father said, huffed, "Oh my god. What do I always tell you? Health first, and then work. You've barely even recovered, and you're already back at it again. What do you think will happen if you continue like this? You'll pass out again."

Her father said, "Yes, honey. I know that. It was just one day, which I couldn't miss because I do have patients that need me, some of them trusting only me with their surgeries."

Mrs. Zhou sighed and nodded, but Anya, who was sitting right next to her mother, heard her quietly say, "But you're still a patient."

Mr. Zhou returned the conversation back to Anya, saying, "So, Anya. What did you want to say to us?"

Oof. Okay, so this isn't how I wanted the conversation to start. But it's okay, at least I have their attention now. "I wanted to talk about Camelia."

As soon as that name was uttered, it seemed that cold air washed over the room, particularly when Anya saw the look on her mother's face. *Right, I haven't talked to my mother about Camelia in months because I've only been talking to Dad about it. I've been purposely avoiding doing so, as she hasn't brought her up once. Even after Camelia had just left, she didn't say anything.*

Realizing that the room had been dead silent for the past ten seconds, Anya added, "I have something new to say about her."

Mr. Zhou spoke up, timidly saying, "Anya, go ahead." He turned to look at Mrs. Zhou, and Anya followed his gaze.

Mrs. Zhou's face was turning more and more pale, as she sat unblinking in her chair.

Anya asked, "Mom, are you okay?" Anya anxiously waited for her response. *She looks like she's going to pass out. What is going on?*

Just when Anya was about to tap her mother's shoulders to see if she was okay, Mrs. Zhou suddenly stood up and said, "I need the bathroom." With that, she left the room without a word spoken about the topic at hand.

After she was out of sight, Anya turned to look at her father. "What the hell just happened" is what she wanted to say, but out of courtesy, she simply asked, "Is Mom okay?"

Mr. Zhou shook his head and buried it in his hands. "I've never told you this, but your mother hasn't talked about Camelia for a reason."

Anya, in despair at her mother's response, blankly asked, "Why? Does she never want to see Camelia again?"

Her father sighed and looked Anya in the eyes. "Look, your mother has this form of anxiety. I'm not exactly sure what it's called, but when we went to the doctor's, he told us that she gets triggered every time she hears Camelia's name."

Are you kidding me? If anyone should be triggered, it should be Camelia with all the stress Mom put on her. "I mean, isn't Camelia safe and all? Why does Mom have to react like that? It's not like Camelia died in a freak accident or something." Realizing that she had spoken too harshly, Anya corrected herself. "I didn't mean it that way. I'm just confused at why she's triggered by the name."

Mr. Zhou sighed again and replied, "Your mother has always been an anxious person. Ever since I've known her, she's always fretting about the smallest things, so much so that she often can't sleep at night. So when Camelia left, she blamed herself. The days following Camelia's disappearance, you thought that she was at work the entire time. But in reality, she was at a hospital."

Anya's eyes widened in shock. "What do you mean she was in a hospital? All of you guys said that she was just busy with her patients, prescribing medicine and all."

"I know... I really didn't want to tell you this. But now that you've grown up, I think it's time for me to tell you."

Anya sat forward in her chair.

"She started profusely vomiting after Camelia left, so much so that when we brought her to the ER, they said that she was in critical condition. And the entire time, she kept on just saying over and over again that it was her fault. She refused to eat or drink anything, and I was seriously worried about her life during that period. Then, when the doctor said that he couldn't help her any longer, we asked him what we should do."

Too appalled by what she was hearing, Anya butted in, "So, what did the doctor say?"

"Well, the doctor just said one thing, which was that we should limit bringing up Camelia. Best of all, don't even bring her up at all. If we wanted her to stay healthy, of course."

Anya, upon hearing her father's final lines, put her head down in despair.

fifteen

Sophie

"I CAN'T BELIEVE that this is all actually happening," her mother whispered.

"What is happening?" Sophie thought. *Why are they being so mysterious again? I didn't even want to snoop around, but this situation kind of begs me to listen in, doesn't it?* Sophie knew in her gut that she shouldn't be doing this spying, especially not when she was just going to apologize for doing so earlier, but she couldn't help herself.

"I know, right? I can't believe she went there, of all places in the world."

Who are they talking about? Are they gossiping about a coworker? A family friend? Sophie instinctively shook her head at the thought, realizing that her parents were most definitely not the type to engage in such gossip. *Plus, one's in architecture and the other's in business, so they barely spend much time together. Come to think of it, they probably don't even have someone in common to gossip about.* These observations only made Sophie more curious to hear who her parents were actually talking about.

Sophie heard her mother's response to her father, saying "I thought we sent her to Costa Rica to rehab, so how the hell did she manage to slip away to an island?"

"Well, Tortuguero is in Costa Rica, I suppose," her father said.

Hearing this familiar word, Sophie stepped back in shock. *Isn't that where Camelia went to? Why are they talking about that place? And rehab? They sent someone off to rehab?* At this point, Sophie felt like there could only be one possible answer, yet she didn't want to accept it. *No, my parents wouldn't do this to me. Would they?*

Her mother snapped back, "I know that Tortuguero is in Costa Rica, for goodness sakes. But we sent her to San Jose, not there."

"Goddammit, what are we supposed to do now? Sit here and wait for her to come back?"

Sophie could feel the immense tension in the air even when she was outside of the room. By now, she was on the verge of breaking in and demanding to know who the person they were talking about was, but she knew that doing so would just make her parents shut up and never reveal themselves.

But Sophie didn't even have to break into find out, as moments later, her mother said, "No, I know Mackenzie. She would never return if we simply just asked her to. Unless we go there ourselves, she never does."

Even though Sophie had already suspected it, her mother's verbal confirmation pummeled her head and sent a wave of nausea over her. *What. the. actual. fuck. Everything makes sense now. Why my parents have always been whispering about Mackenzie. Why I wasn't even allowed to see her body after begging and crying to do so.* Everything was so twisted that she had to hold onto the doorknob to stabilize herself, and she didn't even know what to do anymore. *It's all been a lie. Does Uncle Wang know about this? If he does, he's been hiding it from me as well. Oh my god.* Sophie really felt like she was about to collapse.

For a while, she just stood there in absolute shock. Her parents' voices became a jumble of incomprehensible words, all making Sophie feel like she was going to throw up. She couldn't even feel anger at her parents; it was just this insisting throbbing of her head that wouldn't dissipate. Too many thoughts bombarded her all at once: thoughts of her parents' betrayal, thoughts of how stupid she had been all this time, and thoughts of how she was going to confront everybody. *Should I even confront my parents? I want to scream at them so bad, but...*

Sophie decided that she had to take a couple of deep breaths before she started going berserk at her parents. *No, if I confront them now, who's to say that they won't just hide Mackenzie away again?* As soon as her thoughts flitted to Mackenzie, another wave of emotions hit her, this time filled with joy and hope. *Oh my god. Mackenzie's alive. She's actually alive. That means... Maybe I can see her again.* Sophie wanted to scream again, this time for a different reason than before. *My sister, she's alive.* Sophie kept on repeating that phrase to herself, letting it sink in. She had never truly accepted her sister's death, so even when Mackenzie had "died," Sophie had made sure to keep everything in her room exactly as how it had been. *And now she might be able to live in it again.* All her previous anger dissipated, and her thoughts began to become more rational. *Okay, so I definitely cannot confront my parents until I know the real story about what is happening. After all, I cannot lose Mackenzie again. But... who should I talk to?*

Her first thought went to Anya, as that was perhaps the only person she could trust as of now. *I would tell Lyla, but then I would have to explain to her so much. I haven't talked to her about Mackenzie in who knows how long. It could be a month or two by now. And I can't trust Uncle Wang, so the only option I've got is Anya.* As Sophie thought it over, she realized that it would be quite a shock to Anya as well. *Who the hell just hides their daughter away and then tells everybody that she's dead? My parents, I suppose. And the fact that Mackenzie is in the same town as Camelia? If I were Anya, I would never believe me.*

Sophie didn't even have to ask her parents to know why they did it. *They didn't want the world to know the addiction problem their daughter had. So they sent her off to rehab and decided never to tell me. Not even their own daughter.* Sophie consoled herself that at least her sister was still alive. *As long as I'm able to see Mackenzie again, everything will be okay. I mean, I don't know if I'll ever forgive my parents, but I'll have Mackenzie by my side again.* Even just the thought of it made Sophie giddy with joy. She pressed her nails into her arm to make sure she wasn't dreaming, as it all seemed too good to be real.

Her thoughts were suddenly disrupted when she heard her parents coming nearer and nearer to the door. Their voices once again came into focus.

Her father said, "Okay, that's enough said about Mackenzie today. Let's talk more about what we should do tomorrow. Also, I just realized."

Her mother, in an anxious tone, replied, "What did you realize?"

"Mackenzie doesn't have an infinite amount of money; she might not even have any at all. So she can't stay at Tortuguero for long. She will have to go back to San Jose soon."

"You're right. What should we even do about that?"

"Just wait it out, I suppose. At least that means we don't have to worry about her staying on the island of Tortuguero forever."

At this point, Sophie *really* wanted to burst into the room and scream at her parents. *I mean, how could their biggest worry be her returning to the rehab center? Are they not even worried about her well-being? They haven't even shown a hint of remorse.* But Sophie decided against it. As her parents' footsteps got closer, she quickly headed back to her room and shut the door before her parents could find out that she was snooping around again.

Sophie splayed out on her bed, just letting her thoughts process. *These last few days have really tried to wipe me out. First, I get caught spying on my parents to find out that they're undergoing therapy. Then, when I'm feeling so guilty I might have died, the atomic bomb came that Mackenzie is fucking alive. I still can't believe it, not at all. Am I dreaming? My sister is alive.*

After all the chaos, Sophie checked her bedside clock and saw that it was already almost 5:30 pm. *Okay, so it seems to be around time to tell Anya. That's kind of the only thing I can do right now.* Sophie took a quick moment to calculate the time difference, which was almost instinctive at this point. *It's 8:30 am, her breakfast time. And I basically know her school schedule at this point, and she has a free period in the morning. This means she should be at home and that if I call her now, I only have a short period of time to inform her of everything.*

Sophie decided that the situation called for action, so she quickly texted Anya, sincerely hoping that she would check her computer before she went back to class. *Or else I most definitely won't be able to sleep a wink tonight. I need to get this information off my chest.* Sophie had never felt this kind of burden before, and it both exhilarated and scared her.

As her texts were sent out, Sophie anxiously paced her room, making sure to keep quiet in case her parents heard. Even though she had a huge English test tomorrow that she hadn't even studied for, nothing in the world could have stopped her from pacing until Anya's reply five minutes later. *Thank goodness.*

It was short and exactly what Sophie had expected. It read, "You have got to be kidding me."

Sophie immediately replied, saying, "Call now."

Before five seconds even passed, they were already facetiming.

Anya first spoke, saying, "There is *no* way. Tell me straight up that you're not lying. There is no way that Mackenzie and Camelia are on the *exact* same island."

I wouldn't believe myself either. "Nope, I'm telling the absolute complete truth. I'm just as shocked as you are, believe me." *Well, I can't say I didn't have my suspicions before, but Anya doesn't need to know that. Or else I'm going to have to tell her about me spying on my parents. And then explain why I didn't tell her about it.*

"If you are telling the truth..." Anya paused, perhaps trying to scrutinize Sophie's face for any sign of a lie. Perhaps finally convinced, Anya's attitude changed one hundred eighty degrees, as she started bouncing up and down and exclaiming, "That is such good news! Omg, I'm so happy for you! This is the greatest thing ever!"

Sophie smiled but thought back to her doubts. "I know, I am so happy right now. I feel like I could honestly be happier, but it just doesn't seem to be real. Like I've tried to process my thoughts multiple times now, but each time I do so, the events just seem crazier and crazier. I mean, I have my sister back. After I thought that she was dead for *months*. What could be crazier than that?"

"That is so, so crazy. Your life seems unreal, like it's out of a movie or something."

"Uh huh. I don't even think I've seen this play out in the movies before."

Both people took a moment to reconvene their thoughts. Then, Anya asked, "So, what are you going to do now? Are you going to confront your parents?"

"Well, for one, I'm definitely not confronting my parents. That would just lead to absolute disaster. And on the broader scale, I really don't know what I'm going to do." *I was kind of hoping that you would have an answer.* But as Sophie looked at Anya with her head in her arms, she realized that Anya was probably more at a loss than her. "And don't bring up Uncle Wang. I'm pretty sure he was in this whole scheme as well. After all, my mother and him are like best buddies. They tell each other everything."

Anya thought about it for a moment and sat back to drink a sip of water. "Hold on, are you sure that he knows about this?"

"What do you mean? You think that my mother hid this secret from essentially her best friend?"

"Well, kind of yeah. If your mother hid the true story from you, what's to say that she didn't hide it from everyone? You should have been the first one who she would tell, wouldn't you?"

Now that Anya said it this way, Sophie began to see it in a different light. *I suppose that Uncle Wang wouldn't have felt such grief if he actually knew that Mackenzie hadn't died. There's no way that all that grief he expressed then wasn't real. Those were real tears I saw. I'm sure of it.*

Sophie responded, "So you think I should talk to my uncle about this?"

"Well, that's kind of the only option you have right now, isn't it?"

That's true. "But what if he does know? And then he goes and tells my parents?"

Anya smiled. "So that's why we're about to devise a plan. Hurry up though, I only have thirty minutes left to call."

sixteen

Anya

ANYA'S MIND was whirring at 100 miles per hour. Even when she was trying to devise a plan for Sophie, part of her still thought it was all a big prank. *There is no way somebody just comes back from the dead like that. And she's in Tortuguero, which means that she might have met Camelia.* Anya shook her head in disbelief. *There is just no way this is real. And the fact that her parents have been hiding Mackenzie away for months...* Anya had previously thought that her mother was the craziest person she knew, but everything paled in front of Sophie's parents.

I feel so bad for Sophie. I mean, she has every reason to be happy that Mackenzie's alive, but I would never be able to trust my parents again if I were her. I would've probably gone psychotic on them by now. Anya looked at Sophie trying to come up with a plan. *How in the world is she so calm right now? She's definitely got some sort of otherworldly willpower that I do not have.*

Realizing that her thoughts had gone off track, Anya went back to thinking about the plan. *This situation seems kind of familiar somehow.* She grimaced. *Perhaps that's from all the times I've lied to my parents. What would I do in this situation?*

With this mindset of talking to her parents, Anya almost immediately came up with a plan.

She told Sophie, "Okay, listen up. I think I've got a plan."

Sophie looked up at the computer screen and said, "It better be good. I'm relying almost everything on this, so if it messes up..."

"It won't, trust me."

Anya then proceeded to tell Sophie about each step that she would take. For once, Anya was pretty sure about this plan, as she had lied so many times to her mother that it seemed almost like second nature. *Plus, she doesn't even have to see him face to face, so it'll be even easier to hide her actual emotions.*

After hanging up, Anya rubbed her eyes, trying to bring herself back into the reality of school. *How did that much happen in such a short time? I feel like a lifetime has already passed, and it's only 8:45 am. And now I have to change and get ready for school. After I just learned the craziest news I have ever heard.* Moreover, a part of her really didn't want to go out of her room, as she wasn't prepared to see her mother again.

Since yesterday when her mother ran out of the dining room, Anya hadn't seen her mother once. After going to the bathroom, she disappeared inside her room, not coming out the entire time. Anya's father had quickly followed after, as he wanted to make sure that Anya's mother was doing okay. Anya had waited and waited for her parents to come out of the room, but nobody had come out. After around thirty minutes, Anya had given up and had left for her room. The sheer disappointment she had felt then was unlike anything she had ever experienced, except perhaps when Camelia disappeared. *I had at least expected her to say something, not just turn tail and flee. I didn't even get to say what I wanted to.* Anya sarcastically laughed to herself. *Imagine what would have happened if she heard that I had actually found out where Camelia is.*

Anya realized that she couldn't be late for school again. *Which means I probably have to see Mom again.* As she brushed and straightened her tangled hair, she tried to rehearse what she was going to say, but she couldn't come up with something that would alleviate the awkwardness.

Whatever. Why should I be the one who's awkward? She should be the one who's awkward if anybody is. So, with that "comfort," Anya left her room.

She prepared to see her mother waiting for her in the kitchen to go to the car, but in her place was her grandmother. *What is happening now? Why is Grandma Wang here?*

Her grandmother's face lit up when she saw Anya. "Hello! I haven't seen you in such a long time. Your mother is always keeping you busy, isn't she?"

Well, I suppose, but that's not the main problem right now. "I missed you, Grandma. How have you been?"

"Ah, you know. Getting old is really quite terrible. My back is always killing me." She patted her back for emphasis.

What do I even say right now? I want to ask her about Mom, but then it also feels like I shouldn't. So, Anya decided to just avoid the topic altogether. "Would you like me to massage your back for you? I have a couple of minutes left before I have to go to school."

Her grandmother clicked her tongue. "No, no, no. I came here to pamper you, not the other way around. Your mother is feeling under the weather, and your father is at work, so I'm going to be taking care of you today. Your grandfather couldn't come because he's busy doing stocks at home. Apparently, there's this new company that's been on the rise or something. Ay, I'm too old to keep up with those frivolous things."

So that's what Mom's explanation was. Makes sense, she probably doesn't want to tell her mother about how she can't even talk about her own daughter without going crazy. Anya accidentally scoffed.

Her grandmother, hearing this scoff, curiously asked, "What happened? Is there something funny I don't know about?"

"Sorry, I was just thinking about a joke my friend said."

"Ah, you're two best friends, Odyssey and Isabel? Are they still causing you the same drama as before? You used to always cry about them, and I would have to console you with lollipops. But then you would start being best friends the very next day."

"Yup, I'm still besties with them, but we have less drama now." *To be honest, I haven't thought about them since what seems like forever. I've been so caught up ever since that letter. And now the whole Mackenzie thing.*

Her grandmother replied, "Oh, that's good to hear. Anyway, I brought some of your favorite breakfast foods over. You've loved them since you were a baby. Let's see here." She took out a large plastic bag, in which were rice balls, pan-fried pork buns, and small, homemade dumplings with shrimp and cabbage.

Even though Anya had lacked an appetite from all the chaos of the morning, the delectable smells wafting from the bag made her hungry again. *Even if I have a terrible rest of the day, at least I'll have had a delicious breakfast.* She looked at her grandmother as her petite and wrinkled hands busily prepared the food, and Anya realized just how grateful she was. *I do really have the best grandmother in the world. She's been here for me through everything, though I don't get to see her as often as I wish to.*

After eating a hearty breakfast, it was already time to go to school. As her grandmother didn't know how to drive, they went on the bus instead. Anya was beyond grateful for the change of scene, and she and her grandmother chatted throughout the entire bus ride. She learned of how her grandmother had just had a huge family reunion with all her sisters, and how they had eaten at least five different kinds of steamed fish. She chuckled when she learned of how her grandfather had gotten into a huge fight with one of the sister's husbands about paying the bill. All in all, she managed to remove her thoughts from her mother.

After Anya got off the bus, she told her grandmother, "See you soon!" *Which I will make sure of this time. I most definitely won't go another month without seeing her.*

Anya's grandmother eagerly waved back at her, her eyes crinkling as she smiled.

Her spirit lifted, Anya turned around and headed past her school's gates.

Right away, she was bombarded by Odyssey and Isabel, who had apparently been waiting for her for twenty minutes already.

Isabel exclaimed, "Anya! Have you not seen our texts? Something huge just happened."

Anya checked her phone, seeing that she did in fact receive all those messages. "Sorry, I was with my grandmother and didn't look at my phone. What happened to make you guys all so excited?"

Odyssey replied, "You might not like this, but... Isabel, you say it."

Isabel gave a death glare at Odyssey, which made Anya nervous. *What the hell are they so worried about telling me about? Did someone die?*

Finally, Anya just said, "Spit it out. What happened?"

Isabel, giving another dirty look at Odyssey, said, "Fine, I'll say it. But you have to promise that you won't get mad at me, okay?"

Anya sighed, exasperated and unnerved by how much tension her friends were building up. "Okay, I promise. But tell me now."

"So, Liam got a girlfriend." Isabel and Odyssey glanced at Anya.

THAT'S what they were so worried about telling me about? Anya knew she should be upset, as she had liked Liam since forever. *And it's not like I don't like him anymore, it's just that...* Anya wasn't sure how to complete that sentence.

Odyssey, perhaps anxious for an answer, asked, "Hello? Anya?" She waved her hand in Anya's face. "Aren't you shocked? Why are you not saying anything? Are you so stunned that you can't even reply anymore?"

For goodness sake, give me some breathing room. Anya brushed away Odyssey's hand and answered, "There's no point in freaking out. It's not our decision who he likes, right?"

Both Odyssey and Isabel stepped back in shock. Isabel asked, "So you aren't even the least bit upset about this? Do you not actually like him?"

Anya shrugged her shoulders. "No, no, I do like him. And I can't say I'm happy. But I'm just okay. It doesn't really affect me."

There was a moment of awkward silence before Isabel said, "Oh, my baby. You're probably so sad, but you're just hiding your emotions really well." She went in to hug Anya, whispering the entire time that "it'll be okay."

Odyssey also added on, "You don't have to hide your emotions in front of us. We understand." She also embraced Anya.

Anya wanted to scream, "What are you guys doing?" and "Why can't you believe me?" but she decided to just play it off cool and pretend to be sad. *It probably makes more sense to all of us that I would be in a meltdown right now.*

As Anya sat in Chinese class, she let her mind drift off. *Why was I not upset about Liam?* She looked at him sitting in front of her, realizing that she hadn't thought about Liam in quite a while. *I suppose this week has been too hectic for me to think about him. Or maybe...* Anya thought for a moment about how she might have lost feelings for him, but she immediately retracted the thought. *There's no way I lost feelings in such a short period of time. Yes, it must have been from all the mayhem that I just stopped thinking about him for a while.*

Before she knew it, her thoughts had again drifted, this time back to her mother. *What in the world am I going to do now? I can't tell my mother I've found Camelia, or else according to Dad, she'll go berserk. And then I definitely will be barred from searching for her. I wouldn't even be shocked if my mother locks me away in my room to stop me from searching for her.* Anya could already imagine how her mother would nearly pass out and then tell Anya that if she wanted her mother to be in good health, she wouldn't go halfway across the world to find Camelia.

Then Anya thought about telling her father. *How would that play out? He would probably be super nice as that's just his character. But he would be obliged to tell my mother. Especially after seeing how worried he was about her yesterday, he definitely wouldn't do something that would risk damaging her health.* Anya audibly sighed, feeling like she was completely out of options. *I suppose both Sophie and I are dealing with this kind of problem.*

The school day passed relatively slowly, as Anya kept on making sure to keep a "happy" face on in case anyone thought that she was depressed about Liam. Finally, the end of the school day came around.

Once again, Anya didn't see her mother, as her father had come to pick her up. *Shit. This conversation might be awkward as well.*

"Hi Dad. Aren't you supposed to be at work?" *I'm not bringing up Mom until he does.*

Luckily, Anya didn't have to wait long, as her father replied right after, "Well, your mother is still feeling unwell, so I decided I had to come pick up my sweet daughter. How was your day?"

"I'm good, and thank you for coming, but why is Mom still feeling unwell? It's already been almost a day."

He sighed. "I know. She's been especially sensitive these past few days because it's nearing her birthday time. And a family "friend" commented on how she never let Camelia rest on her birthdays. So she keeps on quietly blaming herself."

"But is she still doing this? How long is her freak out going to last?"

"Well, truth be told, she's probably fine by now, but she's probably embarrassed to see you again. So she might just be avoiding you."

Ah, that sounds more like my mother. Anya slightly laughed. "That's funny. I was nervous the entire day to see her as well."

Her father laughed along with her. "You know, sometimes you and your mother really aren't that different. You always complain about your mother, and she always complains about you."

"Haha, that's very true, though I wouldn't say I'm like her." *She's batshit crazy.*

Her father didn't say anything, just winking at her through the rear-view mirror.

Noticing that she was on the way home, Anya asked, "Don't I have English tutoring today?"

"Oh yeah, I forgot to tell you. Both your mother and I agreed that we should cancel your class today. It's only right after what you had to go through yesterday."

Anya smiled. *Perhaps seeing my mother won't be as bad as I had imagined.* They pulled into the parking lot.

seventeen
Sophie

HAVING JUST WOKEN UP, Sophie quickly checked outside her room. *Okay good, nobody's there. They probably haven't woken up yet since it's only 6 am.* Sophie had made sure to set an alarm for an earlier time, as she wanted to make sure she could call her uncle before going off to school. *He has probably finished work by now and is getting ready to go to bed. So it should be perfect timing.*

Quickly, Sophie rehearsed in her head about what she would say to him. Even though she had practiced it long into the night, she wanted to make sure that her plan was absolutely perfect. *I cannot afford any mistakes.*

Sophie pressed the dial button on the video call, and her uncle almost immediately answered.

"Hey, Sophie. What's up?" Her uncle's face seemed surprisingly energetic for it being his nighttime.

"Hi, Uncle Wang! Oh, nothing much. I just wanted to check in so that we don't go without saying a word to each other for *months* again." Sophie comforted herself that she wasn't completely lying.

"Ah, how nice that my niece is thinking about me. So, what did you want to talk about?"

Okay, this is where I have to lie perfectly. "Well, I started thinking about Mackenzie more and more these past few days."

An awkward pause occurred before he asked, "Why is that?"

"Well, it's nearing summer, and we would always have this big celebration on the last day of school." *Not a lie.*

"What would you guys do?"

"We would do *everything*. We would always get something audacious from Amazon a few days before so that it arrives the day of the last day of school. Like once, we got a water trampoline, which took up our entire front yard. When Mom and Dad got home, they were so mad, but then they started playing in it as well." Sophie chuckled and her uncle did so as well.

"So now you miss this kind of experience?"

"Yes, very much so. And I'm quite afraid that it'll get worse as summer comes because I won't have anything to do to preoccupy my time."

"Ah, I'm sorry to hear that. What would you like me to do to help?"

Sophie smiled. *He fell into the trap.* "Do you think it's possible that... no, it's too much to ask for."

"No, just ask. I'll try to do whatever I can."

"Well, if it's not too much of a burden, would it be possible for you to bring me to see Mackenzie's grave?"

Another pause. Her uncle replied, "I would be happy to do that, but might I ask why you can't just tell your parents?"

Okay, critical point time. Sophie put on her most innocent face and nonchalant voice she could do. "I already asked them, but they said that they were too busy to take me." *Actually, they've never told me where she was buried. Nor have they even brought up the idea of holding a funeral for her.* Sophie internally kicked her younger self for being so naive. *How could I have not seen right through them?* Sophie looked to her dwelling uncle and anxiously waited for his response. *Please don't ask my parents for confirmation that I asked them. And please, please don't be in on my parents' secret.*

He responded, "You know what, sure. But I've never been there either. Where is it?"

Sophie smiled at this response, but she just needed to confirm it. "Has Mom never told you about where Mackenzie was buried?"

"Nope. Not one word... Come to think of it, I can't remember her saying anything about a funeral. I suppose she was in too much grief to hold one." Sophie could hear the confusion starting to arrive in her uncle's tone.

YES. Having received the exact answer she had wanted, Sophie felt like she had scored the grand prize at the arcade. *He's absolutely oblivious to the truth, which means that he probably won't rat on me if I tell him what's happened.* Sophie did realize that there was the possibility that her uncle could spill everything to her parents, but she took it on the bet that he probably wanted to see Mackenzie more so than he cared about his sister's temporary feelings. She was also betting all her cards on how her uncle would be quite upset at his sister for hiding such a large fact, so he would have a desire for revenge. And finally, she was betting on something else, which was that she knew her uncle inside and out.

I've known that guy since forever, so much so that at one point, I was calling him "Dad." So if I know him right, then he's the type to love a good challenge. Sophie thought about what would have to be done. *And practically nothing would be more challenging than this.*

So, she decided that it was time. *If I don't say it now, then I'll never end up saying anything. And who knows how long Mackenzie will be in Tortuguero before she's whisked away back to the rehab center, of which I'm not even sure of its location?*

But as Sophie prepared to tell her uncle, her indecisiveness started to come through. She started to stall for time, talking mindlessly about her life. As she ranted, her uncle nodded along, but Sophie could tell that this call wasn't going to last long before he had to go to bed.

Okay, I need to think straight. I literally just told him all of those lies so that I could get to this point. Considering that I had just lied the most I've ever done, I need to tell him now if I don't want him to be upset at me.

But... Despite her own comforting words, Sophie couldn't bury the feeling that telling him now would be an impetuous decision. *I don't even have a plan yet, so if I tell him now, and he asks me for a plan, I'll have to say that I don't have one because he definitely won't believe me if I make one up on the spot. And even though he likes challenges, he doesn't like doing something that will have an almost 100 percent failure rate. Added on to how I don't even have any proof of what I'm saying...* Sophie took a moment to do some calculations in her head. *That means I only have around a 50 percent chance of success, if not less.*

Realizing that the odds weren't in her favor, Sophie disappointedly decided to call it quits. *That doesn't mean I'm giving up though. I just need to talk to Anya and come up with a plan.* As Sophie hung up the call, she made a silent vow to herself that she would carry out the rest of the plan in under two days. *Which means I don't have long to think of a plan.*

But for now, it was school time, meaning time to see her parents again.

Walking toward the living room, where her mother usually waited to drive her to school, Sophie at first gulped in fear. *What if they're still mad at me?* But then, on second thought, she realized with irony that she should be one upset at her parents. *They're the ones who hid the biggest news possible, while I was just snooping around. We're on completely different spectrums of terrible.*

Sure enough, when she got to the living room, her mother was right there waiting for her. Sophie was about to say something out of courtesy, but she held her tongue. *Nope. Not giving her that pleasure.* Looking at her mother's stone-cold face, Sophie wanted to reveal everything right there and then. *I can just imagine the shock on her face if I told her. She would be the one apologizing to me, not the other way around.* Just thinking of the idea made Sophie delighted, which lasted all the way until she reached the car.

By then, Sophie had realized amid the awkward silence how strange the situation was. *I should most definitely not be happy right now that I can get revenge on my parents. I mean, I should be mad at them, but they're honestly probably going through so much more than me.* Right after she had learned the truth, she had envisioned her parents as these monsters hiding someone away in their cave. But Sophie, seeing how her mother's eye circles were even darker than usual, realized that her parents were just human as well. *While they might not be the best people, and I certainly won't forgive them for a long time, I don't want to see them all depressed. I haven't even begun to process how my parents are seeing a literal therapist.*

So although Sophie still couldn't wrap her head around why her parents had to go to such large extents of hiding Mackenzie, she took back her earlier thoughts of revenge. *Plus, I should instead focus on fixing this family. I don't even know how we got so messed up. Like sooo messed up.* Sophie thought about all the people she knew. *Not one family is as crazy as mine. Not even Anya's kind-of-crazy family.*

But how do I even begin to fix everything? I suppose I should start with fully apologizing to my mother, which I haven't even truly done. I had just thought that they wouldn't forgive me anyways, so I hadn't said anything.

Quietly, Sophie said, "Hi, Mom."

Her mother barely took notice of her greeting, just staring off into the road.

"Okay, you don't have to respond, but I just wanted to say that I'm sorry. Like *actually* sorry. I was suspicious of you because you hid your phone when I heard the word "Mackenzie," but that doesn't give me an excuse to spy on you. I won't do that again in the future, I promise."

Well, I got my apology across. Finally, Sophie waited for her mother's response, but there was none. Not even after twenty seconds had passed. *What the hell? It doesn't even look like she registered what I had just said.*

Annoyed at this reaction, Sophie shouted, "Hello, Mom!"

This time, her mother seemed to take notice, turning around and saying, "Huh? What's up?"

Sophie wanted to punch the seat in front of her out of frustration. "Have you not heard a single word I said earlier?"

"Sorry, I'm a bit tired. Could you repeat what you wanted to say."

What even is the point of talking to her? "I said..." Before she could say the rest of her sentence, however, they had already arrived at school. "Never mind, I'll tell you later."

Her mother just nodded.

Exasperated, Sophie entered her school.

When she walked in, she could already sense that something was off, as people were silently whispering to one another. *What happened now?* Just as Sophie was about to enter her first class of the day, someone snatched her arm and dragged her around the corner.

It was Lyla. She was talking in a quiet but urgent voice. "Do you know what's happened?"

I don't particularly want to know right now. "No, is it about Ashley and her two friends?"

"Yes, it is. Ashley's moving away!"

"What? She's moving? Does her family need to move or something?" Having known Ashley since the day she arrived at her school, the sudden news about her departure surprised Sophie to say the least.

"Well, she is moving, but not because of her family. At least, I think."

"What do you mean?" *There's no way this is because of her argument with her friends, right? They've had so many arguments, and they've reconciled each time better than ever.*

But Lyla reflected Sophie's doubts. "I think it might be something to do about her and her friends' relationship. Ever since the birthday party, it seems that something has been wrong between them."

"I suppose that's true. But I can't imagine how a fight could lead to such drastic measures. We're also already in the middle of high school, which means that if she transferred schools now, she would be entering into a completely different environment where everyone already knows each other."

Lyla nodded and said, "I have a feeling that it's something bigger, but I'm just not sure what it is."

The bell rang, so Sophie said, "Let's discuss this topic later. For now, it's frustrating, but we can't do anything yet." *And that's true for my secret as well.*

eighteen
Anya

ANYA PREDICTED CORRECTLY, as when she walked into the house, there was a delectable table of food laid out in the dining room. There was king crab, each one peeled so that the delicious flesh could be taken out in one movement of the chopsticks. There was fresh-caught shrimp and clams, steamed rather than braised. There was an *entire* chicken and so much more. And most of all, there were her favorite handmade shrimp crackers that her mother only made for special occasions.

Seeing this scene, Anya looked to her father, who looked back at her in shock.

He mouthed the words, "I wasn't in on any part of this."

Anya quietly mouthed back, "Why did she go all out? You know how much she hates having to fry those crackers."

"To apologize, I think."

Anya and her father awkwardly stood there, waiting for Mrs. Zhou to come out of the kitchen.

A few moments later, she stepped out, and Anya internally gasped again. *Why is she dressed like that?* Clad in a matt red dress that nearly touched the ground as well as with her hair intricately done in a tight, traditional bun, she seemed to be on her way to a formal dinner at a

Michelin star restaurant, not just eating at home. Once again, when Anya looked at her father, he seemed shocked as well.

Mrs. Zhou spoke first and said, "Welcome home everyone!"

Anya just stood there gaping.

Mr. Zhou, sensing the awkwardness in the room, inquired, "Honey, is there an occasion or something? We never have dinner like this unless on very special occasions. And..." He looked at her outfit.

Mrs. Zhou laughed. "Oh my goodness, look at all your shocked reactions. Haven't you all forgotten what date it is? It's '*Mahjong* Day!'". And before you say that we usually just go out to a fancy restaurant, I want to say that I haven't forgotten. But I also wanted to apologize to Anya today, and I think the dinner at home would better show my apologies. That was probably very surprising yesterday for Anya when I just turned and left. I will explain why I did so another day when I'm feeling all good and healthy, but for now, let's just dig into this food."

Still at a loss for words, all Anya could muster to say was "thank you."

As they sat down at the table and began to eat, Anya finally took recognition of what was happening. *If she doesn't want to talk about why she left the room, then I won't push her. Let's just enjoy this dinner in peace.*

Anya asked, "Mom, didn't you say you weren't feeling good? How did you have the energy to cook up all this food?"

She responded, "Oh, it was nothing. I just didn't want to just laze around the house and do nothing. Plus, cooking makes me feel better."

That's so typical of her; she can never fully rest, can she? Anya ate a piece of the chicken and licked the sauce off her lips. "Did you get this chicken from that very expensive marketplace you always go to on *Ma Jiang* Day?"

"Of course I did! It's *Mahjong* Day after all."

Anya lightly chuckled but then cringed inside. *I had nearly forgotten that it was Mahjong Day; I haven't picked up those poker cards in ages. And seeing how Dad reacted when he walked into the house, he also probably forgot among all the drama.* "So, are we going to play *Mahjong* later?"

"Yes, we are. It's an absolute must so that we don't lose that skill of yours when you grow up. You know, being a good *Mahjong* player is more important than most people think. It's a must-have social skill here."

Laughing, Anya said, "But I don't have skill. It was just beginner's luck."

Her father pitched in. "No, no, no. You beat all the experts that day, including your aunt. There is no way that that was just beginner's luck."

Anya responded, "She was definitely just going easy on me. There's no other way."

Her mother clicked her tongue. "You always say that, but when I talked to your aunt later, she told me in confidence that you had actually won."

Mr. Zhou said, "And you've won all the ones afterward."

Anya jokes, "Well, if I'm not good at anything, then at least I'm definitely good at *Mahjong*."

Her parents both chuckled, and Anya was glad to see the light come back into her mother's eyes. *This might be a dumb tradition, but it's certainly quite nice.*

Yet, when she saw her mother happy, she realized all the more that she didn't want to tell her about Camelia. *If I do so, she's going to be overloaded with worry. Especially if I show her that vague note, she might as well implode.*

So, Anya kept her mouth shut, deciding that there had to be another way. *There's a thousand million ways that people can get to Costa Rica. It doesn't just have to be with your parents. Tons of people travel all the time; I'll be just fine.* With those comforts, she ate her shrimp crackers and commenced beating both her parents at *Mahjong*.

As Anya laid in bed, however, she realized that getting to Costa Rica was not as easy as she thought. It was, in fact, nearly impossible. *First off, I'm only fifteen years old, which means that I can't fly alone. So I would need someone to bring me. But there is absolutely no one who can.* She thought about the possibility of asking her grandparents but soon realized that they were way too old for this kind of trip. *They barely want to go to Beijing as it is, so asking them to take me halfway across the world is a definite no. And I suppose I have my aunts and uncles, but I'm nowhere close enough to them for them to agree to bring me. I literally only see them two or three times a year. They would go straight to telling my parents.*

The more she thought about her lack of options, the more frustrated she got. *Why is there nobody that I can ask for help from?* Wanting to scream into her pillow, she nearly did, but she was distracted by a "ding" from her computer.

Completely wide awake from her frustration, Anya decided to check it.

It was Sophie, and it read, "Hey, want to call sometime?"

Yes, perfect timing. I need some distraction. Anya plugged her nearly-dead computer into the wall and started a video call.

To her great relief, Sophie picked up.

Waving hello, Anya asked, "Why did you want to call? What's up?" She could see that Sophie was still in bed and hadn't changed into her school outfit yet. *Is she having trouble sleeping as well?*

Sophie responded, "Okay, I first want to tell you the good news, which is that my uncle wasn't in on the secret."

"Yay, that's wonderful!" exclaimed Anya. "So he's okay with being the one to take you to Costa Rica?"

"Ummm... that's the bad news. I kind of haven't told him yet."

What??? "You haven't? But wasn't that the whole point of testing him?"

Sophie sighed. "I know, but I wimped out. I was too scared that something would go wrong. I think I need a plan first before I tell him. What do you think?"

Tapping her feet, Anya realized what she said was true. *It's definitely a lot safer with a plan than without one.* Thinking back on how she almost just spilled everything to her mother without even having a plan behind it, she scolded her previous self. *What was I even thinking? Did I just think that she was going to immediately agree and go with me?* Not wanting Sophie to make the dumb mistake she had almost made, Anya said, "Yes, I think that's a great idea."

Sophie smiled and said, "Good, thanks for saying that. I was regretting it so much earlier, as I kept on thinking about how I was running out of time before Mackenzie leaves. Also, what about you? What happened after your mother just left?"

"Well, we kind of reconciled. But I decided that I can't tell her. It would just end up in disaster, and I might end up ten steps back from my starting point of receiving the letter."

"That's very true. But do you have no one else who can bring you?"

"Nope, no one at all. I don't have someone who's that close to me, like your uncle is to you."

"I see."

For a little while, both people just sat there. Anya thought about a plan for Sophie. *It's nearing summertime, which means that she can make an excuse to get away. But how would she tell her parents not to come? And if they know that Mackenzie is there, would they even let her go?* Anya doodled on a piece of white paper, urging herself to think of a plan.

No, the words of Sophie leaving needs to come out of her uncle's mouth. If he says he wants to go on a solo trip with Sophie, there's a much greater chance the parents will agree. And about the Mackenzie part... the uncle will have to say that they're going somewhere that's in the complete opposite direction of Tortuguero. And they'll have to give the parents an outline of what they'll do there. Hmm... about convincing Uncle Wang...

Sophie suddenly interrupted by saying, "Hold on. I just came up with a kind of crazy plan for you that might just work."

"Really? I was just in the middle of thinking about a plan for you."

Sophie took a deep breath. "Okay, what I'm about to tell you might sound a bit crazy, and it's okay if you completely disagree. But hear me out first, alright?"

"Okay." *What kind of crazy plan is she going to come up with?*

"So, you've met my uncle before."

"Yes, I have. But what does that have to do with the story?"

"Hold on, let me finish."

"Sorry, I won't interrupt again. Go ahead."

"No worries. Okay, so since there's this crazy coincidence of both Mackenzie and Camelia being on the same island, I was thinking, 'What if we went together?'"

Anya gasped but didn't say anything.

"I know it's shocking, but if you were willing to, you could tell your story to my uncle. And since you've met him before, he knows who you are and that you're my friend. So he'll probably agree, and then we can go together. How does that sound?"

Anya's mind was whirring. Despite how crazy the plan sounded when it first came out of Sophie's mouth, she was beginning to think that it was a good idea. *This might be the only option I have.* "Yeah, I think that it's a possible plan."

"Really?"

"Yes, it's a bit of a far reach, but it might actually end up being helpful for you as well."

Sophie cocked her head.

"You see, if your uncle hears that you want to go to Costa Rica to find your sister, he'll most likely be convinced. But on the off chance that he isn't, hearing that not one but two people want to go to Costa Rica to find their sisters should be more than enough to tip him over the edge." *At least I hope that it is.*

Sophie exclaimed, "You're so right!"

Anya paused for a moment. "But how will I ever convince my parents?" *There's no way they'll ever agree.*

"That's easy. I was already thinking about it."

"Huh?" *She thought that far ahead?*

Sophie continued, "Remember how you found out in that meeting with Uncle Wang that your mother is close to my aunt?"

"Oh yeah..."

"Then that's perfect! My uncle can just have his wife tell your mother. And since they're so close, your mother should be just fine with it."

"I see." Anya's mind was whirring with ideas. *It might actually be possible.*

Sophie echoed what Anya was thinking, "But we need a plan first."

"Right. Here it is..."

Together, they began to mold a solid plan in place.

nineteen
Sophie

SOPHIE LOOKED at the written plan with pride, realizing they had come up with everything in under thirty minutes.

Their plan was as follows: (1) Ask uncle with entire plan laid out (2) say to parents they want to go to Costa Rica because of its beautiful nature and that their uncle is coincidentally going there for a business trip, making sure that the uncle verifies this part (3) tell parents they want to go on a friends-only trip with minimal adult supervision so that's why they're only calling their uncle over (4) give parents detailed descriptions of where they will be, of which are mostly lies (5) meet up at LAX to fly to Costa Rica, meaning that Anya and Sophie's uncle would first have to go to LA (6) get to Costa Rica and then make way to Tortuguero.

They didn't have a plan yet of what would happen after they made it to Tortuguero, as there were too many unknown factors. *We'll just have to see what happens there and think of what to do then.*

Anya said, "Okay, now that we have the basis of what we're going to do, do you feel ready to tell your uncle?"

Even though Sophie wasn't exactly confident about telling her uncle, she knew there was no reason not to anymore. "Yes, I'll do it tonight, so right before he goes to work."

Anya nodded. "Make sure you give him the specifics so that he doesn't start doubting the plan. And also make sure to tell him to not breathe a single word to your parents."

"Yes, I'll make sure to do that. In the meantime, don't worry too much and just go to bed. Summer vacation is coming up in just a week, so we need to be in our best condition when we get to Costa Rica" *If we get there. I really hope this plan works.*

Yawning, Anya replied, "Yes, now that we've talked it over, I feel a lot calmer than before."

"Me too, let's call soon to discuss further."

With that, they ended the phone call, and Sophie got ready for the day.

It was quite an uneventful school day, but Sophie did notice that she wasn't being the star student that she once was. It wasn't that she didn't try anymore, but it was just that she didn't crave the perfection she once did. Her thoughts no longer centered around impressing the teachers; instead, she was more focused on other factors, such as finding her sister.

So, when Sophie got a B on her history test, she was first shocked but then gradually accepted it. *I really haven't put any effort into school recently, so there is no reason why I should expect to see results.* Her thoughts flipped to the darker side. *Maybe with this grade, my parents will talk to me again. When they check my grades online, they'll surely be surprised, if not angry, when they see that their straight A student got a B.*

Yet, even when her parents came home late from work, they said nothing about it. In fact, they barely even turned to look her way. They came home, put down their keys, took off their shoes, disappeared together into the office without eating dinner.

They're probably brainstorming what to do about Mackenzie right now. Sophie sighed and was about to return to her room when she suddenly stopped. *Hold on, what if they're talking about something of importance? What if by the time I get to Tortuguero, they will already have sent Mackenzie back? No, I have to hear what they're saying.*

Sophie slightly retracted her steps and was soon again at the office's door. Unlike last time when she had broken out in a sweat from fear of being caught, she wasn't nervous at all. *This is already my third time sneaking around in under five days.* She made a silent promise to herself that she would stop after getting her sister back. *I'll go back to good old honest Sophie. It's just that right now, I need to listen in, or else I could lose everything.*

She first heard her mother's voice. "Okay, calm down. The rehab people finally responded. They say a friend took her away for a mini trip. But it was okayed by the hospital."

Her father responded, "What friend though? She doesn't have any friends there."

"Don't think of the worst-case scenario, for goodness sake. She was always a popular girl at school; maybe she made a friend at the rehab center who just took her out for some fun. The rehab center wouldn't have let her leave until she consented, so it wasn't like she was abducted or something."

"My god, what if she was tricked?"

"Please, stop kidding around. She's a fucking adult, not the little kid we once knew. She knows not to follow candy and get tricked by someone." Despite this wording, Sophie could hear the worry in her mother's voice. *She definitely doesn't trust Mackenzie that much.* Even Sophie, as she heard what her mother had said, began to worry. *Why would the hospital even do that? Mackenzie's grown up, yes, but she's still... She's still a patient.*

Hearing this made Sophie want to go to Costa Rica even more. *I need to see if she's okay.*

After a short bit of silence, her father said in a sarcastic tone, "Okay, so if we're so sure that she didn't get abducted, then what are we going to do? Just let her stay with her so-called friend?"

Her mother let out a scream. "Stop saying it like that! I've already planned out what we're going to do."

Sophie leaned as close as she could to the door without making a sound.

Her mother continued, "So we obviously can't drag her back. That would be an absolute disaster."

"Why would that be so bad?" Her father's voice was urgent.

"Do you not get it? She's literally an independent person. The last thing she would want right now is someone dragging her away right in front of her friend."

"Well, that's better than her being abducted."

"She's not being abducted, so stop saying that!" Quieting down, her mother said, "Do you really not want to be able to talk to your daughter again?"

There was silence until her father finally responded, "I suppose you're right. Sorry, please continue."

"As I was saying, since we cannot just take her away, I've already sent people there to watch her. They're making sure she's okay every step of the way."

What. They sent people to spy on her? Are they crazy? If Mackenzie finds out they're doing this... Sophie thought she was going to go crazy, but she took a deep breath. *Okay, so if this is what Mom is doing, that means I'll be watching in Tortuguero as well. Which makes my job a whole lot harder.*

Sophie returned to her room, not wanting to hear her parents talk anymore. *If I hear one more word, I might just burst into the room. I mean, how could they literally send someone to spy on their daughter?*

Once she returned to her room, she immediately wanted to tell everything to Anya. But she couldn't. *I have to spill the news to Uncle first.*

Sophie dialed the call button, and her uncle picked up.

"Hi Uncle!"

In a groggy voice, he replied, "Sophie? Is that you?"

"Yes, it is. Did you just wake up?" *Shit. Is this bad timing? Oh well, no time is good timing according to my standards.*

"I woke up around thirty minutes ago. But I'm not much of a morning person."

Sophie gulped in fear as she heard him say this phrase. *Please, please don't be in a bad mood when you hear what I'm about to say.*

"So, you've been calling me a lot. Is this call just to check up on me again?"

Okay, here goes. "No, it's actually for a different reason."

"Oh?"

"Yes, it's about Mackenzie, and you might need to brace yourself for what I'm about to say."

He chuckled, "I think I'll be fine, but sure."

You will most definitely not be fine. "Okay, so the thing is that Mackenzie's alive." Sophie said the last part of the sentence extremely quickly, as she wanted to get the hardest part over with.

Her uncle's voice wasn't groggy anymore. "Sorry? Come again, I think I heard you say your sister is alive. I must have been not hearing things right."

Oh dear. "Nope, you heard things exactly right. My sister, Mackenzie, is alive. And she's in Costa Rica. In a rehab center."

Silence. Finally, he said, "You have got to be joking with me. There is no way. Weren't you just asking me about going to visit her grave? Is this some prank you're pulling on me? If it is, it's not funny at all."

"So, I might have lied to you earlier."

"You, Sophie, lied?"

Sophie gulped. *I keep surprising myself as well.* "Yes, I lied to you to test if you knew the truth. And you passed, so I'm telling you now. Otherwise, I was scared you would tattle to my parents."

"I see. Hold on, give me a second. I'll call you back in five."

Before Sophie could respond, her uncle had already hung up. As she waited, terrible thoughts began to spiral in her head. *What if he's taking this time to tell my parents? What if he's so hurt by my lying that he doesn't want to talk to me again?*

But, to Sophie's great relief, her uncle's call came after five minutes.

He said, "Sorry, I just had to get some water to gather my thoughts. Everything was too much to comprehend all of a sudden."

"I completely understand. That was me when I heard Mom and Dad talking about this in their office."

"So you mean that your sister never actually died and that your parents just sent her to a rehab center? That's insane."

"Exactly right. And so I'm going to go find her."

"What?"

"Yes, I already have an entire plan to do so."

"But you're only fifteen years old. How in the world are you even going to get to Costa Rica without your parents?"

Sophie cringed. *He might be even more shocked at the next part.* "That's why you're going to bring me!"

"What? I'm going to bring *you*? What in the world..."

"Wait, before you start freaking out, I already have an entire plan laid out for you, so it shouldn't be that difficult." Sophie awkwardly chuckled, trying to ease the tension.

"Uh huh," her uncle said in an unsure manner.

Sophie then proceeded to tell her uncle every detail of the plan. At first, he was more than skeptical, questioning her at everything she said. But toward the end of the call, he began to nod as she talked, which made Sophie feel more confident in the plan's success.

After finishing talking about the plan, she asked her uncle, "So, what do you think?"

He rubbed his chin. "Hmm... it's actually not as bad of an idea as I had originally thought it would be. I can't say that I'm all in, as I still think it's quite dangerous. We don't want to risk upsetting your parents."

"But..."

"Wait, let me finish. Even though we don't want to upset your parents, they did hide away that your sister is alive for way too long. So, give me a few days, and I'll get back to you about it, okay? I'll also tell my wife about Anya's situation."

Sophie nervously rubbed her forehead. *He better not back out after thinking it over.* "Sure Uncle, summer vacation is coming up in just a week, so can you get back to me before then?"

"Yes, I will. And before you leave the call, I just wanted to tell you that you're quite strong. If it had been me, I would have burned the house down when I heard the news. And I'm not joking at all." His voice was comforting, which made Sophie feel a whole lot better.

"Thanks. I'm more happy than angry at my parents, though. I miss Mackenzie so much."

"Me too."

With that, the phone call ended, and Sophie laid back in her bed. She felt lighter than she had before, having taken off the huge load on her shoulders. It was once again waiting time.

twenty

Anya

ANYA WAS EXCITED, to say the least. Finally, the reach to her sister didn't seem like a mile away. She could almost imagine seeing her sister's smile, revealing her sparkly white teeth that she always treasured. *The only thing remaining is for Aunt Want to talk to my mother. They've been best friends for years now, so it should be completely fine.* Anya silently thanked the world for giving her such a lucky coincidence. *Or else Mom would never agree to such a thing.*

She also thanked the world for letting her go to an international school in Shanghai, as only her school started summer vacation in June while all the others started in July. *Mom will probably want me to do summer homework during the break, but I'll tell her that I'll keep up with all my work by working extra-long hours when I come back.*

Anya was in the middle of her math tutoring when she got her mother's text, which read, "Auntie Wang is coming over for dinner. Before you come home, go to the little market next to our compound to buy some peaches. And tell them to wrap it up as a gift."

Gulping in fear and excitement, Anya could barely concentrate on the numbers in front of her as she tried to learn derivatives while simultaneously thinking about how her mother would react. After ten minutes of receiving his text, Mr. Yen finally caught on that something was off.

Tersely, he commented, "Anya, your mind is everywhere but here right now. Your eyes are barely even looking at the whiteboard in front of you."

Shit, nothing escapes Mr. Yen's observational skills. Anya, sheepishly tucking her hair behind her ears, replied, "Sorry. My mother texted me a rather surprising message, and I've been thinking about it ever since."

"Uh huh." Anya once again gulped as he fixed his spectacles and cleared his throat. *He better not rat on me again. Every time I don't pay attention in this class for just one moment, he tells Mom. And if he tells her right now, she'll be pissed and say I'm wasting money. If that happens, I might as well kiss my dreams of going to Costa Rica goodbye.*

Trying to save the situation, Anya lied, "I'm really sorry, Mr. Yen. It's just that my mother has been sick as of recently, like really sick. She just started getting better, so when she texted me saying she felt sick again, I just can't help but worry, you know? Again, I'm sorry for not paying attention." Anya cringed at herself practically losing all her dignity toward Mr. Yen, but she believed in the saying that "desperate times call for desperate measures." And this was indeed a desperate time.

After pausing for a moment, during which Anya held her breath, Mr. Yen responded, "Fine. Seeing that your mother is sick, I'll let you off the hook. But I don't want to see this kind of nonsense anymore. This is the one and only time, understand?"

Thank god. "Yes, I promise this is a one-time thing. Never again."

"Good. Well, since you can barely focus now, you might as well leave class five minutes early. Come back to class next time with a better attitude, understand?"

"Yes, of course. Thank you so much." As Anya excited the doorway, she let out a huge sigh of relief. *That was completely unexpected from Mr. Yen. If it had been normal times, he would have pointed out how many times I have lazed off in class, but he acted like this was my first time or something.* Anya shook her head. *He probably has something he needs to do elsewhere, so he might have been just saying those words so that he could get out of class early as well. That sounds more like the Mr. Yen I know.*

Having called a taxi, Anya stopped right next to her compound and entered the market.

Almost immediately, she was greeted by the sweet aromas of Chinese bayberry, one of her favorite fruits that she only had a chance to truly enjoy when it reached the summer season.

A voice soon followed after, which was that of her favorite grocer Sandra. Having known Sandra since she was a baby, Anya treated her like family and vice versa. Whenever Anya came over, which usually always landed on Saturday mid-afternoons, Sandra would give her a small carton of fruit to take home. Anya would always politely reject it out of courtesy but would always end up walking home with the box. Anya's mother also loved Sandra, giving her boxes of gifts whenever returning from a foreign country.

Sandra said, "Anya? Why are you here? You're not usually here until Saturdays!"

Anya chuckled and replied, "I just couldn't wait one more day to see you."

"Ay ya, that means I haven't had the time to prepare your assortment of fruits to bring back yet."

"No, no. You're always too kind." Giving Sandra a side glance to tell her not to always give her so many free things anymore, Anya continued, "I'm actually here today to buy a gift for a family friend."

"Hm... what would you like? The bayberry is very in season right now. The lychee is too, and the peach..."

"Let's see." Walking around the display of fruits, Anya said, "If it were me, I would definitely take the bayberry, but I think this family friend likes peaches. So I'll take the peach and come back tomorrow for the bayberry. Otherwise, it's too much to carry."

"Smart, smart. Alright, I'll pick out the sweetest and juiciest peaches for you and wrap them up with a bowtie, how does that sound?" Before

Anya responded, Sandra had already started gently testing the peaches to pick out the best ones.

After receiving the packaged fruits finished with a pink ribbon on top, Anya checked the time and realized that she didn't have enough time left to sit down and chat with Sandra. *I definitely cannot be late today. Otherwise, I'm really screwed.*

So, Anya said a quick goodbye, promising to be back tomorrow. Walking toward the house, Anya's pace quickened as she thought about Mrs. Wang and her mother sitting together at home. *I need to get there quickly, or else who knows what they might be talking about before I arrive? What if Mrs. Wang has already revealed the news to my mother, and my mother is pissed? What if my mother has already rejected Mrs. Wang's proposal?*

Anya's stomach sank at this thought, but she comforted herself that she was just overthinking. *No, Mrs. Wang wouldn't have already told her, not without me there. They're probably just chatting about life right now, so there's nothing to worry about. Nothing at all.* Despite herself-reassurances, Anya broke out into a sprint to return home.

Taking her shoes off before she entered the doorway, Anya could already hear her two women's voices. They were laughing and cheery, which made Anya calm down. *That probably means Mrs. Wang hasn't told her yet.*

Anya walked into the house and, glancing to her left, immediately saw Mrs. Wang was sitting on the sofa, with her mother sitting right across from her in the armchair.

Mrs. Wang first looked up at the sound of someone entering, and, upon locking eyes with Anya, exclaimed, "Why, hello Anya! You've grown so much since I last saw you, and it's only been a few months!"

Although nervous, Anya put on her calmest voice and responded, "Hi Mrs. Wang! It's so nice to see you again."

Mrs. Zhou added, "Anya, did you get the thing I asked you to buy?"

"Yes, yes, of course I did." Walking closer to Mrs. Wang, Anya said,

"Here, Mrs. Wang. I got you a box of peaches, as it has just reached the season, and my mother tells me they are your favorite type of fruit."

Mrs. Wang broke out into a smile. "You're too kind, really. Now I feel bad for not bringing anything. I'll make sure to bring you some of your favorite shrimp crackers from that store in Xiamen next time, okay?"

Anya laughed and responded, "Okay, it's a deal!"

Mrs. Zhou chuckled and just said, "Alright, since Anya's back, let's get ready for dinner."

Mrs. Wang stood up and replied, "Let me help you."

Both adults looked to Anya, who, after a moment of confusion, realized what was going on. "Count me in as well!"

All together, they prepared the dishes, most of them already done and just in need of a reheating. Afraid that Mrs. Wang had forgotten about her mission of coming over to visit Mrs. Zhou, Anya pulled Mrs. Wang to the side when her mother wasn't looking.

Anya whispered, "You're still telling her, right?"

Mrs. Wang, taking a glance at Mrs. Zhou, replied, "Of course, I am. I was planning to do it over dinner, as that seemed like the most appropriate time to reveal the news."

Thinking it over for a second, Anya nodded and said, "Yes, that's probably the best idea. Anyhow, thank you so much for doing this."

Mrs. Wang just smiled and returned back to the preparations.

Once the food was all laid out on the table, Mrs. Zhou said, "I don't know when Mr. Zhou is coming back today, so let's just eat first."

Everyone sat down, and Anya took a deep breath. *Okay, this is it. This is the deciding moment.* She picked at her food, too nervous to eat.

Finally, around five minutes after they had begun eating, Mrs. Wang cleared her throat. "Ehm, I was just thinking."

Mrs. Zhou looked at her. "Yeah, what is it?"

"Well, my husband is going on a business trip next week, and he's bringing Sophie, my niece, along. Sophie's told me all about how close she is with Anya, and I suppose Anya thinks the same?"

Anya nodded and replied, "She's my best friend."

Pausing for a moment, Mrs. Zhou responded, "Ah, the one you were talking about on that day we ate ice cream together?"

Anya nodded.

Mrs. Wang continued, "I was thinking that because it's a fun location, Anya might want to tag along." Chuckling, she said, "Otherwise, it would just be Sophie and her uncle, and I'm sure that Sophie would be bored out of her mind."

Mrs. Zhou replied, "Where is this place, though?"

"It's in Costa Rica, so the kids could just play on the beaches or explore the wildlife. I heard that everybody, especially teenagers, wants to go there these days."

"Costa Rica? But that's so far..."

"Indeed, it is. But that's half the fun, isn't it?" Mrs. Wang winked at Anya.

Recognizing this cue, Anya added on, "Yes, Mom. That sounds delightful. Everyone, and I mean everyone, has been wanting to go to Costa Rica at my school."

"Really? I've never heard anyone say that."

"That's because you don't hang out around teenagers. Costa Rica is the new *Sanya* right now."

"Hm... I see. But is it safe there?"

Mrs. Wang pitched in, "Safety is definitely the least of your concerns. My husband works in IT, so he's extremely, extremely detailed."

"I see..." Mrs. Zhou tapped her chin. "Alright, I'll think it over. I suppose that Anya deserves to go on vacation somewhere this summer, but I need to talk to my husband first."

Mrs. Wang replied, "Of course, you do. Just get back to me within a few days, and there's absolutely no pressure to say yes at all."

"Alright then, I shall do that."

With that, the conversation about Costa Rica ended, and Anya felt her entire body loosen. *Based on how my mother seemed pretty accepting, she probably will let me go. Plus, if she's not convinced now, my father will definitely be on my side.* Anya smiled at the thought.

twenty-one
Sophie

BACK ON HER HORSE, Sophie was determined to ride better this time. She counted her strides to each jump, making sure that she nailed all her distances and that her horse never had to help her.

Indeed, her concentration paid off, as her coach commented on her significant improvement from last class. Sophie smiled and patted Cassie, who just snorted in response.

But, when Sophie got off her horse and no longer had to concentrate on something else, all she could think about was her uncle's response. It had already been two days, and he still hadn't said a complete answer. One comfort she had right now was that her uncle had already agreed shortly after their call to ask his wife to talk to Anya's mother. *If he's already telling his wife about it, then it should be just fine, right?*

Sophie anxiously tapped her feet on the stone ground, deciding that she would ask him today. *I've already given him a few days, so it's only right that I ask him about his decision today.*

On the road home, she was thinking about what she would say if her uncle said no when her father suddenly said, "You haven't called your grandparents in a long time. They probably miss you a lot."

Sophie realized with a pang of guilt that she truly hadn't talked to her grandparents in over two weeks and that she had nearly forgotten all about them until her father had brought them up. She replied, "Yes, I will call them as soon as it hits the weekend."

"Good."

There was an awkward silence as Sophie did not know what to say afterward. It had nearly been a week since the "incident," but it was still extremely awkward for Sophie to be around her parents. It didn't seem to Sophie that her parents were still mad; rather, it was like they also didn't know how to reopen the conversation.

Finally, Sophie opened her mouth and asked, "So, Dad. How has golf been going?"

He cleared his throat. "Well, I can't say that it's been going spectacular, but it's been getting better."

Trying to lighten the mood, Sophie asked, "Should I start to learn? That way, our entire family can go play golf together."

"Haha, I've always wanted you to learn, but you've always been in love with horseback riding."

"I could do both?"

Chuckling, he jokingly replied, "Do you want to make me broke?"

Sophie laughed, happy she was normally talking with her father again. *I hope this means he'll be more accepting of me if I tell him I'm going to Costa Rica.* She placed a silent prayer into the air that the puzzle pieces would all align and let her see Mackenzie. *First, though, I need to talk to my uncle. And before that, I need to reconcile my relationship with my mother like how I've reconciled with my father. Or else if my mother doesn't agree, it won't even be of any use if my uncle does.*

Upon returning home, Sophie saw her mother folding the laundry, which was her task every Sunday afternoon. On the other hand, Sophie was usually solely in charge of the washing process.

But, seeing that this could be the perfect opportunity to finally start a conversation, Sophie took off her boots and, instead of immediately going to shower, went to help her mother fold the clothing.

Her mother, upon seeing what Sophie was doing, exclaimed, "Sophie! What are you doing here?"

Sophie smiled and replied, "I'm here to help you, of course!"

"Help me?" Her mother gave her a side-eye. "Are you sure? You never fold the laundry. You probably don't even know how."

Sophie scratched her head. *Well, I suppose it's true that I have no idea how to fold any of these clothes.* "Well, I'll take this as an opportunity to learn, then!"

Mrs. Zhou chuckled and replied, "Alright, if you so insist. You can first start by folding the pants; those are easier than the tops."

"Gotcha." Sensing that her mother was no longer terribly upset, Sophie smiled and commenced folding the laundry. Only after she had spent thirty minutes folding did she realize just how tiring it was. *Damn, washing clothes only requires me to throw everything in. I never realized how much energy it took to organize them.* Looking at her mother's neat stack compared to hers, Sophie quietly decided that she would continue to help her mother out with this task in the future.

Returning back to her room, Sophie let out a big sigh. She had already finished all her homework the day earlier, so besides reading, she really was quite at a loss of activities to do. As she patted Potato on the head, she fell into a slumber. The nap was a fitful one, as Sophie tossed back and forth in her bed, She transitioned between dreams of her uncle denying the trip, her parents screaming at her for even bringing up the idea, someone finding out that she was going to Costa Rica to find Mackenzie, and finally, Mackenzie refusing to see her. It seemed like she was running between different realities, each one scarier than the next. Surrounding her was complete black, and no matter in which direction Sophie ran, she couldn't escape the vision in front of her. It was torture.

Finally, when Sophie snapped out of her sleep, she was soaked in sweat. *What the hell? The dream felt like ten thousand nightmares all put together.* She shuddered at each thought that had popped up in her dream, realizing that they had manifested her deepest fears. *If all of this happens, I don't know what I'll do.*

Checking the time, she realized that it was already dinner time and that she had been in that fitful sleep for nearly four hours, *Alright, Sophie. Snap out of it. I better not be all wound up when I'm talking to my parents later. Or my uncle.*

The dinner went quite smoothly as everyone made small talk. To Sophie, it seemed like her parents had finally gone back to normal, which she was grateful for. Although Sophie had never fully apologized for her spying that day, nobody brought it back up, so she avoided the topic as well. *If they find it awkward to talk about it, then I won't add fuel to a fire. They probably know by now how sorry I am without me saying it,*

Before she knew it, it was time to call her uncle. Sophie wasn't sure how to approach it, but she decided to just be blunt and ask.

When her uncle picked up, she began with a few courtesies but almost immediately dived into the heart of the subject. "So, Uncle. Have you made your decision yet?"

"Haha, I knew you were going to bring that up right away. Well, I've talked it over with my wife, and she agrees. She's already gone to talk to her friend, you know that right?"

"Yes, you told me." Timidly, Sophie inquired, "So, that means yes?"

"Well..."

"Please say yes!" Sophie was desperate at this point.

He chuckled. "Hold on, let me talk. I told my wife to first ask for permission from Anya's parents because I knew that I could still retract the offer if need be. But I've been waiting to give you the final decision because once I say yes to you, that means it's definitely happening."

"Well, what is the reason for your hesitating?"

He paused. "I was thinking about how we would end up finding Mackenzie and Camelia, even if we do go to Costa Rica. I mean, based on what you're saying, there's people watching Mackenzie now, right?"

Realizing that what he was saying was true, Sophie begrudgingly replied, "Yes."

"Exactly. So I didn't give you the 'okay' earlier because I knew that we had to find a solution to this problem, or else going there will be of absolutely no use."

"Mhm. Wait... so... if you said 'earlier'... does that mean you found a solution now? And it's a yes?" Sophie held her breath in anticipation.

"Okay, fine. It's a yes."

"Yes!!!" Hit by a wave of relief, Sophie got up and started dancing around the room. "You are the best uncle ever. Like ever. Thank you so, so much. I mean it, I really do."

He laughed. "Well, don't thank me, thank your aunt. She's the one who really convinced me."

"Really?"

"Yup. She literally told me that I *had* to do it, or she wouldn't talk to me ever again. Apparently, it's my duty or something."

"She's the best, then. Tell her that I love her so, so much."

"I will, but I think you should call her yourself to thank her."

"Yes, I will do exactly that. Actually, can you give her the phone right now? I want to thank her right now."

"I can't do that right now, as she's currently away from home. But I'll give you her number so that you can call her afterward."

"Okay, sounds good." *I'll make sure to call her right after calling my grandparents.* "So, what was your plan to deal with the people watching Mackenzie?"

"Ah, yes. I thought it over, and I think that the best plan is just to blend into the crowd."

"What do you mean?"

"Alright, so it's pretty sunny there, so we'll wear sunglasses at all times. And hats, preferably. We won't stick out because everyone will be doing that."

"Uh huh."

"And, most importantly, we have to not act suspicious. Mackenzie's watchers don't know we're her family, so they won't be especially looking out for us. So as long as we don't do anything out of the ordinary, they won't catch on."

"I see... that's actually a good idea. Okay, then. How are we going to break the news to my parents?"

"Well, that's the hard part. I was thinking that we should do a group meeting so that I can talk to all of you guys at once."

"Right, so I tell them that I want to call you and that we haven't talked together as a family in a long time?"

"Exactly right, just use any method so that we're all seeing each other face to face over the screen. And then I'll begin talking first while you back up my statements. How does that sound?"

"Yes, that's probably for the best so that they think it's your idea, not mine."

"And since your summer vacation is coming up soon, let's plan to tell them tomorrow, perhaps when they are off of work."

Sophie gulped. *That soon? I suppose that it has to be that soon, but it just feels like everything's happening at once.* "Alright then, I'll see you tomorrow."

"See you."

The phone call ended, and Sophie sat back in her chair. It felt like she had already done so much, but she knew that things had just started and that the next step might be the hardest one yet.

twenty-two

Anya

A NIGHT HAD PASSED since Mrs. Wang had given the news to her mother, and Anya was anxiously waiting for an answer. She knew that her mother had already told her father the news the night before, but they had gone to bed right away without discussing the decision.

Now that it was morning, Anya knew that she had to get the answer. Seeing them eating breakfast, she approached.

"Hi guys. How did you all sleep?"

Her father responded, "Well, what you really want to know is our decision, right?"

Anya sheepishly nodded.

"So, after discussion with your mother last night, we decided that you are allowed to go. Isn't that right, Anne?"

Anya eagerly looked to her mother, who slowly nodded.

Oh. My. God. Thank the heavens. "Thank you guys so, so, so much!!!" Anya ran around and gave each person a tight hug. "I love you all so much. You are both the best parents ever."

Her mother chuckled. "Okay, hold on. Before you get too excited, we have some prerequisites that you need to meet before we actually send you off."

"Uh huh. Anything is fine."

"Okay, so first of all, I need to talk in-person with Mr. Wang to go over the logistics."

"Done."

"Second, I need to talk to Sophie as well."

"No problem."

"And third, I want you to buy a gift for Mr. Wang. If he's spending all this effort, it's only right if we give him something in return."

"Of course."

"Okay, then that's it. If you meet those, you're free to go."

"Yay!" *Those should be pretty easy to meet; I do need to hurry though.* "Alright then, I'll get in contact with them right away."

"Yes, you do that."

Before leaving off to school, Anya gave both her mother and father one more hug.

To say the least, she was on cloud nine for the rest of the day. It felt like she had passed the greatest obstacle, and she was finally at the brink of succeeding. *If everything goes according to plan, I'll literally be leaving in under five days.* Part of her thought about telling Odyssey and Isabel but then decided against it. *Even though I've known them since forever, I can't trust them to keep their mouths shut. I must make sure that my parents don't know Camelia's in Costa Rica at all costs.*

So, when Odyssey and Isabel asked her about her plans for summer, Anya simply responded that she would be going to Costa Rica, leaving it at that. Feeling slightly guilty for how much she was keeping her friends in the dark, she reassured herself that she would tell them everything once the dust settled.

After piano class, Anya decided to take a little detour to go visit Uncle Wang, as she wanted to thank him first before doing so in front of her mother. *I owe him so much; without him, I would probably be completely out of options.*

This time, when Anya got there, she was no longer as intimidated as before. The office workers no longer seemed terribly stern, and the guards just seemed like regular people.

Arriving at Mr. Wang's door, Anya gently knocked and asked, "Is there anyone there?"

A female's voice responded back, "Come on in!"

Who's that? Anya opened the door. It was Mrs. Wang, and right next to her was Uncle Wang.

Mrs. Wang must have seen the surprised look on Anya's face, as she quickly said, "You must be wondering why I'm here. I was actually discussing with him about how you were all going to get to Costa Rica, so it's pretty perfect that you're here now."

Wow. What a coincidence. "Great! It's so nice to see you again." Turning to face both of them, Anya said, "Actually, I came to thank Mr. Wang, but since you're here as well, I want to thank you as well."

They both chuckled. Uncle Wang replied, "I'm very flattered, but it's quite unnecessary."

"No, no. I insist. Without the both of you, I don't know what I would be doing right now. I would have probably had to kiss my dream of seeing Camelia goodbye forever."

Mrs. Wang replied, "Oh, my dear. You don't need to thank us. It was only right for us to do this, no matter the consequence. Otherwise, we simply wouldn't be human."

Uncle Wang nodded.

"Still, I really want to thank you. And…"

"Yes?" asked Mrs. Wang,

"I'm really sorry to burden you guys again, but I have another favor to ask."

"Go right ahead," said Uncle Wang.

"My mother wants to go over the logistics with you guys before I go, so she can ensure that the trip is safe and all. I know it's asking a lot, but would you guys have some time to meet in person with her sometime this week?"

"Of course, that's no problem at all!" said Mrs. Wang.

Uncle Wang nodded and added, "That's what I was going to do, even if you hadn't asked."

Smiling from ear to ear, Anya said, "Thank you!" Realizing that she had nothing to give them, she sheepishly said, "I prepared a gift for you guys, but I didn't bring it today. Can I give it to you guys when you all come over?"

They both chuckled again, and Mrs. Wang replied, "My, my. You already got me a gift last time, and you're getting me another one? I think I should be the one getting your family a gift this time."

Anya quickly replied, "No, no. I would never allow that. Plus, the last gift was on my mother, and this one will be on me."

Uncle Wang said, "Alright, then. If you so insist. But just know that we really aren't doing you a favor. We are simply doing what is right."

Anya nodded. *They've definitely very kindhearted.* "Alright then, I'll leave you to it. Just text me when you're available to come, and I'll make sure to be there!"

They asked Anya to sit down and eat a peach, but Anya declined, saying that she had to go home to dinner. While walking out of the building, Anya thought that she was floating. It seemed like every step she took was getting her one step closer to her dream. *Now I just need to get Sophie to talk to my mother, which should be pretty easy.*

After helping her mother out with preparing dinner and getting some homework done, Anya decided that it was perfect timing to call Sophie. She brought her laptop out to the living room, where both of her parents were waiting.

Before hitting the call button, Anya told her parents, "She's my best friend, so be nice, okay?" *They better not start grilling her.*

They nodded, so Anya hit the call button.

After a few seconds, Sophie picked up.

I should probably begin with the introductions. "So, Mom and Dad, this is Sophie. And Sophie, here are my parents."

Sophie responded, "Hi Mrs. and Mr. Chen! It's so nice to finally meet you!"

Mr. Chen replied, "It's so nice to see you too! Anya has been talking about you for quite a while now, but she hasn't let us see you."

Sophie chuckled and said, "Well, Anya always likes to be a bit mysterious; we actually knew each other for months before we even saw each other's faces!"

Seeing that the conversation was going quite smoothly, Anya calmed down. Turning to her parents, she said, "Alright guys. What did you want to ask Sophie about?"

Mrs. Chen replied to Anya, "Right. Since we're assuming that you and Sophie will be together at all times, we wanted to know a general outline of what you're going to be doing there, especially when Mr. Wang is at work."

Shit. We haven't exactly discussed this. Panicked over what to say, Anya looked to Sophie, expecting her to be at a loss of words as well.

Contrary to her expectations, however, Sophie was perfectly calm. "Right, so I've actually written out what we're going to do every day, and I can send it to you if you would like."

She: WHAT? She already planned that far ahead? Looking at Sophie, who was typing away at her computer, Anya was in complete shock. *I didn't know she would be thinking that far ahead. Damn, I might be having to rely on her during the trip for guidance, then.*

Realizing that her parents had seen her making a face, Anya quickly laughed, "Sorry. I was just thinking about something else. But yeah, we already coordinated our entire week's plan. I just didn't have time to tell you guys."

"Uh huh," said Mrs. Chen. "It's good to see that you guys are being responsible, but I'll still have to take a look over the itinerary to see if any changes need to be made. After all, this is the first time that Anya will be traveling without us."

"I completely understand," responded Sophie.

Anya chipped in, "Mom. Dad. Since you've gotten what you need, I think it would be good to let Sophie get to her class. After all, it's morning time for her."

"Of course," Mr. Zhou said. "It was so nice meeting you, Sophie."

"Nice meeting you as well!" Sophie eagerly replied. "Just let me know if there needs to be any changes; I'll make them right away."

With that, the phone call ended, and Anya turned to her parents to see their reactions. Seeing that they were all smiling, Anya smiled as well.

"So, what did you think?" *Please have your answer be positive.*

Mrs. Chen responded, "I think she's quite the courteous child. I see why you're such good friends with her."

Mr. Chen nodded. "And she seems really responsible as well, which makes me more relaxed about you going."

Anya beamed. "That's great to hear! I also already got in contact with Mr. Wang, and he'll be coming over with Mrs. Wang sometime soon."

"Okay, good, good. But if you're actually going to go, we probably should start the packing process. We might need to buy some traveling supplies as well." said Mrs. Chen.

Mr. Chen added, "How about this? Anya makes a list by tomorrow, and then we go buy them either online or at a store. The shipping here is extremely fast."

"Sounds good!" replied Anya.

"Okay then, it's a done deal," said Mrs. Chen.

Leaving the living room, Anya began to think. *Alright, so if I'm going to go around five days, and the temperature is going to be quite hot and humid, then I'll have to pack extra clothes. Bug spray and sunscreen as well.* She remembered what Sophie had texted her earlier. *If I want to disguise myself, then I should bring sunglasses and a hat. And the hat shouldn't be too big so that it doesn't catch attention. Just a normal cap should do.* It was time for Anya to finally start the search for her sister.

twenty-three
Sophie

IT WAS 6 PM, which meant her parents would be home relatively soon and the call was about to happen. *Anya's family is already confirmed to be going, which means that I'm the last missing piece. I need to convince my parents, or else this entire plan will fall apart. My parents shouldn't have any reason to refuse, as I've gone on solo trips with my uncle before. As long as they don't catch on that I'm going where Mackenzie is...*

Sophie's train of thought was cut short by the sound of a car pulling into the driveway. Peeking out the doorway, she saw that it was her mother. Seeing that she had brought a lot of food, Sophie rushed outside to help, which also inadvertently distracted her from the daunting task she would have to do later.

Around thirty minutes later, her father also returned home, and they all sat down at the dinner table.

Taking a deep breath, Sophie said, "So guys. Do you have time to call Uncle Wang with me later? We have something we want to ask you guys."

Her mother responded, "Sure. But why can't you just tell us now? Why does it have to be with your uncle as well?"

"It's kind of a big decision, so we both thought that it would be best hearing it from the both of us."

Giving her a weird look, Sophie's father replied, "Are you up to some mischief and having your uncle cover it up for you?"

"No, no," replied Sophie. "It's actually exciting news, and I'm super excited for this opportunity."

"Hm... I wonder what it could possibly be," questioned her father.

Sophie timidly smiled. "You'll find out soon enough!"

Perhaps Sophie's parents were in a rush to find out, as they ate dinner much faster than usual. The entire time, both her mother and father kept giving her weird looks, and Sophie just kept on smiling back. *I would tell them, but I need to keep with the plan.*

Finally, it hit eight o'clock, which was the time that Sophie had scheduled to call with her uncle. Circling around the dining table, the call began.

"Hi Uncle Wang!" started Sophie.

"Hi everyone!" responded her uncle.

Sophie's parents waved hello, and everyone said a few words to catch up.

Eventually, Mrs. Zhou asked, "So, what is it that you two were planning on telling us together about?"

Uncle Wang responded, "Ah, yes. That's the key point of today. So, as you all probably know, I go on a business trip almost every summer.

Her parents nodded.

He continued, "This time, the business trip is to Costa Rica."

"Costa Rica?" exclaimed Mrs. Zhou.

"Yes, Costa Rica. What's wrong with that?"

"Sorry, nothing. Please continue."

"Anyhow, I'll be going to the southern part of Costa Rica, mostly conducting my business on the Osa Peninsula."

"Ah, I see," responded Mrs. Zhou. Anya could right away tell that her mother had calmed down. *Okay, good. This is exactly what we wanted.*

Uncle Wang continued, "I was thinking, since Costa Rica is also known for its beaches and wildlife, I could bring Sophie along. She's always told me about how much she loves wildlife. Isn't that right, Sophie?"

Sophie vigorously nodded to show her approval. "Please, Mom and Dad, please?"

Mr. Zhou responded, "Yes, I know Sophie has always loved nature. But Costa Rica..."

"Why, what's wrong with Costa Rica?" inquired Sophie. *I know exactly why they're hesitating, but I have to act like I'm completely oblivious so that they're not suspicious of me.*

Mrs. Zhou quickly replied, "No, there's nothing wrong with Costa Rica. We think it's a wonderful place. But..."

Sophie said, "Oh, come on, please? You let me go places with Uncle before, so why not now?"

Mr. Zhou sighed and looked at Mrs. Zhou. "Honey, do you think it's a good idea? I don't see why not."

Mrs. Zhou, after taking a moment's pause, reluctantly said, "I suppose that Sophie won't have anything better to do over the summer."

Sophie perked up. "So it's a yes?"

Mrs. Zhou replied, "Yes, fine. You can go. But don't bother your uncle too much, okay? He's already brought you to so many places."

Uncle Wang chuckled, "She's really not the bother. I mean, she used to be, but she's all grown up now. Plus, it works perfectly because you two are always too busy with work to bring her out, but I'm always going on business trips to fun places. After all, a child needs to get out and about before she's like us, stuck with work all the time."

Sophie—smiling so much that her jaw started hurting—replied, "Don't worry, Mom. I'll be on my best behavior. Thank you guys so, so, so much." *I'm so happy right now I could die.*

Mr. Zhou chuckled and said, "Take a lot of pictures, okay? And make sure to call. You always forget when you go on these trips and leave us hanging."

"Yes, yes," replied Sophie.

After a few ending words, the call ended. Sophie, wound up with adrenaline, prepared to bound off to her room to tell Anya. Before she did, however, she made sure to hug her parents. A wave of relief hit her. *For some reason, I was so sure that they were going to see right through me. Now that I think of it, it's probably more likely for them to believe me than to think I somehow found out about Mackenzie and then schemed up this whole plan.*

Once she got back to her room, she immediately called Anya to tell her the good news.

"Anya, Anya! Guess what? My parents said yes!"

Anya exclaimed back, "Yay!! That means we're definitely going!!"

Both Sophie and Anya got out of the seats and started jumping around like they were little kids again.

After jumping around for a full minute, Sophie sat back down and said, "Okay, I'm super, super excited, but we still need to do a bit more planning."

Anya replied, "Yes, for sure. I saw that you made a plan, kind of?"

Right... that fake plan I created just in case. "Well, I sort of made one. My uncle already planned that you'll first come to the U.S. to pick me up, and then we'll go to Costa Rica from there."

"Yes, that sounds like a good idea. And I suppose we're going to Tortuguero right after we get there so that we can have as much time as possible to find our sisters?"

"Exactly. We should also have another call sometime soon with my uncle so that we can go over the logistics in detail."

"Good idea. "Anya paused. "Oh yeah, by the way, have you thought about what you're going to do if we actually do find them?"

So, that's exactly what I've kind of been avoiding. "Um... I'm not too sure. I was just thinking about finding her, but I've never thought about what I'll say once I actually do see her." *Like, do I say that I'm so glad she's alive? That I thought she was dead for months and that's why I haven't been reaching out?* "What about you? Have you thought about what you're going to do?"

"Well, it probably won't be as surprising for Camelia to see me as Mackenzie to see you, as Camelia is the one who sent me her address. At least, I hope it is." Anya nervously chuckled and rubbed her forehead. "But besides that, I'm not too sure. She didn't send a letter to my parents, so she probably won't agree with coming back to Shanghai. I think the most important thing for me now is just to see her. I don't really care whether or not she comes back. Of course, if she does, I'll be over the moon."

"And if she does, how will you explain it to your parents?"

"So... that will definitely be an awkward conversation, but I'll probably say that I accidentally saw her or something."

Sophie nodded. *I probably don't even have the choice to bring Mackenzie back to the U.S., as she's still registered at the rehab center.* "It's alright. Let's not worry too much about what will happen afterward. We should probably concentrate on finding them first."

"Right."

Even though the conversation shifted back to what they were going to do in Costa Rica, Sophie could tell that the energy was off after talking about what they would do with their sisters. *I don't need much, but I just hope that Mackenzie will be happy to see me. It's been so long that I don't even know what I'm going to say anymore.*

The call ended on a more dispirited note than it had started, as both girls fretted about the future. But no matter how scared Sophie was of what would happen when meeting Mackenzie, the trip was happening, and she had to get ready.

twenty-four

IT WAS the morning of the big day, the day that Anya would finally leave Shanghai and embark on her journey to Costa Rica. Her bags were all packed and ready, and Uncle Wang was waiting right outside. The only thing left to do was say goodbye.

Anya knew from the get-go that it would be an emotional goodbye, as she had never been separated from her parents before for such a long period of time. But she didn't expect it to be as emotional as it was, especially not for herself to be so emotional.

As she was about to leave the house, she hugged her parents tight and whispered, "I'll miss you guys so, so much."

Her father whispered back, "Us too. You have fun, okay? And make sure to call us every day, okay?"

"Okay, I'll FaceTime you guys all the time."

"You better," choked out her mother.

The car honked outside, and Uncle Wang's voice rang through the door. "Say your goodbyes quickly, or else we'll be late to the airport!"

Realizing that they were kind of on a time crunch, Anya gave her parents one last big hug. "See you guys in a few days!"

Her parents waved goodbye, and Anya turned to go to the car. When Uncle Wang drove out, Anya looked back, her parents were still waving.

Sophie was at the park, waiting for Lyla. *How did I even end up here when I need to go to the airport in just three hours?* When Sophie was about to leave school the day before, Lyla had told her to meet her and that she apparently had big news to tell her. Sophie had tried to get it through Lyla's head that she had to leave the next day and to say whatever she needed to say right then and there, but Lyla had bounded off, saying that they had to meet in the park one last time before Sophie left.

Sophie texted Lyla, telling her to hurry up, but there was no response. Finally, just when Sophie was going to give up and leave, Lyla came running over.

Panting, Lyla said, "Sorry. I was delayed preparing your gift."

"No worries, I just got to go in a little bit." *What in the world could she have prepared?*

Lyla said, "I was thinking that I've been too wrapped up in all the Ashley stuff, so much so that I didn't even know about you going to Costa Rica until yesterday. So I decided I needed to get you something to make up for that. After all, you're my bestie."

Touched, Sophie responded, "There's no need to be sorry. I've been wrapped in a lot of things as well, which I'll tell you all about once I get back."

"Yes, you better tell me everything once you get back; I will be expecting an hour-long update, okay?"

Sophie chuckled and nodded. It felt so good to have Lyla back. "Since I didn't get you a gift, how about we exchange gifts when I get back? That way, I don't feel bad about not bringing anything today."

"Fine, fine, if you so insist. But we NEED to hang out over the summer, okay?"

"Yes, let's hang out as soon as I get back."

Sophie went in to hug Lyla, who hugged her tightly back.

On the walk back home, Sophie was smiling ear to ear. Not only was she going to Costa Rica, but she had finally gotten close to Lyla again. *It feels like forever since we last fully talked together. I almost forgot what it feels like to talk to Lyla about anything other than Ashley.* When Sophie thought about Ashley, however, she all of a sudden thought about how she was doing. *I hope she's okay, wherever she's going.*

But for now, she needed to go home, get her bags, say goodbye, and head to the airport. *My uncle and Anya were waiting.*

Returning home, Sophie began zipping up her large suitcase. A few minutes later, both her mother and father both walked into her room.

"Hey Sophie," said her mother. "Do you need any help packing?"

Taking one last glance at her room, Sophie responded, "No, I think I've got everything."

Her father piped in. "You be careful, okay? Make sure to tell us if you need anything. I'll be checking my text messages."

Feeling a sense of warmth, Sophie responded, "I will, but don't worry too much about me. I'm going to be with Uncle Wang, so I'm not worried at all about the trip." *Well, I'm worried about other aspects, like finding my sister.*

In a movement that slightly surprised Sophie, both her mother and father embraced her. Though feeling a bit awkward, Sophie hugged them back, her mouth parting in a smile. *This is definitely strange, but it's nice.*

A couple minutes later, Sophie's bags were in the car, and it was time.

Seeing Sophie's familiar face walking into the airport, Anya ran to go greet her. "Hi Sophie!"

"Oh my goodness, hi Anya! It's so nice to actually see you in person! You're taller than I imagined," Sophie chuckled.

Anya laughed. "I know, right. We've only been seeing each other's faces the entire time, so I only recognized you coming in by your face."

Uncle Wang shouted out, "Okay, girls! It's time to go check-in!"

Anya smiled and replied back, "We're coming!" Helping Sophie out with her suitcase, they hurried to the check-in aisle.

The entire flight, Anya and Sophie chattered like birds despite Uncle Wang's incessant reminder to get in some sleep before they reached Costa Rica. They talked about their dreams, fears, passions, sisters, and everything else imaginable in that six-hour period of flying. Throughout the entire conversation, Anya couldn't help but notice that she had *many* similarities with Sophie, perhaps not based on hobbies, but more so her way of thinking. It was like two lost twins separated at birth.

And, while Anya had envied Sophie a little bit before because of how much freedom her parents gave her, she soon began to realize based on Sophie's words just how much her parents' lack of parental care hurt her. *I always thought she was the luckiest girl in the world, not having to worry about her parents saying this and that, but it's actually quite sad not having someone guide you throughout your life, especially when the times get difficult,* She made a silent note to appreciate her mother a bit more once she got back home.

Soon, before she knew it, the pilot announced that they were descending.

The dream was becoming all too real, and Anya couldn't wait.

Hot, humid air blasted Sophie in the face as she walked out of the airport doors. Unused to this kind of humidity due to living in L.A., Sophie immediately began profusely sweating. "Hey guys, is there anywhere indoors we can go? Perhaps call a car?"

Her uncle chuckled. "Not used to this weather, huh? Well, Anya and I are perfectly fine because we're used to Shanghai summers, aren't we?" He turned to look at Anya, who nodded and said, "Yup. It's pretty much the exact same."

Damn, so I guess I'll just have to be adapting to the weather a LOT more. Sophie saw the taxi line. "There're the taxis! Let's go there."

Sophie led the way, making her path through a huge crowd of people. She kept on bumping into people, and each time she did, she would apologize in Spanish. Everyone was quite nice, either nodding their heads or saying that it's okay, but Sophie was beyond embarrassed of how many people she was bumping into. *Why did I have to bring such a large suitcase? Oh right... I bought a bunch of props.* Unsure of what the people in Costa Rica would dress like, Sophie had brought nearly everything in her wardrobe so that she was prepared for any style necessary. But now, she realized that everyone practically just wore t-shirts, shorts, and sometimes sunglasses and a hat. *I overthought so much that I literally ended up bringing sundresses.* Sophie cursed this bad habit of hers as she painstakingly made her way to the cab.

Finally getting in the car, Sophie took a moment to cool down before she began talking. "So, our plan is to first get to a hotel, stay the night, and then travel up to Tortuguero tomorrow morning?"

Uncle Wang responded, "Yes, that is the plan. Otherwise, we would all be too tired when we reach Tortuguero, and we wouldn't be thinking straight."

Sophie nodded her head. "I agree. We should take tonight to get some good sleep, as we've just flown quite far, and you two probably have jet lag coming all the way from Shanghai. Anya, what do you think?"

Anya was staring out the window, taking pictures of the scenery around. Sophie tapped her shoulder and whispered, "Hey, Anya. What do you think about going to Tortuguero tomorrow?"

Anya turned around and replied, "Sorry, I was just admiring the beautiful landscape, But yes, sounds like a good plan to me."

Realizing that she hadn't even taken a moment to admire the scenery yet, Sophie edged back to her seat and put her face near the window.

The view was amazing. They were surrounded by mountains on both sides, which were swathed in vines, palms, and dotted with blooms of orange and purple flowers. Sophie had never seen anything like it, each speck of land covered in dense green. *Wow, this is something else. I'm so used to the yellow mountains of L.A. that I've always just thought of mountains like that; I didn't know they could be so... majestic.* She could tell that Anya was equally as amazed, perhaps even more so based on how her eyes didn't leave the window once. *She's probably grown up only in Shanghai, where there really aren't even mountains. This place is definitely the complete opposite of the city life she's so used to.*

When they made their way out of the mountains and toward the ocean, it became even more beautiful. It was like a dream; on their left side were rolling green hills, and on their right side was turquoise water that came onto shore in ferocious yet soothing waves. Although Sophie had been worried earlier about how they would execute the plan, all her worries were carried away by the waves.

twenty-five

THEY ARRIVED AT THE HOTEL. It was quite quaint, not the seventy story ones that Anya was used to. But it was this exact contrast that made Anya obsessed with every part of it. She especially loved the vibrant hammocks placed out in front of each room and the central eating area that was open-air and connected all the rooms together. *I could seriously stay here forever and just never leave.* Looking at everything made Anya want to sit down and draw, a feeling that she hadn't had in quite a while. *I always thought of myself as more of a city girl, but perhaps I find more peace and comfort here.*

After checking into the room, which she would be sharing with Sophie, Anya took a quick shower and changed into clothes that would keep her cool. Filled with excitement at the prospect of being somewhere new, Anya forgot all about the previous conversation of resting and instead asked Sophie, "Do you want to go explore?"

Sophie, who was lying on her bed, replied, "I do, but..."

"It's fine if you don't want to; I will just explore in the hotel!"

Sophie paused for a moment, and Anya could tell that she was thinking over a dilemma. *She's definitely more responsible than I am.*

Finally, Sophie responded, "Okay, it can't hurt to go out for a little bit, let's go!"

Anya smiled and put on her sandals. Together, she and Sophie walked to the hotel's edge. It was almost like a little enclave, as there was a short walkway through some forest, which then led to the ocean. Once they got to the ocean, Anya smiled and took her sandals off. "Come on, Sophie!"

Sophie, after taking a sketchy look at the water, took her sandals off as well. "Okay, coming!"

Anya waded into the water, Sophie not far behind. The water was the perfect temperature, not too cold so that she didn't cringe going into the water but also not too warm so that it was just the perfect level of refreshing against the hot air. As the ocean waves tickled Anya's feet, she laughed, and Sophie did as well. *I haven't been this free in so long; I think I could just sink in the sand here and never leave.*

Looking at Sophie, Anya could also tell that while it was leaving her comfort zone, Sophie was having a good time as well.

Pretty soon, an hour had passed, and the sun was close to setting. *Okay, as much as I want to stay here, we should probably start heading back soon.* When Anya asked Sophie about it, she agreed, so they both dried off and returned back to the hotel lobby

There, Uncle Wang was already waiting for them. He said, "I see you girls have been up to some fun, how about we go grab dinner now?"

Both Anya and Sophie immediately nodded their heads, and Anya realized with a startle of just how famished she was. The exhaustion was also close to setting in, and Anya could feel her eyelids starting to droop. She tapped Sophie on the shoulder. "Hey, Sophie. What do you say we go to bed after dinner?"

Sophie replied, "Yes, for sure. We need to get up bright and early tomorrow if we want to make it to Tortuguero before nighttime. It's quite a long journey."

The dinner was short but delicious. It was one of the staple kinds of

Costa Rican foods: chicken, rice, and a little side of vegetables. Anya scarfed it down, and before long, she was fast asleep.

Waking up in the morning was definitely a difficult task, but, with the help of five alarms, Sophie was finally able to drag herself up. Groggily, she woke up Anya, who was still dead asleep after all the alarms.

After getting ready for half an hour and repacking their suitcases, they headed to the lobby, where her uncle was waiting for them.

Her uncle said, "Hey guys! I already rented a car, so quickly grab some breakfast and then we can be on our way."

Sophie wanted nothing more than to sleep, so she just grabbed a piece of toast from the hotel's buffet for the road. *How in the world does Uncle Wang have so much energy right now? It's literally only 6 am in the morning. At least Anya isn't crazy like him. She looks just as asleep as I am.*

Thankfully, as soon as they got on the road, the rapid changes of scenery managed to wake her up. It transformed from mountains, to beaches, to cities, and back to mountains again. There were also wondrous colorful birds flying every which way; showing off their glorious feathers with splotches of green, red, and yellow.

They barely stopped along the way, only stopping once to grab some lunch. By the time they reached the marina, it was already well into the afternoon. By this time, Sophie began to feel nervous, as they were nearing where Mackenzie was supposed to be. *This island isn't small, so it's highly likely I'll see Mackenzie quite soon. Or...* Sophie thought about the possibility of not finding her sister but quickly dismissed that thought. *No, I will find Mackenzie, or else all of this will have been for nothing.* She looked to Anya, who had gotten quieter in the last hour or so. *She's probably nervous as well; we've been preparing so much that we haven't really thought about what we would do to find them, but we can truly only hope for the best now.*

~

The ferry boats taking them to the island were small, fitting around five to ten people. Anya took a seat next to the water, as she wanted to lean out against the rim and touch the cooling water. She was definitely nervous about finding Camelia, but she tried her best to hide it. *I don't want to get all wound up and then end up making the other two nervous as well.*

Everyone had already put on their costumes: Uncle Wang was wearing khakis and a white flannel shirt, Anya was wearing a tank top with jeans, and Sophie was wearing a light floral T-shirt with white jeans and a cap. Everyone was wearing large but natural sunglasses that covered nearly all their facial features just in case the people sent there to watch Mackenzie recognized any of them, particularly Sophie. All in all, Anya thought they looked just like three tourists on a trip. *We definitely don't look like people going to secretly find their sisters behind their parents' backs.* Anya thought about the idea of themselves wearing completely black costumes and lightly laughed to herself.

As the engine of the boat started, Anya leaned closer to Sophie and asked, "Do we go straight to the hotel or start searching around?"

Sophie put her mouth close to Anya's ear so that she could hear. "We're gonna first put our stuff down, maybe take a shower, and then start asking around. How does that sound?"

Anya nodded. "Okay, sounds like a plan." Louder this time, she asked, "Do you want to feel the water? We can switch spots if you want!"

Sophie shook her head. "It's okay! I would rather stay dry for now."

"Okay, but tell me if you ever want to switch!"

Having expected the boat to be slow and peaceful, Anya was surprised by just how fast they were going. Especially when other boats coming from the opposite direction came close to theirs, there would be a great splash as the ripples caused from each boat collided. Anya enjoyed watching these moments, as it offered an almost uncertainty to whether or not the water would hit her.

Around an hour later, they began to pull into the island of Tortuguero. From where Anya first started seeing the island, the first thing she noticed was that there were wooden buildings lining the entire dock, and there was a vast crop of just green land to the right side. All the buildings were quite colorful, with just a few colors fading due to time.

Seeing that Sophie looked quite anxious, Anya tried to cheer her up by pointing out all the animals she was seeing. At first, Sophie seemed quite out of it, barely taking her eyes off the dock. But finally, perhaps on the third animal that Anya was pointing out, Sophie began to gain interest, looking for animals herself as well. In under ten minutes, they were able to locate and define—with the help of the locals on the boat—a white-faced capuchin, a sloth, a crane, a cayman, and a morpho butterfly. Anya took pictures of all of them and reminded herself to search up later. Each time she saw a new animal, she began to understand more and more of why Camelia decided to come here.

As they pulled into the dock, Sophie had calmed down a lot compared to the beginning. Yet, she couldn't stop but look at each person's face helping them get off the boat. She knew that Mackenzie wouldn't be among these people, as they were all inhabitants of Tortuguero that worked the boats, but she didn't want to miss any opportunity.

Once everyone had successfully gotten off the boat, Sophie, her uncle, and Anya all gathered up together next to a granite table. They pretended to be tourists just casually talking.

Sophie spoke first. "So, we're headed to the hotel right away, right? We haven't asked any people questions yet?"

Uncle Wang replied, "Right. We need to be patient. We should continue with the plan that we lost someone and that we are searching for them. If we randomly start asking now right after we get off the boat, everyone won't believe us that we lost someone. Plus, I bet Mackenzie's watchers might be looking at us, as they need to make sure that

Mackenzie doesn't leave this island. So we should get more inland to ask questions, not at the dock."

Anya commented, "Yes, that is probably for the best. We can't risk making any big moves when we don't even know what the island looks like yet."

Sophie nodded her head. "Okay then, it's decided. Let's go to the hotel."

Having expected a need to drive, even for just a little bit, to get to the hotel, Sophie was quite shocked when she put the location of the hotel in her phone and found that it was only a five-minute walk away. *Is the island that small?* Everyone else was shocked as well, and her uncle made sure that she had put in the correct location. Deeming that it was correct, they exchanged surprised looks and began the short walk.

twenty-six

H AVING PUT THEIR STUFF DOWN, Anya was more than ready to get out and start asking around. But she knew better. *No, we said that we would begin tomorrow; everyone is far too tired today.* So, Anya returned back to her room, where Sophie was sitting on the bed and reading.

Anya gently tapped Sophie on the shoulder, "Hey, what are you reading?"

Sophie looked up. "Oh, nothing much, just *Little Women*. I've read this book like a thousand times, but it helps calm me down when I'm nervous."

Anya nodded. "I get you, I'm super nervous as well."

"What do you usually do when you get nervous?"

Thinking it over for a moment, Anya responded, "Well, I'm not sure, actually. I mean..." Anya paused. *Is art even considered one for me? Like I love it, but...*

"It's okay, you don't need to tell me if you don't want to."

"No, no. It's art."

"Really? That's so cool!"

Skeptically, Anya responded, "Really? I always just use it as my pastime. I mean, I used to do it a lot, but then my mother told me to stop after a while."

"Why? Did you not like it anymore?"

"No, not that. It's just that in China, they don't look at any of your extracurriculars to determine your acceptance; it's all based on one grade. So, my mother thought that as I got busier with school, doing art would be a waste of time when I could be studying. Which makes sense, I suppose." Anya picked at her nails.

After a moment's pause, Sophie responded, "Well, the system is definitely different in the U.S. for colleges, so I can't be one to judge. But... I still think that if you truly love something, then it doesn't matter whether or not it 'helps you.'"

"Really? I've never thought about it that way before." *Mom has just always told me that studying was number one, so I've always prioritized that over any hobbies. Come to think of it, I did quite a lot back when I was young, but then they all dropped off once my studies started taking up my time.*

Sophie kept on talking. "Yes, like, take for example, reading. It does absolutely nothing for my college admissions and definitely takes up a *lot* of my time, but I love it, so I just keep on doing it. It helps me calm down and relax, which I think is equally as important as my outward success."

"I suppose that's true. But with all the classes that my mother assigns now for college, I barely have time to draw or paint."

"Hm... perhaps you could ease this topic of art into a conversation with your mother? Maybe you can start by just talking about a recent piece, and then start diving more into your passion for it. I'm not sure how receptive she'll be, but it's at least worth a try, right?"

I guess she has gotten more accepting as of recently. "Alright then, I'll ask her once I get back."

"Great!" Sophie pulled out her laptop. "Since we probably shouldn't go anywhere without Uncle Wang, what do you think about watching a movie? Even though this trip isn't meant to be exactly a vacation, I thought that it would be good to have a little fun once in a while, so I bought face masks! We can do facemasks and watch a movie, how does that sound?"

"Omg, really? Let's do that!" *This will be such a good way to destress before tomorrow; Sophie really does quite think ahead.*

Plopping back on her bed with the facemasks and offering one to Anya, Sophie asked, "So, what movie do you want to watch?"

Together, they decided to rewatch the Notebook, a movie which Anya had already watched at least three times but was her comfort movie. During the length of the movie, Anya relaxed, but she also thought about what Sophie had said earlier. *She made a really good point.*

Sophie woke up the next morning and immediately thought about how it might just be the big day. *This is it. There's a very high probability that I will see Mackenzie today.* The more Sophie thought about this idea, the more afraid and excited she got. *I really, really want to see her, but I have no idea what I'm going to say if I do.* Sophie had tried with Anya the night before to plan what they were going to say if they saw their sisters, but they hadn't come up with anything. Well, they had come up with a *lot* of ideas, but none of them had seemed appropriate, so they scrapped all of them and decided that it would be best to just go with the flow.

Sitting down at the hotel lobby for breakfast, Sophie asked her uncle, "So we're first starting by looking around, right?"

Her uncle replied, "Yes, this island isn't too big, so it's probably best to first scope out the place before we start asking around. As to not draw attention, we should seem like we're shopping every once in a while."

Sophie nodded. "Yes, that sounds good." Turning to Anya, she asked, "Are you good with that plan?"

Anya paused for a moment before saying, "That sounds good, but there's just one thing."

"What is that?" asked Sophie.

"I know this is for later and if we don't find them in the first round, but when we actually have to start asking around, I don't know if I can. See, the thing is that I'm not exactly fluent in Spanish, and Uncle Wang isn't either, so only you can be the one to ask."

Sophie gulped. *I haven't really thought about that yet. Thank goodness for the Spanish classes I take at school.* "So I just say that I lost Camelia and Mackenzie, and kind of give a description?"

Anya replied, "Hold on. I can kind of write down a script for you; I'm pretty sure it will work."

At first, Sophie looked at Anya skeptically but then remembered how Anya had plotted how she would approach her uncle. *She's got this.* "Okay, I'll translate and say whatever you write down."

Anya took out her phone and started typing away, while Sophie thought about all the things that could go wrong. *What if we're walking around and get spotted by the people sent by my parents? What if I mess up when I'm talking to a person, and the person suspects something? What if everyone refuses to tell us anything? What if nobody has any idea? What if... Mackenzie and Camelia have already left Tortuguero?* Sophie shuddered at all of these thoughts.

A minute or two later, Anya was done. "How does it look?" she asked.

Looking it over, Sophie responded, "It looks pretty good, but are you sure I should pretend that we're just friends instead of just saying they are our siblings?"

"I thought this point over, and I think it's for the best in case they know Camelia or Mackenzie and find that it's weird how they have siblings if our sisters have never told them."

"But don't we and our sisters look alike?"

"Yes, but that's not what people will think at first, especially since you guys are quite some years apart. Overall, it'll be a lot less awkward if you say you guys are friends. They'll probably just think that Camelia or Mackenzie brought some friends over."

"I suppose that makes sense. Okay, I'll go with that. But first, let's go check out the island."

Uncle Wang added, "Alright, I'll stay here so as to not make it weird and disrupt your 'searching for your friends' act. Call me if anything arises, and I'll check in with you guys in an hour if the initial scouting hasn't worked out."

Sophie and Anya nodded, gave each other a look of excitement as well as nervousness, and headed outdoors.

Anya's initial thought was that there were *way* too many shops and buildings to look into. Not knowing how large the island was, it seemed from her perspective that it was stretching on forever without end. For a while, she thought about splitting the island between herself and Sophie, but then eventually decided against it. *I should probably stick around Sophie if I have absolutely no idea how to speak any Spanish. Well, I tried to learn a bit of Spanish before I came, but all last-minute studying is truly not helpful. All I remember is how to say hello and goodbye.*

Giving up after a while on trying to determine how large the island was, Anya turned her attention to the people, trying to distinguish who Camelia would interact with. She looked particularly hard at places advertising anything to do with animals, particularly consisting of tours to see animals. *She definitely likes these places for how they emphasize taking care of the environment on these tours.* But no matter how much Anya looked into these places, she could not find Camelia's face.

Just as Anya was about to ask Sophie if she wanted to sit down and rest for a little while, she thought she saw someone familiar. She suddenly disappeared, but it was the streak of red hair that caught Anya's attention in addition to the seemingly familiar face. *I remember clearly how Camelia told me she always wanted to get a red highlight but never could. What if this is her?*

Without telling Sophie, Anya quickly sprinted in the direction of which she last saw the girl. The entire time, her mind was flooded with thoughts of seeing her sister. Now that she believed she was on the verge of finally finding her sister, she almost couldn't imagine her face anymore. *What if she's changed so much that I can't recognize her?* Pushing down her worst fears, she wrapped her way to the back of the brick building she had seen the girl disappear behind.

There, sitting on a granite table, was the girl. Her back was turned, so Anya could only see the back of her head. She walked closer.

Sophie had been looking into a clothing store for her sister and had just turned around to return to Anya when she discovered that she was gone. Thinking that she couldn't have gotten far, Sophie peered into the surrounding buildings, just in case Anya had decided to move further ahead.

But no matter where she searched, it seemed that Anya had disappeared into thin air. *Where the hell could she be? I had only gone into the clothing store for like thirty seconds, so she couldn't have gotten that far.* Sophie reached out her phone to call Anya, but just when she was about to hit the call button, she saw Anya running towards her.

Once Anya got closer, Sophie could hear her heavy breathing, each breath making Sophie more and more anticipatory. *Did something happen? Did she...?* Sophie didn't dare say it out loud. Instead, she asked, "What happened? I've been searching for you everywhere."

Catching her breath, Anya responded, "Nothing, I just thought I saw something, and I went to go check it out. Sorry for worrying you."

"Uh huh, no worries, as long as you're okay." Sophie glanced at Anya, whose facial expression was familiar. *I've seen that look on her face before. It's a look of disappointment. Something must have happened, and she's not telling me about it.* It didn't take long for Sophie to realize that Anya had probably thought she had seen her sister, only to realize it wasn't her.

Knowing how disappointed she must be, Sophie jogged to Anya's side and said, "Hey, I think we've been searching for quite a while. What do you say when we stop to drink a coconut? I heard they're the freshest here."

Anya smiled and enthusiastically replied yes, but Sophie could tell that it was forced. *I would feel the same way if I were her. To have such hopes only for them to be crushed.* Sipping on her coconut, Sophie sincerely wished there would be results soon. It had already been forty-five minutes since they started searching, and there had been nothing.

Thinking it over, Sophie decided they had to change their game plan. *There's no point in blindly searching for them; we could be on the opposite side of the island as them for all we know. Or we might get somewhere, only for them to just have left.*

Sophie turned to Anya. "I know we said we would search the whole island first, but I think it would be more efficient and effective if we started asking around now. Or else we might be searching until nightfall with no success."

Anya's face visibly brightened. "Yes, that's what I was thinking as well. That way, we can follow actual clues to see where they are."

Sophie nodded. "Should we tell my uncle?"

Anya nodded and called him immediately. Based on Anya's nodding, Sophie could tell he had already agreed. Her mind started spinning.

Okay, Sophie. Just follow the script and you'll be fine. Do not, do not make it awkward and have anyone suspect you.

twenty-seven

Anya hung up the phone, feeling a new energy she had been missing. She comforted herself that it was normal to have mistaken someone else for her sister, that anyone could have a streak of red hair, and that to have found her sister on the first try would have been too good to be true. *Still, I would be lying if I said that I feel completely confident right now. I had been so sure, so completely assured I was right that seeing her face was like a bucket of cold, dirty water.* Anya shuddered when she thought about how she had felt when the girl had turned around, looking confused at why a stranger was tapping her shoulder. It had taken all Anya's strength to not immediately run away in embarrassment and disappointment; instead, she had uttered a meek apology for mistaking her for someone else.

The more Anya thought about it, the more naïve she realized she had been. *Why was I so sure that my sister had dyed a part of her hair red? How am I so sure that her thinking hasn't changed in all these months?* Anya was frustrated, to say the least, but at least things were getting in motion. *We have to find them now; the first resort didn't work, so now we're going to the second.*

Anya stood up, and Sophie did as well. Anya gave Sophie a look of encouragement, as she knew that it would be mostly up to Sophie now. Yes, Anya had learned a few words of Spanish in a last-minute preparation, but she could only muster the sheer basics. She had faith in Sophie, though, as she knew how much it meant to her. *Seeing Mackenzie for her is probably so much more crucial to her than I can imagine. She's been planning everything out so methodically; I can only hope it pays off.*

Together, Anya and Sophie left the coconut stand and began searching for where to start.

Sophie, pausing at a clothing store, said, "Hey, this place kind of looks like where Mackenzie would buy her clothes from. How about we start here?"

Having nowhere better to start from, Anya replied, "Sure, let's head in."

Sophie gulped. Nervous was one way to describe her at that moment, but she was more apprehensive. There were so many factors that could go wrong, yet also so much that could go right and lead her to finding Mackenzie. The store had first caught her eye because of its dark colors and oversized clothing, all of which Sophie remembered Mackenzie wearing almost every day. *I hope she's stopped here for perhaps buying some clothes, especially if she's here on "vacation."*

Almost as soon as she walked into the store, the bells jangled and from behind the counter walked out a young lady. She was wearing similar clothing that Sophie remembered Mackenzie wearing, and she had a smile on her face that made Sophie almost immediately calm down. *Okay Sophie, just think about this like talking to your average clerk person from Zara; don't think about any of your second intentions behind it.*

"How may I help you?" asked the clerk.

With a jolt, Sophie realized that she was speaking in English. *How could I forget? Tortuguero is known for its tourism, which means that everyone here probably knows how to speak some English. Why did I think that they could only speak Spanish?* Realizing that it would be weird now if she spoke Spanish, she decided to switch the script back to English.

"Hi there, I'm Sophie." Just as Sophie was about to begin the crucial line, a wave of nerves hit her. *Why did I say my name? That was not following the script at all. Shit. What if she thinks I'm weird for introducing myself? I mean, who introduces themselves when they're at a shop?*

Anya must have realized that something was off, as she immediately stepped in to help. "Hi, there! Sorry, we lost a friend of ours. We tried to contact her on the phone, but she didn't pick up. It's been quite a while now, and while we're not exactly worried, it would still be really nice if we could find her sooner rather than later. We have an activity planned, you see."

The clerk responded, "Ah, so you're looking for your friend. Can you give me a description? Maybe I can help."

Sophie, giving a grateful look to Anya, replied, "Yes. Her name is Mackenzie. She's Chinese, and is quite tall..." Pausing, Sophie realized that she couldn't exactly say what her sister looked like anymore. *For all I know, she could have completely changed her style.* But, realizing that she didn't have much of a choice, Sophie continued, "She wears quite heavy makeup, with usually very long lashes. And her style... well, it kind of looks like what you are wearing right now." *Please, please have worked.*

There was a bit of a pause before the clerk replied, "It's hard to say; I've seen a lot of customers today. But anyone in particular, I'm not so sure."

Wanting to give it one last try, Sophie added on, "Are you sure? She's quite noticeable; she had a black bowtie in her hair today." Sophie cringed as she said that last part out loud. *I actually have no idea what she was wearing today, but I have to go off of something. And she did wear it almost every day back when she was in LA.*

At Sophie's last phrase, the clerk brightened up. "Wait, I think I've seen who you're talking about. Was she wearing a black hoodie as well?"

"Yes, yes," responded Sophie enthusiastically. She looked to Anya, who was also nodding in agreement.

"Okay, great. I'm not exactly sure when I saw her today, but she definitely bought something. And she was with another girl as well, though I can't clearly remember what the other girl looked like."

Anya pitched in, "That's so great to hear. I know the other girl as well; she's Mackenzie's friend, and they told us they would go off to explore. Do you by chance have any idea of where they left off?"

There was another pause. Then, the clerk responded, "Well, I'm not exactly too sure on that point, but if they went off to explore, then they are probably visiting some of the more touristy places, like the canoes or the forests."

Knowing they had managed to squeeze out all the information possible, Sophie said, "Thank you so much, and sorry for taking up your time. But is it possible to alert us if you do see them walking around? We can perhaps exchange phone numbers?"

"Yes, yes. Of course. I'll let you know if they pop up."

Smiling, Sophie thanked her one last time, and Anya did so as well. As Sophie exited the building, she was happy to hear that there was a very likely chance that Mackenzie had just been at the shop, but she also knew that more information was needed. *It would take forever if we searched all the tourist areas; there are just too many here.* Conferring with Anya, they were both in agreement. There had to be more asking around before they could pinpoint a location.

Okay, we got some information; where should we go now? With Sophie by her side, Anya looked around, trying to find something that sparked her attention. Since they had started on the trail of finding Mackenzie, Anya decided to follow that path instead of diverting to Camelia's.

The clerk had told them before they left that most of the tourist sites were at the ends of the island, so Anya and Sophie had begun to walk there. The two girls stayed relatively quiet, trying to focus just in case Mackenzie walked by.

Around twenty minutes later, Anya could discern they had reached the tourist area. Almost all the wooden shops had signs atop of them describing activities they could do, such as learning about the creation of cocoa.

Anya nudged Sophie. "Hey, what do you think Mackenzie would be interested in if she was just coming here for vacation?"

"Hm... I know she has always liked the water; we used to go to the beach a lot."

Looking around, Anya's eyes latched onto the canoe. She pointed to it. "Perhaps she would like that activity? Just guessing based on what you said about her affinity towards water."

Sophie walked closer to the shop, stopping at its entrance. "You might be right. This is probably one of the places she would most want to visit if she came here."

Anya nodded. "Should we go inside and ask around then?"

"Let's go."

Walking into the shop, Anya was stunned by how many people there were. Upon initial observations, they all appeared to be tourists, as they were speaking in various languages. The line to the counter wrapped around a cabinet full of merchandise, and little kids weaved in and out of the sundresses that decorated the borders. *Wow, this activity must be really popular here. It's already late afternoon, and this place still seems to be teeming with people.*

Anya and Sophie got into line, enjoying the bouts of cold air as the fan above them rotated left and right.

Sophie asked, "Anya, how long do you think this line will take?"

Anya took a glance at the long line ahead of her, which was moving at a steady pace. "Probably around twenty to thirty minutes. Why do you ask?"

"Uncle Wang has been wanting to call me for quite a while to get updated on the situation, so I was planning on stepping out and talking to him about it."

"Yes, that's a good idea. We haven't really talked to him in quite a while about the general situation. How about I stand in the line, and you can find a quiet place to talk to him?"

"Okay." Sophie stepped out.

Going back outside was like entering back into a microwave. The sun was setting, but the heat that had accumulated throughout the day was now all at the ground level, and Sophie could feel the heat radiating from her skin. *We really need to hurry up and find them. If we stay intensely searching for them much longer, I'm afraid we'll have a heat stroke.*

Her uncle picked up the phone. He said, "Hi Sophie. How's it going?"

Sophie quickly gave him a rundown of what last happened since the previous update.

Uncle Wang paused. "I see you guys are making some good progress. But it's getting kind of late; do you all want to put off finding them until tomorrow or keep on going?"

Without a second thought, Sophie responded, "I want to keep on going. I think we're getting close, and I would hate to give up a lead now."

"Alright then, but make sure you don't take it too late. You'll be tired, and plus, Mackenzie and Camelia will probably be in their rooms by then if it gets past 8 pm. I'm also going around searching until then, so we can all meet up at the hotel room at 8."

So that gives us around four hours more. "Okay, Uncle. I'll get back to you soon with any updates. Keep me updated on your side as well."

"I will. And also, make sure you keep your disguise on. The people following Mackenzie around shouldn't be at where you guys are because Mackenzie isn't there, but it's always better safe than sorry."

"Sounds good."

With that, the call ended, and Sophie hurried back inside the shop, where Anya was nearing the front of the line.

"How did the call go?" asked Anya.

"Overall good, but we only have four hours left, so we better hurry up."

Anya nodded.

Quite soon, they arrived at the front of the line.

Anya spoke up. "Hello. Sorry to take up your time, but we have a quick question for you."

The clerk, an older man perhaps in his fifties, grunted, "Sure, but be quick. There's a lot of people waiting in line."

"We are missing a friend..." Anya proceeded to give the description that Sophie had given earlier.

The clerk responded in an exasperated tone, "Do you see all these people here?" He pointed to all the tourists in line. "What makes you think that I would know the person you're describing? Plus, we have multiple clerks on duty during the day, so it might have been with someone else."

Shit, we didn't exactly think about that. Sophie pitched in, "Is it possible to talk to the other clerks, or are they all busy?"

The clerk sighed. "The clerks rotate, so some of them have left to eat dinner, etc. It would probably be best for you guys to try talking to the boat drivers, though. They stay the entire time."

Perking up at this line, Sophie said, "That sounds like a great idea! Where would we find these people?"

Grunting, the clerk told them to go down the stairs and then turn right onto the dock. "They should all be parked there if they're not currently on the water. You guys can go try your luck there."

twenty-eight

THEY WERE AT THE DOCK, and although Anya couldn't yet see the boats, she could already hear the clamor of people going on and off. The sounds reminded her of the bustling sounds of a market near her house, except in a mixture of different languages.

As the boats came into sight, Anya realized just how difficult it would be to talk to the boat drivers. They seemed extremely busy, helping people off the boat only to receive more customers.

Anya glanced at Sophie, who seemed to be thinking the same thing as her based on the disappointed look on her face. Anya tapped Sophie's shoulder, "Um... I'm pretty sure you've noticed, but I'm not sure if these people have enough time to talk to us."

Sophie despondently nodded. "Do you think there's a chance they'll be done soon? Maybe we can ask them then?"

"I mean... based on the looks of it, I'm not quite sure. But maybe. Should I go back up and ask the clerk?"

"Okay, I'll stay here then?"

"Okay."

Anya jogged back to the room, where the clerk told her that it would be closing at 6 pm. *Which means we have to wait around an hour and a half. That's probably doable.*

Walking back to the pier, however, she saw a familiar back, sitting, crouched over on the ground. It was Sophie.

Anya immediately began sprinting towards her. "Sophie!" she yelled.

Sophie looked up. "Huh? Sorry, I was taking a little nap."

"Oh my goodness, you scared me so much. I thought that you had passed out." Anya could hear her chest beating in her ears.

Sophie stood up. "Oh no, I'm completely fine, just a little bit tired, that's all."

"Can you still continue the search, or do you want to call it for today? I'm completely fine with calling it if you're not up to it." *It can't hurt that much if we wait one day, though I would have loved it if we could have found at least one of them today."*

Sophie seemed to be thinking it over. Finally, she said, "I'll be fine. I really want to find Mackenzie as soon as possible because she will be leaving very soon."

Wow, I would have expected her to say no, though I suppose she is in kind of a time crunch. "Okay, then. We do have to wait around an hour and thirty minutes, so maybe we can go grab some food?"

"Yes, let's do that. What are you thinking?"

"How about that fresh fruit stand we saw earlier?"

"Let's do that."

The sunset looked especially pretty to Sophie as she walked with Anya to the fruit stand near their hotel. Something about the way the Sun dipped into the horizon made Sophie just want to sink into the sand right on her left side. She was tired, to say the least, but she also knew that she had to carry on. *If what my parents were saying was true, then Mackenzie is returning sometime on Sunday, and today is already Friday. I can't risk*

just having only one day tomorrow to find her. And what if she decides to leave early?

So, as not to worry Anya and be convinced by her to wait another day, Sophie tried to emulate a walk that matched her usual one. Anya kept on giving her side glances, as if to check if she was still okay, and Sophie kept on returning it with a smile.

Since it was a relatively long walk, and the silence—usually okay with Anya—seemed kind of suffocating, Sophie said, "Hey, doesn't this ocean remind you of the one I have in my background on the app where we first met? It looks almost the exact same; perhaps the photo was taken here?"

Anya, who had been more glancing towards her right, now looked left. "Ah, yes. Now that you say it, it does look quite familiar. I remember thinking that your profile picture was quite pretty, and wasn't that the first thing I said to you when we started our conversation?"

"Haha, I nearly forgot that, but I remember now. We went on a long tangent about sunsets, whether they were better from the mountain view or from the ocean one. I was fully on the ocean side, but you managed to talk me into liking mountains as well. I even ended up changing my profile picture for a while."

"Yup, but I'm not going to lie, you kind of made me like the oceans as well. I think it's just that I've only ever lived in Shanghai, so there aren't really many oceans. All the places I've visited in China have been mostly mountains."

"That's me, but like the complete opposite! The beach equals LA for me, and while there's mountains here in Costa Rica... they're definitely not like the ones I know." Sophie laughed as she thought about the always yellow and soot-brown grasses that marked the LA mountaintops.

Amidst the conversation that soon led to their most favorite places they've ever been on vacation, Sophie regained her energy, no longer having to fake feeling okay. *Alright, I'm ready for more searching.*

~

Anya thought she was hallucinating. *There's no way; it's definitely just way too hot right now and so I'm not seeing clearly. I'm probably mistaken again, just like last time. But...* Sophie was standing in line to buy the fruit, and Anya had looked around for a place to sit and eat. She hadn't gone far before she found the perfect spot, a table tucked underneath a tree, facing the river.

But, as Anya had walked nearer, she had seen that three people were occupying another table next to the one she had sought out, and one of them looked oddly familiar. The ponytail was the exact kind of curled she remembered, and the back was pin straight. *Nobody sits that straight, except for...* This person was sitting with her face away from Anya, which made her pause. *It's probably nothing; it would be so stupid of me to check again only to fail and return to Sophie disappointed. I need to keep my spirits up, so it would be better not to put such stakes on this.*

Anya turned around, preparing to go back to find Sophie, when she heard a laugh.

Her blood cooled.

She knew to laugh anywhere, even in her deepest of sleep. It was an almost perfect incarnation of the laugh of Will Smith, a type of laugh that came from the bottom of the chest and rose up to make a deep, bellowing sound.

It was the laugh that Anya used to always make fun of Camelia about.

Slowly, Anya turned her head around. She slowly walked towards the group, counting each of her steps as if she walked too fast, she would break the spell.

Perhaps ten feet out, the girl sitting directly opposite of who Anya supposed to be Camelia looked up. She looked Chinese, and Anya remembered seeing her somewhere but couldn't pinpoint the exact place. *I've definitely seen her somewhere, maybe in a store or in a picture?*

The girl looked at Anya weirdly, as if questioning why Anya was walking towards an already full table.

Then, perhaps intrigued by what this girl was looking at, all three of the girls looked up.

Sophie rubbed her face with one hand, the other holding the giant cup of fruit, an assortment of mango, watermelon, and dragon fruit. *What is taking Anya this long to find somewhere to sit? Isn't it just right across this corner? Is she waiting for me there so that she can make sure somebody doesn't take the spot? Perhaps I should go check.*

Walking in the direction Anya had gone, Sophie checked her phone. There was a missed call from her parents, which surprised her. *They're calling me? Did something happen?* Sophie's almost immediate thought was Mackenzie. *Shit. Did the people sent for Mackenzie recognize me? I don't look that similar to her, but I suppose we are sisters.*

Nervously, Sophie looked around her, trying to seek out if anyone looked suspicious. *I just need a little more time, a little more time so that I can find where Mackenzie is. Afterward, it doesn't matter if the spies tell my parents.* Part of Sophie wanted to call her parents back just to ease the burning worry she had. Plus, she just had this tiny figment of hope that her parents, on hearing her desperation to see Mackenzie, would give in and allow it.

Sophie's finger wavered over the call button, but she ultimately decided against it. *If I hear that they have already found me out... then I probably might as well just give up on this whole thing. They'll hide Mackenzie away like they've done before, and I'll never be able to see her again, as they'll only become more careful. No, I can't take that risk, not when I still have a chance.*

Putting her phone back in her pocket, Sophie proceeded to navigate her way to Anya, which wasn't that difficult because they had exchanged locations after Sophie couldn't find her the first time.

Oh. My. God. Even if that face staring at her had become one of an alien's, Anya would have recognized that face anywhere. It was forever cemented in that slight bump on the nose, eyes that seemed to have little stars in the middle, and a mouth that was forever curved a little bit upwards. It was Camelia.

For a while, all Anya did was stand there and gape. Yes, she had come to find Camelia, but a part of her had never truly prepared or fully expected to see her. It had always been this almost imaginative realm in which she tried to convince herself that it was possible but hadn't really believed herself. So now, when she saw Camelia, who she hadn't seen or talked to in months, standing in front of her, Anya had no idea what to do.

Finally, Camelia, who had been sitting there and gaping for some time as well, stood up and walked to her.

Camelia said, almost timidly, "Anya, I can't believe you came! You received my letter after all!"

Just beginning to walk out of her disbelief, Anya answered back, "Camellia? Is that really you?"

Camelia ran to Anya and hugged her tight. It was the same bear hug that she would give Anya whenever they needed each other's comfort. Anya hugged her back, realizing how she was almost the same height as her sister now. *I can't believe all of this is happening. It's been way too long.*

Wiping away a tear from her eyes, Camelia whispered, I've missed you so, so, so much. You have no idea."

Anya didn't respond, as she was so choked with emotion that she was unable to utter a word. Instead, she just held on tight to Camelia as if she would disappear again.

In that moment of embrace that Anya wished could endure forever, her world was complete.

After taking a few minutes to play with a stray dog and her puppies as well as give them a slice of watermelon, Sophie soon rounded the corner, where Anya's location was pinpointed.

The first thing Sophie saw when her phone read that she was only a few steps away from Anya were bushes. There were so many kinds, each offering their own type of border for the tables beyond.

Then, she heard Anya's voice intermingling with that of another girl's. *Who could she be talking to? Is she already asking another stranger?* Wanting to help Anya talk to this person, Sophie quickly walked out through the wall of bushes.

Sophie was shocked, but it was more this sensation in her stomach that stirred up an emotion she had almost forgotten. She couldn't pinpoint what emotion it quite was, except that she knew right then and there that it was all worth it. All her anger towards her parents and her loneliness as she sat waiting for Mackenzie to miraculously return dissipated at the sight in front of her: Mackenzie.

She had definitely grown healthier looking since the last time Sophie saw her. There was a fullness in her cheeks that were essentially gaunt in the last few months Sophie had spent with Mackenzie, and she could no longer see her clavicle protruding.

Sophie ran to Mackenzie, who was standing next to the table, mouth agape in shock. Emotions came back wave after wave as she bounded to her, and they all erupted together when she hugged her sister.

Mackenzie hugged her back, first lightly as if not imagining the situation to be real, then squeezing Sophie tight.

Amidst all the hugging, Sophie did not once realize that Anya was standing right next to her.

twenty-nine

Having cried nearly all of her tears out, Anya finally looked up, and, almost simultaneously with Camelia, saw the scene in front of them.

She only recognized Sophie, so it struck her as odd why Sophie was hugging someone. *I swear I've seen her somewhere, but I also don't really know where. She looks like someone I should know yet different from what I remember.* Glancing at Camelia, whose eyes were still red and puffy, Anya could tell that she was surprised as well and trying to figure out the situation.

That's right; I literally haven't even said a word to the two people who were sitting at the table with Camelia yet. And… Why do they both look so familiar?

The girl sitting at the table walked closer. "Camelia? Mackenzie? Are these your two sisters?"

It was then that it all clicked. *There's no way; that's Sophie's sister? That's why she looks so familiar; I must have seen her in a picture Sophie showed me. How???* Anya had way too many questions about what in the world was going on, but she had no idea how to begin. So she just stood there, a mouth still agape in shock.

Thankfully, Camelia broke the silence by meekly saying, "Wait. Hold on. What is happening?"

Oh yeah. She doesn't even know about Sophie.

The girl Anya, supposed to be Mackenzie, awkwardly said, "This is my sister, Sophie."

Camelia's mouth dropped open. "There's no way. This is my sister, Anya."

Mackenzie replied, "That Anya? The one you always talk about?"

"Yes, that one."

At this point, Anya's mind was going kind of crazy. It was like she was watching a reality TV show, only everything was even too coincidental for that.

Anya tapped Camelia on the shoulder and beckoned to the girl who still hadn't been named.

Catching the hint, Camelia exclaimed, "Oh yes! And this is Olivia, my friend."

Another button clicked. *That's why she looks so familiar. I've definitely seen her photo before on Camelia's WeChat, and she's the granddaughter of the man I talked to. That makes sense; he did tell me that she went to Costa Rica to find Camelia.*

Yet, there was something that still didn't make sense, no matter how much Anya tried to reason it out. *Why in the world are Mackenzie and Camelia together?*

Just having experienced perhaps the most emotion-riddled moment of her life she had ever felt, Sophie's head felt like it was going to explode but in a good way. *Anya found her sister at the exact same time as I did? What are the odds? And... Why were they together when we found them?*

Sophie decided she had to ask. "Why are you guys together? Did you just happen to meet up at Tortuguero, or...?"

Mackenzie chuckled. "Oh... I see. Right, so Camelia and I have been friends for a *long* time."

"Huh? Don't you guys live in different countries?"

Camelia responded, "We met online one day, and we have been friends ever since."

Once again, Sophie was baffled, and she could see the look of intense shock on Anya's face as well. *How in the world did such a coincidence happen? There is no way that two pairs of sisters both met each other online and never knew about it.*

Sophie wanted to ask why Mackenzie had never told her about this friend, but she quickly answered it herself. *She did kind of tell me before, but she just never really went into depth about it. So I just kind of brushed it to the back of my mind like all of her other friends. But... wouldn't she have told me if they were very close?*

Just as Sophie looked to Mackenzie in confusion, Mackenzie answered her unspoken question. "We didn't really grow close until I left L.A. for the therapy place."

At this sentence, Sophie slightly cringed. *Why had she talked to Camelia but not me when she was in therapy? Why did she leave me without a word?* These internal questions opened up a different part of Sophie that she thought she had subconsciously hidden away. All this time, she had pitted all the blame to her parents, not wanting to believe that Mackenzie would voluntarily leave without a single word. But now, as Sophie stood in the five-people circle, she wasn't so sure. *What if she really hadn't trusted me?*

It made sense logically to Anya now that Camelia and Mackenzie had explained the situation, yet it didn't really make sense how in the world all of these events had added up to this. *What are the chances that I met Sophie online, and Camelia met Mackenzie online? And that they're all in Tortuguero together?*

Anya especially wanted to hear more about Camelia's story, as she had way too many burning questions she needed to ask. *Such as why she suddenly disappeared without a trace? And what happened to that boyfriend?*

But, looking at the setting she was in, Anya realized that it would probably be better to ask her in a more private setting.

So, she said, "Guys, this is all a lot. How about we all split up? We can meet back in like an hour. If that's okay with everyone, of course."

Everyone nodded in agreement, and Olivia said, "Since you guys are all going, I should call my grandfather. He's probably worrying about a storm back in Shanghai."

Anya eagerly nodded. "Yes, for sure. When I went to talk to him, he was definitely waiting for your call."

"You visited him?!" exclaimed Olivia.

Right, she doesn't know about that. How do I even start to explain? "Okay, so long story short, I was trying to find Camelia, and remember how you told me about how you might have an idea? I went to visit you but couldn't find you. And then your grandfather told me you were here. So I almost kind of followed after your tracks."

"Ah... I see. You must have been surprised to not find me there."

Recounting the shock she had felt when she heard an old man answering the door instead of Olivia, Anya slightly chuckled. "Yes, just a tad bit."

"Well, I'm glad you're here, and I'll definitely be hearing an earful from my grandfather soon. You guys go, I'll stay here and wait."

The other four agreed and went in two separate directions.

Walking around the more-empty streets of Tortuguero as people were beginning to close up their stores, Sophie turned to her sister but didn't know how to begin the conversation. *The last time we talked was so long ago, probably a few months have already passed. I basically have no idea*

what happened to her, so it's not like I can go into any of the specifics of her recent life.

Mackenzie, who was looking at the ocean, also seemed to not know what to say. Finally, she spoke up. "How did you find me?"

Sophie wondered for a bit about how she would respond. *How do I even begin to tell this dramatic story? I suppose I should just start from the very beginning. But first, I need to ask her a question.*

"Wait, before I answer that question, there's something I need to know."

Mackenzie slowly nodded. "Sure, go ahead. I'm sure you have a lot of questions, with all that's happened and all." She nervously chuckled.

"Did you... did you know that I thought you were dead this entire time?"

Mackenzie paused, and Sophie already knew the answer before she said it. Yet, when the words of affirmation came out of her sister's mouth, it still felt like a punch to the gut.

All Sophie could utter out was "why?"

Picking at her fingernails, Mackenzie responded in a despondent tone, "I was embarrassed. I'm your older sister, so it felt like my duty to protect you from what was going on. So I forced Mom and Dad to say it."

"How... how did you protect me by saying that you were dead?" Sophie choked.

Mackenzie took a deep breath. "See, the thing is I never thought I would return. I was so 'not here' that I thought I would never recover. At one point, I didn't want to see anyone familiar; in fact, I didn't even want to see anyone at all. I... I actually thought I was going to die." Her voice cracked, and she paused.

Sophie wanted to hug her, to tell her that everything was going to be okay and that she was sorry for not realizing sooner, but Mackenzie continued on before she could do so. "So I thought of it as better to not give you false hope. You need to live your life without my presence always hanging around as a burden."

"As a burden?"

"Yes, as a burden. I was really struggling with my addiction with heroin, as it slowed down my brain and made me stop thinking so much. When I left, I was so wrapped up in those drugs that I didn't think I would ever return… and it just wasn't fair of me to leave you forever anticipating something so unlikely. At least, if I said I was dead, you wouldn't be waiting around forever."

Sophie wanted a little bit to yell. In part, she understood Mackenzie's decision, yet another part couldn't comprehend at all. *Isn't that the point of family? To support each other during difficult times? I could have…* But, seeing the sad look on Mackenzie's face, Sophie chose another path of thinking. *I'm her younger sister, and she wanted to protect me. But…* Sophie had another question.

She asked, "Sorry for bombarding you with questions, but I have another one."

"Understandable. Go ahead. But I still would like to know how in the world you found me." Mackenzie's voice sounded more stable now, going back to the same deep voice that Sophie remembered.

"Yes, I'll answer that right after this one." Sophie quickly brushed her hair to the side. "I'm assuming you got better, and if so, I'm so, so glad. I'm assuming you did, right?" Sophie apprehensively looked at Mackenzie. *I really have no idea if she's fully recovered or anything. I just don't know anything.* Sophie quickly prayed that Mackenzie was okay now.

Thankfully, Mackenzie replied, "Yes, I'm better now, which came as a huge surprise to me. I never thought I would recover. And… I suppose your next question is why I didn't contact you?"

Sophie nodded.

"Well, what I'm going to say next might completely shock you. I was actually planning to tell you about it during my little trip to Tortuguero."

"What? You were?" Sophie wanted more than anything to believe this.

"Yes, I swear I was. I even have the text written out. I can show you later if you would like. But the reason I didn't contact you immediately was because I didn't know how to say it. It had been so long that I wanted to say it in a way that wouldn't immensely shock you, though I now know that reaching that goal is pretty impossible."

Sophie awkwardly chuckled. "That's pretty true. I don't think coming back from the dead will ever *not* be surprising."

Mackenzie chuckled and continued, "Exactly. That was one reason, and another was that I wanted to make sure I was fine being outside before I contacted you. I was doing quite well at the therapy center, but I had no idea how I would fend outdoors, when I'm among many other people."

"How do you feel now that you're out here?"

Tapping her fingers, Mackenzie responded, "At first, I wasn't used to it because I had been in this 'bubble' of people for so long. Everything felt so chaotic and loud that I just wanted to stay indoors."

"Oh." Sophie's stomach dropped.

"Yes, it was bad, but that feeling didn't last long. After a few hours, and mostly with the help of talking to Camelia, I was soon over it. Now, I feel pretty much the exact same as how I did at the therapy center."

Sophie smiled and timidly asked, "So... does that mean you had decided to write to me?"

"I had actually just decided this afternoon that I was, but you arrived before I could!" Prodding Sophie on the shoulder, Mackenzie said, "Okay, your turn now. Tell me how in the world you found me. There's no way it could have been an accident."

This is going to be a mighty long story. "Okay, I'll tell you now."

thirty

Anya sat down on the plush chair. For the last five minutes, Camelia had led her to supposedly one of her favorite places in Tortuguero. It was a small courtyard in front of a family-owned hotel, and it was filled with hammocks as well as plush chairs. As the courtyard was only a few steps away from the beach, there was a steady wind that kept the place much cooler compared to the main streets. Apparently, outsiders were not allowed to sit there, but because Camelia had grown close to the hotel owners by being a part-timer there for a while, they allowed it.

Legs tired from all the walking, Anya let herself sink into the cushion. Camelia did the same, and they sat facing each other.

Clearing her throat, Anya said, "Ehm. I have a few questions I *need* to ask you."

Camelia sat up straighter and replied, "Go right on ahead. I'm all ears."

"Okay, first of all. I think I know the answer to this question, but why did you suddenly just disappear?"

Clearing her throat, Camelia responded, "Ah, yes. There definitely needs to be a *lot* of explaining about that. Do you remember my boyfriend, Nathan?"

"How could I forget?" muttered Anya.

"Well, he was one of the key reasons I left Shanghai."

"Uh huh." At this point, Anya wanted to scream at Camelia for letting herself just get taken away by a boy, but she decided to keep quiet. *I should let her tell her side of the story first.*

Camelia paused. "Hold on, I said that part wrong. It might be a bit of a misunderstanding if I say it that way. It was more like he offered me a path out."

Of course, she's still covering for him. Anya nodded.

"I know you don't believe me. I would react the same way. But it's true. You might have already known, but I had and still have a huge passion for animals."

This part is true.

Camelia continued, "But Mom and Dad didn't want that for me. They wanted me to take the traditional route, which was to take the *gaokao* and become a doctor."

Anya thought back to all the nights she spent listening to her parents tell Camelia this, which then brought back a flood of emotions as she recalled how Camelia had always just silently nodded along.

"And I was a good student. I always scored at the top of my class, and Mom would always tell all her friends about how well I did after each test." Camelia paused for a moment, and Anya could see a look of almost nostalgic sadness in her eyes. "The thing is, I was only good at school tests. I've told you before, perhaps lightly, but the reality is that I *suck* at standardized testing. I can't do it at all; something about the way that everything is poured in one giant melting pot makes it nearly impossible for me."

Camelia sighed, and Anya patted her back. In a soft tone, Anya said, "Honestly, I think it's for the better. Mom was always so annoying about the test, and you finally broke free of those expectations."

Slightly smiling, Camelia responded, "Yes, I'm happy about finally being able to do what I love; I won't deny that. But there's still a tad, tad part of myself that wants to be the daughter that makes her parents proud." She seemed to reminisce for a moment, then she abruptly said, "Okay, now to answer your question." She slightly closed her eyes for a bit. "By the time the *gao kao* came around, I knew I couldn't do it. I knew that if I took it, I would just disappoint everyone with the score, and there was no way I would get into those top colleges in Beijing that Mom and Dad wanted me to get into. And also... even if I did well on them, I knew I wasn't going to be happy. Trust me, I had *tried* to convince myself that I could be in a hospital all day, operating on sick patients. Yet, no matter how much I thought about it before I went to sleep each night, I knew I was lying to myself. I would be miserable if I continued down that road. And that's when Nathan came in. He offered me a new path by showing me the job opportunities in Costa Rica. In part, he also wanted to escape, mostly due to his parents. We had always dreamed together of going somewhere, somewhere far away from it all." Anya could see little stars glistening in Camelia's eyes. "When I saw the chance to work with wildlife as a tour guide but at the same time continue studying for free about biology's interaction with nature, there was a gut feeling that it was right."

By this point, Anya was already deeply moved by Camelia's story, which seemed so daring from her usual life. Yet, she still had this pestering question—an almost selfish one—that Camelia hadn't answered. She asked, "I completely understand your decision, but why did you leave so quickly without a word? And breaking off communication?"

The sky was turning dark, casting a shadow over Camelia's face that made her seem kind of distant, almost like she was trying to go off into the distance. After around a minute, she answered, "I was selfish. I left quickly because I knew that if I didn't, I would never. I loved you guys way, way too much, and hearing you guys tell me not to go would just break my heart. If you just uttered one word for me to stay, I know that I would give up all my dreams and go back to studying for the *gaokao*. I just wouldn't be able to take it, having to tear myself away from you. And so I left without any of you guys knowing, only leaving a note." Her voice cracking, she added, "Then, afterward, I still never contacted you guys because I knew that if I did and saw your texts or even heard your voice, I would immediately return. But for myself, I *needed* to stay."

At Camelia's response, Anya was shocked at the impact it had on her. It was like a sudden wave washing over her, cooling her from all the anger she had previously felt. Everything felt so sad she thought she was going to cry, and a tear did start forming, but everything also felt so *right. If I had been in Camelia's position, I would have definitely not been that brave. The immense courage and dedication it must have taken, as well as the desire for change. But my goodness, do I understand her. Sometimes... sometimes I think the same way, even when I'm not under half the pressure she is under after Mom realized her mistake.*

For a while, Anya and Camelia just sat in silence, watching as the ocean in front of them started losing visibility in an almost peaceful way. Anya had one more question, though she also was pretty sure that she knew the answer to this one.

Turning to Camelia, whose eyes were starting to droop, Anya asked, "Why the letter, though? Why then, and why only to me and not Mom or Dad?"

Camelia's voice as she responded to this question was less shaky. "Ah, right. The letter. Did you see the specific signature I had?"

"Of course, how could I forget?"

"Right, so I used that signature specifically so that Mom and Dad wouldn't find out. And I chose this time because I felt ready. In this past month, I have finally felt the sense of security I had been lacking, and I am now comfortable with who I am. So I wanted to reach out. You were actually the only person I was going to write to, but I decided to include Olivia as well just because of how long I've known her. But I didn't want to show Mom or Dad yet because I was, and yes, this is going to sound kind of contradictory to what I said about my stability earlier, but I wasn't ready to hear their words of criticism yet. Especially Mom's. I know that they're probably extremely upset at me, and I can already imagine what they would say." Camelia nervously chuckled before continuing. "I think I'll talk to them soon, but not now. I still need to ground myself a bit more."

"I see, though I don't think they would be upset at you." For some reason, Anya was sure about this. "Yes, I think they would actually be ecstatic to hear from you. They miss you so much that just hearing from you would send them to the clouds."

"Really?" Camelia's tone was surprised, a bit hopeful. "You don't think they'll start trying to convince me to come back?"

This, I'm not so sure about. Candidly, Anya responded, "I can't promise that, but I really do believe that they won't be angry. I can just envision their excitement." Images of her father jumping up and down and her mother holding her hands over her mouth flooded in Anya's mind.

"I really do hope so. I miss them so, so much." Camelia, who, in a sudden movement that shocked Anya, gave Anya a big hug and whispered, "I'm so glad you're here; you have no idea how much."

Anya embraced her back.

Sophie took a deep breath and exhaled. She had just finished telling the story of how she had found Mackenzie, and the recap had left her realizing just how crazy everything had been. She looked at Mackenzie's face, which was etched with lines of what Sophie could tell were sad ones.

Mackenzie responded, "Wow. That is one hell of a rollercoaster you must have been on over this month. I... as your older sister... I'm sorry for causing you all this anxiety." She looked downward, which made Sophie break.

Sophie, in a voice louder and more assertive than her usual one, said, "No. You should never, ever be sorry. Don't ever say that, not when you've been through this much. You are not responsible for any of this. You are solely responsible for recovering, okay?" Sophie put her arms around Mackenzie, who almost melted into the hug. Sophie let herself melt as well. *I'm just so glad that I have my sister back, even if it's only for a short time.*

Eventually, once Sophie's tear ducts were completely empty, she said in a placid tone, "Should we head back now? I think they might be waiting on us." She hadn't kept track of time, but she knew that the Sun setting and the night lights coming on in the streets meant that at least an hour, probably more around two, had passed.

Mackenzie nodded and wiped her remaining tears away with her shirt.

On the entire walk back, Mackenzie grasped Sophie's hand tightly, and vice versa.

thirty-one

Anya stood with Camelia at the courtyard, where Olivia had just woken up from a nap. They had spent the walk back talking about Nathan, and Anya had learned that he had gone on a business trip to the other side of Sri Lanka. There, he would be participating in a conference to discuss how to boost the country's environmental awareness while keeping up the economy.

Hearing about Nathan had given Anya mixed feelings, as she still harbored some initial negative feelings, the same ones she had felt all those months ago. Yet, while hearing Camelia talk about him with such passion and remembering the earlier conversation, Anya realized that she no longer thought of him as this "evil" guy. Instead, she recognized how he had probably the same goal as Camelia and that he had probably been the same amount of scared when he had left behind his life in Shanghai to chase his dreams. *Maybe he isn't so bad after all.*

After waiting around fifteen minutes, Sophie and Mackenzie walked back into view, and Anya waved. She wanted more than anything to ask Sophie to spill everything, and she was quite sure that Sophie wanted her to do the same. It would have to wait until later, though, as they first had to go to dinner and meet up with Uncle Wang. *I wonder how he'll respond to seeing Mackenzie. Have we even told him yet?*

Anya ran up to Sophie and nudged her to the side. "Psst... have we told your uncle about what has occurred yet?"

Sophie, whose eyes were quite puffy, responded in a shocked tone, "Omg, we haven't! Come to think of it, we hadn't updated him when we were buying the fruit. He's probably wondering where we are right now." Sophie pulled out her phone, and Anya did so as well.

As Anya had thought, there were texts from Uncle Wang, all inquiring about how the situation was going and telling them that if they really couldn't find the sisters, it would be better to wait until the next day. The texts got more urgent as time passed on, perhaps invoked by how much time had passed since Anya and Sophie updated him.

Anya asked Sophie, "Should we just surprise him at the dinner? That might honestly be the best way if we want to make him really surprised."

Bunching up her mouth in thought, Sophie responded, "Yes. That will probably be the best way, though I'll tell him now that we should meet up for dinner. We had already planned out a restaurant, right?"

"Yes, I believe it's quite close to here. I can put it on my phone's map, but I'm pretty sure we can just follow Camelia's lead due to how long she's been here."

"Okay, let's go."

Indeed, Camelia knew the exact location, and she had been extremely excited about it, as it was one of her favorite restaurants in Tortuguero. When Sophie had asked why, Camelia had said, "It's a surprise."

Now walking toward the restaurant that was just a ten-minute walk away, Sophie hung close to Mackenzie, still kind of amazed at how her sister was right in front of her. She looked around for any sign of the people her parents had sent but knew that even if she saw them, she wouldn't really care. *It's not like they can reverse time and stop me from finding her. Plus, now that I know the full story, I think Mom and Dad just sent them for security reasons, not to force her to go back. Though it's still wrong.*

Anya, Camelia, and Olivia were up front, chatting away about a funny memory. Mackenzie, on the other hand, seemed to just be staring off into the distance, lost in thought.

Wanting to hear her sister's voice a bit more, Sophie gently nudged Mackenzie's shoulders. "Hey, Mackenzie. What are you thinking about?"

"Huh? Oh, sorry. I was just thinking about... about. Well, the thing is that I'm supposed to go back really soon, like tomorrow's my last day."

"Oh, right." Sophie had tried not to think about that, but it was true.

"And the thing is that I really don't want to go back, not after all this. But...I can't quit rehab yet. I know I still have a way to go before I'm fully recovered, as evidenced by how I reacted when I first came onto this island and how I still sometimes cringe at bustling streets." Mackenzie sighed, and Sophie tried to think about something to say but was also choked up by how soon they would again have to separate from each other. *I wish there were some other way... there has to be something that would allow me to stay with Mackenzie or at least see her a bit more often.*

But, before Sophie could dwell on this thought any longer, they had arrived at the restaurant. Well, it was more so the base of the restaurant, as the actual place where they would sit down and eat was up two flights of steep stairs.

By the time Sophie had reached the top, she was a bit winded and took a moment to catch her breath, but she was also amazed. The restaurant was open-air, displaying a clear view of the Tortuguero River, which was illuminated by the lights that shone at each corner of the restaurant. The overall design of the restaurant brought Sophie back to her family trip years ago to Hawaii, as everything held a slight essence of the ocean.

Absorbing in her surroundings, Sophie also finally noticed her uncle, who was sitting with his head in the menu, probably not having yet noticed the group's arrival due to the loud but beautiful music that was playing in the background.

He is for sure going to be shocked by this but here goes. Sophie called out, "Uncle! We're here!"

Her uncle looked up, and the shock on his face etched a permanent memory in Sophie's mind. His mouth was completely open, and for a moment he did not stir from where he sat. After an awkward silence and pause as everyone took turns looking at one another, he stood up and walked over.

Rubbing his eyes, he said, "Mackenzie? Is that you?"

Her face gushing, Mackenzie responded, "Yes, it is! Oh how I've missed you, Uncle! Sophie told me all about your adventures coming here."

Uncle Wang didn't say anything for a moment, and Sophie could feel the tangible emotion that he felt then as he hugged Mackenzie tight. Then, Sophie decided to join in on the hug, and soon, starting from Anya, then Camelia, then Olivia, everyone was in a big hug. Sophie realized later that many people were probably watching, but unlike her usual self, she didn't care. She was just happy that everyone was together again, finally after so many months.

Anya rubbed her stomach, full after eating a delicious plate of curry, tacos, fries, plantains, and so much more. During the dinner, she had thought about bringing up what the next steps were going to be, as they really only had one day left before Mackenzie had to leave, meaning that Sophie and Anya would go as well. But, as Anya had looked at all the smiling faces, she decided she didn't want to be the cruel person who cut everyone's attention back to reality. Plus, she wanted to enjoy the dinner as well without having to worry about the future.

Checking his watch, Uncle Wang announced, "Alright guys. It's getting kind of late, which means that we should probably get going soon. We can all meet up again tomorrow, I'm assuming?"

Mackenzie responded, "Yes, let's do that. It's been such an exciting day that I think we all need some good rest."

Anya nodded in agreement, and everyone else did so as well.

As everyone stood up to leave, Anya hurried over to Camelia and waved goodbye. "See you tomorrow for breakfast?"

Camelia eagerly nodded and chuckled. "Yes, I'll send you the directions to the breakfast place, and then we can all head over to this wonderful place for breakfast. I'm sure you'll love it."

"Okay, see you then!"

"See you!"

Sophie was now finally back in her hotel room, and, having taken a long shower, proceeded to plop on the sofa and say to Anya, "Oh my goodness, I am so tired."

Anya, whose head was already in her pillow, muttered a groan. "I know, right? I didn't even feel it until now due to all the adrenaline."

"Me too, I was so caught up in the day's excitement, but I think I'm going to pass out for like ten hours now."

For a little while, there was no response, and Sophie thought that Anya had fallen asleep. Just as Sophie was going to close her eyes and settle into a deep slumber, however, Anya quietly said, "I was thinking about the day. And I know I should be happy, and I really am, but I'm also so worried about what's going to happen. I feel like just as I have everything, I'm about to lose it all over again. Do you know what I mean?"

Sophie was stunned by how accurately Anya's worries mirrored hers. "I feel the exact same way. Like one part of me is over the moon at finally seeing Mackenzie again, but it also feels like it's going to be ten times harder to say goodbye. I already feel like I'm saying goodbye, and we still have a day left."

Sighing, Anya turned over on her bed, now facing the ceiling. Sophie did the same. Anya asked, "Do you think there's anything we could do? So that we don't have to wait an eternity until we see them again?"

"Well, I suppose they're definitely going to start texting us after this, so we'll at least know what they're up to. But besides perhaps Facetiming them, I'm not really sure. It's kind of up to them, as it is their lives. And it's not like we can move all the way here, either." *I just wish that we could freeze time and stay here with them forever.*

Anya sighed again and said, "I think I'm going to bring this topic up to Camelia tomorrow even if she doesn't. I just need to know what's going to happen, even if the news is good or bad."

Sophie thought about herself asking Mackenzie about it and imagined the disappointment she would feel with the answer she knew would be coming. Yet, just as Anya had said, Sophie realized that she needed a concrete answer, even if it was bad. *I cannot leave here not knowing when or where I'm going to see her again.* Making up her mind, Sophie said, "I think I'm going to talk to her tomorrow morning about it. I don't want to put it off any longer."

"Me too, then."

With that, the conversation ended, and Sophie soon drifted off to sleep.

thirty-two

Anya half-woke up to the sound of incessant knocking. *What the hell?* Still not fully awake, she stumbled to the door and was shocked when she saw Uncle Wang standing there.

Anya uttered out, "Huh? Why are you here so early?"

He laughed. "Is this early for you? It's already 9 am! We were supposed to head over now, and not hearing any movement, I decided I had to check up on you guys."

There's no way. Anya quickly hurried to her phone, and, seeing the time, realized that Camelia was actually telling the truth. *How did I over-sleep this much?* Rushing back to the door, Anya said to Camelia, "Sorry! We'll be at the breakfast place in thirty minutes, just give us a little time to get ready! You should first head over!" Without waiting for his response, she quickly shut the door and proceeded to shake Sophie awake.

"Sophie! Wake up!"

Sophie, who was also still in a slumberous state, was finally dragged up by Anya, and they both hurried to brush their teeth and change into their outfits for the day. Today, they no longer had to disguise them-selves, so they could go back to wearing their "normal" clothes. For Anya, this meant that she could finally wear her beach outfit that she had bought ages ago and had not been able to wear due to not having a beach anywhere near her house in Shanghai.

Anya usually took at least an hour to get ready, but perhaps invigorated by wanting to spend as much time with her sister as possible, she was ready in just twenty minutes. Sophie was waiting at the door, and they both set off for breakfast.

Once again, the breakfast area Camelia chose wasn't far away, and they were there in around a five-minute walk. The entire time of the walk, however, Anya had been deep in thought about how she would ask Camelia. *I agree with Sophie that we should ask them sooner rather than later, though I'm still unsure about how to approach the question without making it seem like I'm pressuring her to do something after I just came.* Without any concrete way, Anya decided that she would just go with the flow. *It's Camelia; I'm sure it'll be fine. Right?*

The breakfast place was once again extremely beautiful, though it was very different from the previous night's. It had almost a jungle vibe that mimicked the Tortuguero National Park Anya had seen a sign of the day before. All the ceilings were covered with plants, sometimes having a spark of color in a vibrant hue of pink or orange.

In the center of the room—which was essentially empty—was Camelia, Mackenzie, Uncle Wang, and Olivia.

Anya and Sophie walked over and sat down.

Camelia spoke first. "Good morning! You guys must have been really tired yesterday."

Anya looked at Sophie, and they both chuckled. Sophie replied, "Yup, I was about to set an alarm clock for 8 AM so that we could have ample time to get ready, but I must have been so drowsy yesterday that it completely slipped my mind."

Mackenzie responded, "That's okay, we already ordered for you guys. Camelia said she knew what is the best to have in this restaurant."

Camelia nodded. "I've been here a thousand times; it's basically like eating at home now."

Almost as soon as Anya had sat down, the food arrived. Everything was delicious, consisting of a mixture between sweet, salty, and even some hints of sour in the drinks that Camelia had ordered. Indeed, everything seemed to have an essence of being homemade in that nothing was exactly perfect, yet it was spectacular for that very reason.

As the plates started to be cleared, Anya gave Sophie a look to say, "It's time."

Sophie nodded, and Anya could see from the look on her face that she had been thinking about it the entire breakfast time.

Alright, here goes. "Mackenzie, could I perhaps talk to you for a little while? Maybe just thirty minutes?"

Quickly, Anya added, "Me too. Camelia, could I perhaps talk to you for a while as well?"

Mackenzie's face scrunched up in confusion, but she quickly responded, "Sure, let's go somewhere else."

Sophie smiled. She had spent the breakfast time emotionally preparing herself, as she knew this conversation would probably end in a fashion that would cause them to be once again separated for a long time. *But that's okay, she should focus all her attention on recovering.*

Once they reached the main streets and had found a quieter and cooler place, Mackenzie stopped walking and turned around to say to Sophie, "Hold on, I think I know what this conversation is going to be about. Is this about tomorrow?"

Sophie stepped back in shock. *How did she already know?*

Mackenzie let out a laugh. "Ah, I see I guessed right. I could pretty much tell from the way you seemed to be in a state of worry the entire time while eating breakfast. Perhaps others couldn't tell, but I knew pretty much right away."

Batting her sister on the shoulder, Sophie responded, "Okay, fine. You got me." Though slightly annoyed at how easily Mackenzie had seen right through her, the fact that Mackenzie already knew what she was going to talk about helped alleviate much of the anticipation she had about having to bring it up. "I just... I just wanted to know what's going to happen next? Are you going back to the rehab center?"

Mackenzie paused. "Yes, probably. But at the same time, I'm not so sure."

Sophie's heart skipped a beat at the last part of the sentence. "Really? What do you mean by that?"

"Well... the main reason I went to Costa Rica was so that I could get away from everyone, as that is what I needed back then."

"Uh huh. I completely understand that. But...?"

"But I think I'm ready to come back."

"What?" Sophie half-shouted. *There's no way.* "Did I hear you right? Like you're going to come back, like back back?"

Mackenzie calmly replied, "Well, it's not going to be back, back. Like I'm not going to start living at home again. But I think I'm ready to find somewhere closer to you guys. A rehab center in LA."

At this point, Sophie could barely believe hear anything, as she was lost in this trance of sheer happiness. Just a few minutes ago, she had thought she wouldn't be able to see Mackenzie again for months, but this revelation meant that she would be able to visit her all the time if she wanted. Sophie jumped to Mackenzie and hugged her tight. "Oh. My. God. I am so happy to hear that. You have no idea how worried I was."

Mackenzie chuckled. "I must say, I am quite surprised by this thought as well. I really hadn't given it much thought, but when I saw you yesterday, it got me thinking last night. I'm at a better place now, and I really don't want to be separated from you again. And it would be pretty nice to see Mom and Dad again."

So she was thinking about this last night as well? I suppose sisters do think pretty similarly. Sophie smiled to herself, a sense of warmth filling her as she thought about how Mackenzie no longer wanted to be distanced from her family. *I never thought I would even see Mackenzie again, and now she might actually be returning. For real.*

"Have you told Mom and Dad yet?" asked Sophie. "Because I know that they would be out of this world in joy."

"No, I haven't. I have just made this decision, so there would be a list of procedures I would need to follow before even being allowed to go to LA. And plus, I need to first find someplace suitable there before I can even go."

"Ah, I see. That makes a lot of sense." Despite realizing that the waiting period would be a while, Sophie still let out a sigh of relief. *Even if the procedure takes weeks, I know that she's recovered enough to be back, and once she actually gets to LA, I'm going to be at the hospital literally every single day visiting her.* Sophie could already imagine it, and she smiled wide.

Anya led Camelia out to where the boats had been the day before, as she had seen a quiet sitting area near the docks. The entire walk there, Camelia had pestered Anya to tell her already, but Anya had consistently declined. *I need a quiet space to talk to her, as I can't be screaming over the noise while trying to literally get her to make such a huge decision.* What that decision was, Anya still didn't know, but she knew that this conversation would either end up with her not being able to see Camelia again for *months*. So, naturally, she wanted to make sure that they at least got to talk in a quiet, peaceful area.

When they at last arrived, Camelia turned to Anya and asked, "Okay, can you say it now?"

Anya took a deep breath. "Yes, sorry. I wanted to find a quiet place."

Camelia, half looking very confused, responded, "Okay. But what is so important that you wanted to bring me all the way here? Do you have a boyfriend, or...?"

"What, no!" exclaimed Anya. "Of course, I don't, who do you think I am?"

Camelia threw back her head and let out a laugh. "No, no. I was just kidding. You are *way* too scared to ever date."

Anya scoffed and mock punched Camelia on the shoulder. "Whatever. The guy I like doesn't like me back anyway."

"Really? Is it still that Liam guy?"

Knowing that Camelia wanted to tease her, as she had known about this crush since forever, Anya diverted the subject. "That's not the central point right now."

"Okay, okay. Whatever you say." There was a slight twinkle in Camelia's eye.

Anya cleared her throat. "Alright, so the thing I'm going to say next is very important, so listen up."

"Mhm."

"It's about what's going to happen tomorrow. When I leave, I mean."

Camelia chuckled. "You brought me all the way here to discuss that?"

"Yes, of course! I might not be able to see you for months again!"

Camelia let out a laugh, which frustrated Anya. *Why can't she take this seriously?* "Hello?" Anya waved her hand in front of Camelia's face. "I'm actually worried here."

Perhaps hearing the urgency in Anya's voice, Camelia turned more serious. "Right. I am serious about this subject, but also, why did you worry so much? Of course, now that I've seen you all, I'm not just going to leave you again for months!"

"Huh? So...?" Anya looked at Camelia half in confusion, half in hope.

"I already decided quite a while ago. I'm going to come visit Shanghai."

"Really?!" Anya stood up from her bench in shock and examined Camelia's face, trying to see if she was joking.

"Yes, really. I'm not going to move back, though. I would love to be around you all the time, but I need my life here. It has been my dream all along."

Anya nodded. "Yes, of course. But you'll come visit?"

"Yes. I will definitely come visit. I was actually planning on coming in like two weeks. That's when Nathan will be back, and then we'll come visit together."

"Two weeks?!" Again, Anya was in shock. "That's so soon!"

Camelia chuckled. "I know. That's why I wasn't really freaking out about you leaving. I know I'll see you again really soon. And plus, we can Facetime all the time, so whenever you miss me, just give me a call. Of course, with jet lag in mind. Please don't call me in the middle of the night."

Anya laughed. "We'll see about that."

The rest of the day pretty much passed in a blur of activity. Right after their separate "meetings" with their sisters, Sophie and Anya had reconvened back in the breakfast area, and they had excitedly exchanged the good news. Sophie could still barely believe that what she had heard was real and that Mackenzie was truly going to be back, but she didn't have much time to process the realization before Camelia whisked them all away to go on the kayak. Apparently, as she had quoted it, "You need to kayak in the morning because that is when the Sun hasn't quite begun its glare yet, but at the same time has already risen to provide the perfect view."

During the entire kayak ride, Camelia talked nonstop about all the animals they were seeing as well as pointing out how they coexisted with the dense plant life that extended far beyond the human eye. Each time Camelia pointed out an animal that Sophie wouldn't have even seen for an hour, Sophie was shocked by just how much Camelia knew. *She's definitely smart, that's for sure. And a lover for animals.* It seemed to Sophie that Camelia and Tortuguero were one.

Next up, Camelia brought the entire group to learn how to make chocolate with pure cacao beans. The experience was truly one of a kind, as Sophie literally got to see an entire cacao bean become rich, delicious chocolate. The whole time, Anya kept on snapping photos of each person, and, at the end of the chocolate-making process, everyone gathered around the stone mallet on which they had broken down the cacao beans. With all six of them together, they all posed for a group photo.

Though some people's faces had a bit of chocolate smeared on them, the picture was perfect for Sophie. And, telling by the bright, chocolate-stained smile on Anya's face, Sophie could tell that she was perfectly content with it as well.

thirty-three

WHY IS SAYING goodbye so difficult? Anya knew that she would see Camelia again in two weeks, yet she still didn't want to leave. The boat taking them back to the mainland of Costa Rica had just arrived, and right after all the passengers' luggage was loaded, she, Sophie, and Uncle Wang would be off.

Realizing she only had a couple of minutes left, Anya leaned in to hug Camelia, whose face seemed generally stoic but was revealed through the slight tear in her left eye.

Camelia, in a quiet voice, said, "I'll see you soon, okay?"

Anya nodded. "I know, you better come to visit soon, or else I will literally fly back and yell at you. And you'll never hear the end of me."

Laughing, Camelia said, "Okay, I'll come, so please spare me your wrath. I'm planning to tell Mom and Dad sometime in the next few days. Once you get back."

Anya just nodded and smiled, not wanting to let go of her sister.

"Hey! We need to go!" called out Uncle Wang.

"Coming!" yelled back Anya. Turning to face Camelia again, she said, "Okay, I think I need to go back now."

"Yes, you don't want to miss the boat." Camelia wiped away a tear, and they hugged one last time.

"See you in two weeks?"

"See you!" Anya walked towards the boat, waving goodbye the entire time.

As the boat left the harbor, Sophie leaned her face against the back of her seat, trying to catch the last glimpses of Mackenzie's waving hands. Anya, who was sitting next to her but on the inside this time, was doing the same thing. Sophie's heart was heavy at the thought of not seeing Mackenzie again for a while, but it was also laden with hope. This trip had been so much more than she could have ever asked for, as not only did she successfully find Mackenzie, but she also learned that Mackenzie was willing to move back to LA. She was also extremely happy for Anya as well as Uncle Wang, as this trip had been a success for both of them.

Now, though, it was time to return back to L.A. And, though Sophie felt like throwing up every time she thought about it, she knew that it was time to confront her parents. *They'll either be super shocked and happy or super shocked and angry. I'll just have to wait and see.*

thirty-four

After a six-hour flight back to L.A., during which Anya and Sophie talked nonstop about how excited they were at everything that had occurred yet also sad about leaving, it was finally time for Anya to say goodbye to Sophie. Having only been with Sophie in-person for a few days, Anya didn't expect the goodbye to be as difficult as it was.

I didn't realize we had connected this much. It feels like she's almost become my sister, my partner-in-crime. Everything will be so... empty without her around. As Sophie's parents—who Anya had just introduced herself to—helped with the luggage, Sophie ran to Anya.

She exclaimed, half-sniffling, "I'm going to miss you so, so much. You have been the best friend ever. Like ever."

Holding back tears, Anya leaned in to hug Sophie. "We need to have a reunion sometime soon. And in the meantime, we'll Facetime all the time."

Sophie nodded. "Yes, I will literally be spamming you with texts all day, and we need to plan sometime for a big get together."

"Yes, for sure." Realizing that Uncle Wang also needed to say goodbye, Anya let herself fade more into the background and just watched as the family all came together to say their goodbyes. Sophie's parents both took turns exchanging words and smiles with Uncle Wang, and they all seemed to be at a place of extreme content. *I really do hope that Sophie's parents aren't too upset when they hear the truth, and I hope they won't see me in a bad light either, especially after I had just introduced myself to them.* With a gulp, Anya thought back to her parents. *I'll need to confront them as well once I get back. I can already picture the look on Mom's face.*

Sophie's exclamation of goodbye knocked her back to reality, and Anya ferociously waved goodbye. As she watched Sophie and her parents walk off together, she could already feel like she was missing something by her side. *I know we said that we would meet again sometime, but with all this distance between us and our busy high school schedules, I really doubt it's possible, at least not for a long time.* Anya's eyes welled up, but she quickly wiped her tears away as Uncle Wang came back. *Time to go home.*

Okay, time to tell my parents the truth. Finally, There's no point in putting it off, as that will only make things worse. Sophie's eyes darted between her mother and father, who were both eating their dinner across the table. She took a deep breath, trying to console herself that all would be alright. *It's fine; I don't even care if they get mad at me anymore. I have nothing to lose, really. I've already seen Mackenzie.*

Sophie cleared her throat. "Mom, Dad. I have a confession to make, and you guys will probably be *quite* upset."

Both her parents put their utensils down. Her father spoke first, in a worried tone. "Why? Did something happen in Costa Rica?" He exchanged a nervous look with Sophie's mother.

Right. They are probably worried about the whole Mackenzie thing but for all the wrong reasons. "Well, yes. Something did happen in Costa Rica. But really, something happened before then. Something big."

"Uh huh," commented her mother. "And what could this be?"

Shit. I'm just going to say it. Sophie closed her eyes and very quickly said. "I know Mackenzie is alive. I heard it through your office walls. And, before you ask, yes. I was eavesdropping."

A gasp. Sophie saw her mother look to her father with her mouth wide open, and for a while, nobody uttered a single word. Then, Mr. Zhou spoke up. "So, you're saying that you went to Costa Rica...?"

Sophie nodded. "Yes, I lied to you guys. But you also lied to me."

Her mother's mouth was still open in shock, but she managed to utter out, "Oh my goodness, I don't even know where to begin."

"Me too," Sophie replied. "Though I think I've learned a lot from seeing Mackenzie."

"You saw her?!" cried Mr. Zhou.

Sophie nodded. "Yes, she told me everything."

Mrs. Zhou held her head. "Oh my goodness," she repeated. "I'm sorry for not telling you all this time. I know it was the biggest lie ever, but you know that...?" She paused, and Sophie knew what was just waiting at the tip of her tongue. *She doesn't want to say anything bad about Mackenzie, so she's testing me.*

"Yes, I know. Mackenzie told me it was all her idea. And I'm sorry as well. For lying all this time, I mean."

Mr. Zhou nodded his head. "I can understand why you did what you did. You were probably confused at the time, right?"

Sophie nodded. "Yes, I thought that if I told you, you guys would..." *I don't particularly want to say what I thought.*

Mr. Zhou nodded. "I see."

Mrs. Zhou, perhaps having slightly recovered from her daze of shock, added on, "Well, Sophie. Thank you for coming clean to us. Seeing that you saw Mackenzie, did she say anything? It's just that she really hasn't talked to us much, and we're quite worried about her."

Should I tell them the good news? Sophie looked at her parents' faces, which were so full of curiosity and hope. *As much as I want to tell them, I shouldn't. This is Mackenzie's story; it's her life, after all.* "She did say something, but you guys will have to wait until she tells you. It's good news, though, that I can tell you."

Letting out a sigh of relief, Mrs. Zhou responded, "Okay, as long as she's fine." She reached for Mr. Zhou's hand and gripped it tight.

Wow, I didn't expect them to react that way. I thought they would be so much more... angry? Perhaps I've got them wrong. Perhaps... Thinking about how she had thought of them as these heartless creatures, Sophie finally started to realize how much stress her parents were under. *If I was that stressed out this past week, imagine how it must have been for them to have been hiding this secret for that long. And not knowing if their daughter would ever recover.* Meeting eye contact with her mother, Sophie let out a smile and excused herself from the table, saying that she had to go shower after getting back from the airport.

As Sophie was about to put her plates back in the kitchen sink, however, her parents stopped her. Mrs. Zhou said, "I know Mackenzie told us to do it, but we're still sorry, nonetheless. It was unfair to do that to you, especially at such a young age."

Mr. Zhou nodded and said, "Yes, we do owe you an apology."

Unused to this attention from her parents, Sophie wasn't sure what to say except nod and reply, "It's okay, really." As Sophie got to process the development of her parents, however, she realized that it was perhaps time for a big change. *No one in this family is evil; we're all just a bit broken. Which means we can mend it.*

thirty-five

When Anya walked out of the airport, the first view she saw was her parents waving their hands, standing in front of the entire hundred-person crowd. *How long ago must have they arrived to get this far up in the crowd? One, maybe two hours?*

Anya ran into her parents' arms and said, "I missed you guys so much, and I have *so* much to tell you."

Her father chuckled. "I'm very excited to hear all your stories, one by one. You have always been the best storyteller in this family."

Anya smiled and responded, "Well, I think this one will be the most interesting of them all." She winked at her parents, and her mother softly batted her on the arm. "Ay yah, not even back a few minutes and already causing trouble."

Anya laughed. *That's usually true, but this one won't be a problem. I promise.*

After Uncle Wang talked to her parents for a while, Anya realized that it was also time to say goodbye to him. Throughout the trip, she had grown really close to him, as he had almost served as a parental figure for her. Now that he was leaving, she was saddened at the prospect of not seeing him for a long time.

So, she turned to him and said, "Okay, this is goodbye for now. But we need to stay in touch, okay?"

He patted her on the shoulder. "Yes, feel free to come around to my office anytime. I'll always have a plate of pears on my table in case you do come around."

Anya laughed. "I'll come around often, then."

With that, they said goodbye, and Anya and her parents turned to go home. As Anya walked out of the airport, she thought about Camelia's phone call that was supposed to be coming soon. *Camelia did say that I could tell them about what had happened before receiving her phone call, but that also means that I have to face the brunt of my parents' reactions.* Anya thought about what she should do, and for a moment, she was quite sure that she would just keep quiet about what had happened until the phone call. But then, the more she thought about it, the more she realized that she trusted her parents now. *Even if they're really mad at me, I know that at the end of the day, they'll understand. And plus, if I don't tell them now, it's only going to be worse for them to know that I didn't trust them.*

So, after conversing with them for a while about the trip, Anya decided to tell them right then and there in the car.

She cleared her throat. "Ehm. Mom, Dad. Do you guys remember how I used to keep a journal of all my drawings?"

Her mother, who was sitting in the passenger's seat, nodded. "Yes, but why do you bring that up now? I thought that you hadn't wanted to draw in forever."

"Well, about that. Um... I actually still like drawing."

"Really?" questioned her father. "I haven't seen you pick up a notebook and start drawing in ages."

Anya replied, "I... I've been drawing in secret, that's why. Not secret, secret. But like trying to avoid you guys seeing."

Her mother turned around now, looking Anya in the face. "Now why would you do that?"

"Erm, do you remember how you used to say that art was useless?" replied Anya. *Oof, that was a bit blunt.*

"Ah," replied her mother. She paused, and Anya could see her racking her brain. "Right, I remember now. It feels like nothing to me, but it probably meant a lot to you, didn't it?"

Anya nodded. "Yes, it really did."

Her father pitched in, "Anya, I wish you had said something to me about this passion of yours. And I truly should have noticed it earlier. But now that we've brought this to light..."

Her mother completed his sentence. "Yes, we need to do something about this. I'm trying to right some wrongs, and this is one of them. So tell me, what is it you would like me to do?"

Anya smiled, thrown aback by how receptive her parents had been. "Well, if you insist."

A few days had passed, and Sophie was still amazed at the messages that would pop up on her phone a few times during the day. She knew that Mackenzie had said she would contact her, but for some reason, Sophie had always thought—perhaps out of fear—that everything would just return back to before she went to Costa Rica. So, every time she received a message from Mackenzie that updated her on the ongoing situation, Sophie would jump up from her chair and click on it immediately, reading it over and over again.

The progress had been slow but good; Mackenzie was already talking to the administrators there, and her parents were busy finding someplace suitable in LA. From the looks of it, Mackenzie would probably be back to LA in the next few weeks. The prospect made Sophie extremely excited, but she also realized that she had to talk to her parents. *I've been putting this off, but I can't anymore.*

It was the weekend, and Sophie had specifically requested the day before for her parents to not go work overtime and instead spend it going out to the beach as a family. Although they only lived around forty-five minutes away from the beach, they hadn't gone in months, not since Mackenzie had gone. Thus, Sophie had thought that this would be a good change of scene.

Sitting on the beach on the mat which they used to always use before, Sophie said to her parents, "Hey guys. I have something I need to discuss with you guys."

Sophie's mother nodded. "Yes?"

"Well, it's going to be kind of hard to hear."

"That's okay," replied her father.

"Okay, so the thing is that sometimes, I just wish that we could spend more time together.

And I know you guys are really busy, but I can't help feeling that it's more than that." She looked to her parents, trying to see their reactions. They were nodding. *Okay, here goes.* "I feel like you guys sometimes avoid me, perhaps out of grief for Mackenzie. I don't want to accuse or anything, but the sudden change from when Mackenzie was here to when she wasn't was just huge, you know?"

Her mother grasped Sophie's hand, which surprised her. She said, "Oh Sophie. I... I know. You aren't wrong."

Mr. Zhou reluctantly nodded. "Yes, you're right. Sometimes, sometimes it just comes easier to work away at the office than sit in a home that feels like it's missing someone. And then knowing what has happened to that person, who you love so very much." He cleared his throat. "But that's no excuse for how we've been treating you. We love you so very, very much, and we need you to know that."

Sophie nodded. "I know, but I just wish you both would be closer. So we could be family."

Her mother, wiping away at a tear, responded, "You're very right. We haven't been the best parents, and you need us. We also need you. We're both going to change."

Caught off guard by how accepting her parents had been of what had just happened, Sophie once again didn't really know what to say but just hugged her parents tight. *Wow. Maybe I should have just told them sooner. Maybe I need to trust them more.* Finally, she uttered out, "Thank you Mom. Thank you, Dad. I'm so glad to have you guys back."

Her mother, half-crying, half laughing, responded, "Oh, my precious daughter. I'm so sorry to have put you through all this. You are way, way too young to have had to deal with everything that has happened in the past few months. And we should have been there, but we weren't."

Her father, also on the verge of tears, added on, "We love you, Sophie. And we'll change. Starting today."

Sophie smiled and buried her head into their arms, letting the sound of waves crashing in the background muffle the loud sound of her tears of joy.

"Okay, ready? I'm going to pick it up," Anya said.

Her parents, one on each side of Anya and crouched over the phone, nodded.

"Okay, then. Here goes." As Anya's finger moved toward the button, she quickly let out a sigh of relief that she had already told her parents. *If I hadn't told them, this upcoming phone call would be so nerve wracking. Also thank goodness that they hadn't freaked out when I told them. Well, okay. Mom had kind of freaked out, but Dad had calmed her down immediately. Overall, I would say that it went quite well. But I'm not going to lie, these past few days, they have been constantly pestering me to see Camelia. I've nearly gone crazy, so I'm so glad that we're finally here.*

Camelia's voice of greeting as well as the sight of her face cut Anya's train of thought short.

Almost immediately, Anya heard a scream, which, when she turned around to look, was coming directly from her mother. She was jumping up and down, trying to hold her mouth. Anya looked to her father, who appeared calmer, but Anya could tell right away that he was freaking out as well. *They haven't seen Camelia in so long, and they had probably given up hope. No wonder why they're reacting like this now.*

Anya said, "Hi there, Camelia! Sorry, Mom and Dad are kind of freaking out. They'll come back to their senses soon."

Camelia chuckled. "It's so good to see all of you guys together. I've missed you all so much, you have no idea."

Looking to her parents for a reaction and not hearing a word come from their mouths, Anya finally nudged her father's shoulder. The slight touch managed to snap him out of his trance, and he said, "Camelia. It is so, so, so good to see you again."

Anya looked to her mother, who finally said, "Sorry, I didn't even know what to say. I came into this call prepared with so much to say, but it all blanked when I saw your face."

Camelia let out a slight smile. "That's okay, the same kind of thing happened to me. It has been months, after all." She paused and asked quietly, "You guys aren't mad, right?"

Mr. Chen quickly shook his head. "Why would we be mad? We are just so, so happy that you agreed to finally talk to us, so please, tell us anything that you want."

Camelia looked to Mrs. Chen for her reply, and she shook her head. "No, Camelia. I was never angry with you. I have just missed you. Way too much." She wiped a tear from her eye, and Anya gripped her hand tightly, afraid that she would fall over from emotion.

"Oh, I've missed you all so much too," Camelia uttered out. "And well, this might come as kind of a surprise, but..."

"But what?" interrupted Mrs. Chen, and Anya gave her mother a dirty look. Realizing the look, Mrs. Chen added, "Sorry, I'm still working on that."

"It's okay," chuckled Camelia. "What I was going to say was that I think I'm coming to visit Shanghai soon."

Now, both Anya's parents let out a scream, and Anya kind of wanted to scream as well. *I mean, I had known, but I hadn't really known. I always thought that she was just trying to make me feel better about leav-*

ing. Anya's mind started spinning with excitement, and she could already envision the gifts that she would prepare.

Camelia added on, "Yes, I'm coming with my boyfriend, Nathan. We'll be coming in a few weeks."

Mrs. Chen let out a yelp. "Oh my goodness, I have so many preparations I need to make. So, so many."

"It's really fine, we're all family," Camelia said with a smile.

Mrs. Chen ticked her tongue. "No, no. You are bringing a guest, and we haven't seen you in so long that it is only appropriate."

Camelia rolled her eyes, but Anya could see the smile underneath.

Mr. Chen, who had also been smiling, now turned more serious. "Wait, Camelia. Your mother and I have some things that we want to say to you."

Ah right, Mom and Dad have told me about this. Anya was still surprised at them actually carrying through, though. *When they told me that they wanted to apologize to Camelia, I hadn't actually taken it seriously. But I suppose they really do want to make amends.* Seeing the earnest look on her mother's face, Anya smiled and excused herself from the room.

thirty-six

A FEW WEEKS LATER...

Sophie sat at a bench in her backyard. She hadn't sat on it for months, perhaps years, even. It was in the thick of summer, meaning that the sun beat down on nearly everything, and almost everyone stayed indoors with their AC. However, this bench was special—quite old and worn down with time—it provided a safe haven from it all. The massive branches of a sprawling oak tree hung over the bench, providing a swathe of shade away from the heat.

Twirling the friendship bracelet that Lyla had made for her recently, with the shells they collected years ago, Sophie wondered why she was there.

This was my favorite childhood place to sit and read. Mackenzie would always sit on one side while I sat on the other. Maybe because Mackenzie started getting busier and staying in her room more, I eventually lost interest in being by myself outdoors, and started to stay in my room as well.

On that particular day, though, Sophie found herself sitting once more on the bench, as she wanted a quiet and peaceful place to digest what she'd just learned concerning Ashley. Earlier that morning, Sophie —on a walk to Starbucks—had found Ashley sitting on the sidewalk. She'd thought that Ashley had already left town, so when she saw her, she didn't believe her eyes.

But it was true, and Sophie, after saying hello, had decided to sit down next to her. Normally, Sophie would have just left Ashley in her alone time, as they weren't that close. However, she also had known that Ashley would be leaving soon, and a part of her, perhaps influenced by Lyla's curiosity, wanted to find out why.

For a while, Ashley had just stared at Sophie, a defeated look on her face. Sophie, having found herself in an awkward position, tried to make some conversation, but Ashley had just meekly answered that she was just picking up some stuff from home and then heading off.

Eventually, out of words to say, Sophie had stood up to leave, but Ashley had suddenly gripped her hand.

In a teary voice, she said, "Sophie. I have something I need to tell you."

Sophie had sat down. "What is it, Ashley? You can tell me anything."

"I... I haven't told anyone at school why I'm leaving. I wanted to keep it all a secret, but I think that I want to get it off my chest now. Can you sit with me for a little longer?"

"Yes, for sure. I don't really have anything to do, anyways."

Ashley then proceeded to tell Sophie something that at first shocked her, but then made sense. She was struggling with addiction. That was what had happened on the day of the party. She had been trying to hide it from everyone, her family included, but at one point, she couldn't anymore.

In the middle of telling Sophie about it, she broke down, tears falling down her face. Sophie had hugged her tight, knowing how difficult it must have been for her to carry such a burden on her shoulders. For twenty minutes, Ashley had just cried while Sophie held her in her arms. Sophie had thought about telling her that everything would be okay, but she also knew that what Ashley needed the most at the time was just some time to listen to her.

After twenty minutes had passed, Ashley had said to Sophie, "Sophie, do you think you could tell our friends about this? I don't have the heart to tell them, but I still want them to know that I didn't mean to hurt them."

"I will," Sophie had promised.

Now, as Sophie thought about the situation, the sadder she felt about Ashley's situation, especially in how it was so similar to her sister's story. But, despite how much she wanted to help, there was nothing she could do about it. So, she turned her attention to a more hopeful thought: Mackenzie's arrival.

She was due to arrive that day, and Sophie and her mother were going to pick her up from the airport. The entire family had prepared a welcome gift consisting of assortments of different items: from Mackenzie's favorite fruit to pictures that she could take with her to the therapy center. *I can't believe she's actually here; it feels like forever since I last saw her even though it's only been a few weeks.* Sophie could envision Mackenzie's face exiting the airport doors and smiled.

"Time to go!" yelled her mother.

"Coming!" Sophie smiled, and headed inside.

"Oh my goodness, those pictures are absolutely beautiful," exclaimed Mrs. Chen. "Did you take all of these?"

Camelia, who was sitting on the living room sofa and was surrounded by the entire family, nodded. "Yes, this is the collection of photos I've taken in the past few months. I've sent them to non-profit organizations in Costa Rica for work on the environment."

"Wow," said Mr. Chen. "I'm blown away. Just shocked."

Anya nodded and playfully slapped her sister's shoulder. "I never thought that you were *this* talented."

Camelia laughed. "Oh, we all have an artistic side, don't we?"

At this phrase, Anya thought about her most recent conversation with her parents. She had told them about her love for art, as Sophie had convinced her through multiple calls that it would be better to be truthful and see what happens than to keep it to herself forever. Plus, seeing that her parents had apologized to Camelia, Anya had felt more assured.

The conversation had gone way better than expected. Anya had gone into the conversation thinking that it would end with perhaps her parents simply acknowledging her love for art, but they had done so much more than that. *Okay, well, at first, Mom did make sure that I was serious about it 100%. And then she had warned me about how she had regretted it back when she was a child. But afterward, she was honestly the most eager. Something must have clicked sometime back, perhaps during the hospital incident? Or perhaps Camelia? I'm not sure. Nevertheless, I'm so looking forward to the art class I have tomorrow instead of my typical math class.*

Nathan's voice echoed from the kitchen. "Is watermelon okay? I'm going to cut some fruit."

Anya yelled back, "That's great, thank you so much!"

Chuckling to herself, Anya thought about how much she had despised Nathan before, seeing him as this evil villain. Now, though, she had fully accepted him and even appreciated him, as he was the one who gave Camelia the route to achieve her dreams. Without him, Anya realized that Camelia would probably have never been able to take those photos that she was now showing her parents, and she would instead have been hunched over, studying. He was also *extremely* helpful with everything and never seemed to stop helping out around the house.

Feeling a wave of gratitude, Anya decided that she should talk to Nathan more. *I still have barely said a word to him; I've been so caught up in chatting with Camelia.*

Anya tapped Camelia on the shoulder. "Hey, Sis. I'm going to help out your boyfriend with the fruit, you guys keep talking, okay?"

Camelia smiled and her eyes twinkled with almost a laugh. "I see that you're finally beginning to accept him. Yes, go help him. I'm going to stay here with Mom and Dad."

Mrs. Chen agreed. "Yes, yes. We can't have Nathan doing everything here."

Anya smiled. *Wow. This is definitely very, very different from when Mom couldn't even talk about Camelia. I see that they've made up, perhaps from the conversation they had on the phone that day.* "Okay then, I'm going!" With that, she bounded off to the kitchen, grinning the entire time.

epilogue
Two Years Later…

SOPHIE COULDN'T BELIEVE IT. Yes, she had looked forward to this day since the moment she entered high school, but everything felt so surreal as she stepped onto the podium and saw the faces of innumerable people all looking at her. She especially couldn't remove her eyes from one person in the crowd: Mackenzie.

As she received her high school diploma—her last taste of high school but also her entrance to college in New York City where she would pursue a life as a burgeoning writer—she blew a kiss to her family. Her mother, father, and sister all vigorously waved back, and her father stood up to record this unforgettable memory.

Another aspect, a closer one than college, was making Sophie extremely excited. In less than a few days' time, she would be off to the airport. The destination?

Shanghai. And the first place she would be going was Anya's house. Apparently, from the latest calls, Anya's social life had experienced some *extreme* developments, and Sophie was ready to hear all about it.

www.ingramcontent.com/pod-product-compliance
Lightning Source LLC
Chambersburg PA
CBHW070743180626
46818CB00007B/2960